Ms. Renfield and the Inheritance Trap

Ms. Renfield and the Inheritance Trap

A Vampire Mystery Romance

Immortal Boss
Book 1

Annika Martin

Chapter One

Harriet

"Whoa," KC the intern breathes, gawking at my latest spreadsheet hack.

"It's really not that big a deal," I say.

"It's next level times infinity," he insists.

Heat rushes to my cheeks. Praise like that always flusters me, especially because I know most people see my devotion to data organization as pitiful if not downright alarming.

A courier appears at the door just then. Saved by the bell.

He's not our normal courier, and instead of the usual plastic or manila envelope, he's carrying something that looks like a prop from the set of *Mission: Impossible*—dark charcoal gray with customs stamps and transit marks I've never seen. A holographic thread glints through the material, and there's even a tamper-evident seal.

I hold out a hand, assuming it's something for Serena. "I can sign."

"Are you Harriet Morgan?"

It's for me?

My heart suddenly pounds against my ribs.

There's only one reason I can think of for somebody to deliver something here for me.

James.

After all these years of fruitless searches and dead ends, I'd always imagined it would happen like this: A letter. A message. Something out of the blue.

We think we found your little brother. We've turned up new evidence, or we matched the dental records you sent. It could be anything.

"Are you Harriet Morgan?" he asks again.

I push up my glasses. "That's me."

"I'll need to see ID."

I rush back to my office to grab my wallet. My hands shake as I pull out my license, sign my name, and take the envelope.

He practically sprints out, like he's afraid I'll hand it back.

The envelope's heavier than it looks. The paper feels expensive, almost alive beneath my fingers. Hope and dread war in my chest.

Hope that James might still be alive. Dread that he might not be.

I can still see the soft shimmer of summer air over the crosswalk. The glint off the monkey bars. "Stay there—I'll be right back!" I'd said.

And James's sweet little "Okay!" tinged with mild annoyance at being distracted from the important business of conquering the monkey bars.

He was tall for an eight-year-old boy. Capable. It would only be a few minutes.

Most of all, I remember how empty the playground looked when I returned.

We never saw him again.

If only I hadn't been so wrapped up in my pre-teen love life, my little half brother would still be here. An adult now, like me.

Jeb, one of the sales guys, wanders over, coffee mug in hand. "That's some ancient-looking mail. Did they send it from the Cold War?"

Serena sweeps through the office, a hurricane in Louboutins. She slows when she sees the envelope. "For me?"

"No, it's... it's for me."

"Really? What is it?"

"I don't know."

Her expression turns serious. "Harriet. Do you think...?"

Do I think it's about James? she means.

"Maybe. I've got feelers out to every police station and morgue from Cleveland to Croatia."

She places a hand on my shoulder. She's one of the few people who doesn't treat my belief that James is still alive like a sad obsession best not humored. She even lets me use company resources to dig into the case after hours. "Do you want me to open it?"

I shake my head. "I got this."

Serena, Jeb, and KC watch as I unwind the string on the envelope. Another envelope slides out: cream-colored, thick, and sealed improbably with dark red wax that's been imprinted with a dragon symbol.

What is this?

Who, outside of crafting influencers and Victorian cosplayers, uses a wax seal in this day and age?

"Okay..." I say.

I turn it over and push up my heavy glasses. My name is written in looping calligraphy across the front:

Harriet Morgan

And below it:

On the matter of the estate of R.M. Renfield

The return address reads:

Namfirescui & Băcilă Asociaţii, Legal Executors

Strada Doamnei 17, Bucharest, Romania

My heart drops.

Renfield. Romania.

So it's not about James at all.

"It's from my deadbeat father," I say. "Or... his estate lawyer."

"I'm so sorry," Serena says.

Because you don't get letters from estate lawyers unless somebody died.

I take off my glasses and rub my eyes. "It's okay. I didn't even know him."

"Still. He was your father," Serena says.

Jeb squints at the envelope. "An estate notice. That means there's a will, Harriet. Maybe an inheritance."

I can feel everyone's attention on me, little sprigs of hope perking up on my behalf. Like maybe something good will finally happen to the stuck girl, the organizational whiz with the pathetic life, the workaholic who keeps her mother, grand-mother, and a failing family antique store afloat.

"Maybe it's one of those long-lost noble estates or whatever, and you're a zillionaire now," Jeb says.

"Spoken like somebody who hasn't met my father," I say.

I didn't know my father growing up. All I had was a name, Renfield, and the fact that my mom met him on a train rumbling through Eastern Europe. After their... encounter, he literally jumped off the train—while it was moving—and disappeared into the Carpathian Mountains.

After years of research and much to the mystification of my friends, I finally managed to track him down. But I've always had a weird gift for seeing things inside data.

That spring break, while my classmates were kicking back on beaches, I was in a café in a village on the southern edge of Karsovia, an obscure microstate located in the mountains between Romania and Ukraine, meeting my father.

The meeting was disturbing, let's just say.

4

Very disturbing.

I stare at the envelope with its bizarro-world, old-timey wax seal, trying not to think about the strange ledgers he was working on while we sat there.

The people around me eventually drift away. I can only guess that Serena gave them one of her famous "get back to work" glares.

She places a hand on my arm, light but deliberate. "If you need to take the rest of the day off—"

"No way," I say, shoving it aside. "I'll open it later."

"So... are you okay to tackle the meeting with the app team?"

"Yeah, of course."

"You sure?"

"I didn't even know him," I repeat. "I definitely don't want anything from him."

Chapter Two

Harriet

I bike home along the river walk. The water's high from recent rains, brown and fast-moving, smacking against the stone embankment. I pass the row of bright benches by the walking path, then cut up to Commerce Street, past the nice restaurants around Gazebo Park, and on to the less glamorous north side of Commerce Street—the part the tourists don't usually wander into.

The brick buildings here are older and more lived-in, the signs hand-painted and sun-faded—Hardware Sam's, Gable's Grocery, Shelby's Consignment.

The bell jingles overhead as I walk into the musty gloom of Mrs. Morgan's Curio Shop. The only brightness is the dust motes swirling in shafts of afternoon light.

I flick on a rose-glass Art Deco lamp in the corner—the one I secretly rewired last year after I got tired of nagging my mom to do it.

"What are we, a brothel?" Mom says without looking up. She's behind the register, surrounded by towers of books and boxes and papers.

"Shopping is aspirational," I remind her. "Nobody wants to

shop at a store that feels gloomy." Deep down, I'm talking as much about her as I am about the store.

And I know it's not fair.

When your child disappears into thin air, you get to be a glass-half-empty person for twenty years if that's what it takes. Who am I to judge?

The envelope burns in my satchel like a radioactive potato.

I decide to hold off on telling her about it. She hates everything connected with my biological father, and who can blame her? Having a guy literally jump out of a train after having sex with you isn't much of a confidence booster.

She was pretty mad when I tracked him down. She didn't want to hear about it at all.

I stop at a set of Red Wing bowls. "Wow! Did you find these last weekend?" I ask even though I already know the answer. I keep near-perfect track of what comes in and out of the store.

Mom and Granabelle go garage sale picking every weekend, and Mom always comes back with a little glow when she scores a Red Wing piece. Now I feel like a total asshole for my gloomy store lecture.

"Not a complete set, sadly," she says.

"Still, this is a real find! Remember when you told me you'd fall over if you ever found a pink spongeware refrigerator jar?"

She shrugs. It's always like this—me trying to point out something good, her brushing it aside.

Granabelle appears in the doorway wearing a turquoise caftan and what I sincerely hope is a wig.

"Quick, get a picture of me by the milk glass!" she says. "Before that harpy LaVerne posts another #GlamTuesday in one of her stupid pillbox hats."

"Didn't you two call a truce last week?"

"She broke it when she declined to reply to or even so much as heart my kind comment on her most recent post."

I take her phone, climb up on a chair, and get a few shots.

Whereas Mom's coping mechanism is cynicism, Granabelle's has been to recreate herself online as a grandmother-living-her-best-life influencer.

I finally escape, climbing the stairs past peeling floral wallpaper and a banister held together by screws that are already loosening. I would stab our inept handyperson with a grapefruit spoon, but sadly, that inept handyperson is me.

The second floor of the old brick building is living spaces, and the top floor is mostly storage and my bedroom, which is barely bigger than a generous walk-in closet. But it's mine. Two-monitor workstation. Dry-erase wall calendar. Noise-canceling headphones. A giant monstera plant named Liz that is the envy of my subreddit. Everything laid out just so.

I shut the door, take a seat, and pull out the envelope. I run my finger over the weird wax seal with a feeling of dread.

I should just open it. I'm always telling people that more information is better than less information.

Why don't I open it?

But I can't bring myself to.

I put it aside and check my email. There's a notification that people have replied to my post on the Northern Ohio True Crime Forum.

My heart does a happy dance.

A strange murder happened just last week here in Ashwood. It was right after a highbrow wedding at a grand old mansion. Town dignitaries were lined up on the majestic curving staircase when it collapsed.

The deputy mayor died. Others were injured.

A remote-control hydraulic device was found in the debris.

It seems that somebody used a wireless device to cause the thing to collapse, with the mayor and his team standing on it.

Everybody in town, including the police, believes it was an assassination attempt.

Everybody except me.

I've followed a string of increasingly dangerous wedding-related disasters that have been happening for almost a year. Poor Granabelle was injured at one of the early ones, where a cart loaded with dirty dishes careened down a hill and smashed into a group of wedding guests.

Nobody could explain how it happened.

I started hearing about other weird wedding accidents over cappuccinos at the coffee shop, in buried social media posts, and through Granabelle's unstoppable gossip grapevine.

So I started a spreadsheet.

That's when the pattern snapped into focus: the timing between accidents, the way each one grew more severe. It was too deliberate to ignore.

It is my belief we have a budding serial killer in town—one who stages accidents at weddings.

This is the first time that person has left evidence behind, however.

Officer Maverick Cooper refused to allow me to examine the device, refused to answer even my most basic questions, and listened to my theory with a pitying and slightly annoyed look on his face, which made me feel more pathetic than usual around him.

So I laid my theory out for my true crime forum peeps. I'd been waiting until I gathered more information, but if anybody would see what I see, it would be them!

I excitedly click onto the discussion.

HarCorman: *LOLOLOL are you serious? I see a pattern in your wedding accident serial killer theory, and it spells CRY FOR HELP.*

Glendale129: *The stairway collapse was a message from the Snag Tooth Riders. Everyone knows it except you.*

MartSamson: *It was one of the bikers going after the mayor... Obvs!!!!! Sometimes a cigar is just a cigar, Rooster5.*

Sherlocksmith: *Nothing suspicious in your data, Roost-*

er5. People fall. People choke. People die at weddings. Doesn't make it a serial killer pattern. Dropping a link to a table "Falls and Accidental Deaths by Setting" for you to study.

TheTorvald: *This might be your most pathetic theory yet. Kudos. Time to take off the serial-killer-colored glasses.*

I start to type a defense. The pattern is so obvious, and yes, I have studied the "Falls and Accidental Deaths by Setting" data.

Instead, I delete it and shut my laptop. The last thing I want to do is get into an internet fight right now.

I know I'm right.

That's enough.

The envelope from the lawyers still sits on my desk, silent and a little bit eerie.

I think about tossing it, but what if it's a check? Summer's coming, and the store's air conditioner is barely functional. Serena pays me well, but most of it goes toward supporting my mom and grandmother and a failing store.

Even if it's a hundred bucks, that would help.

I break the wax seal. It's a letter.

Just a letter.

No check.

The letter is a lot of legalese. Like a mercenary, I scan for words like "account" or "funds."

But all I get is this:

To receive the full details of your inheritance, you must be physically present at the castelul at the time of dispensation. No accommodations for remote attendance are permitted.

No accommodations for remote attendance? If I want to see if I got anything, I have to go to a castle in Karsovia? And I'm informed of this via a letter with a wax seal, circa 1650?

What is happening here? Do any other relatives just want to meet the biological daughter? And if so, why not say it? Though it's hard to imagine my father having any close family. You'd think they would've intervened.

No, I don't want anything from those people.
No way.
I toss it into my vintage Smurfs garbage can.

Chapter Three

Harriet

I'm at work when the call comes: the ceiling's caved in.

"It's only a third-story issue," Granabelle assures me. "Just the storage space."

In other words, the massive, flat, rubber-coated roof now needs replacing. Plus, if my luck holds, a few rotted beams for good measure.

I track down Serena, who owns a big old house herself, and always has the best advice.

She winces when I tell her. "Ouch."

"I know," I say.

"I've got a guy." She's already scrolling through her phone for his contact, mercifully skipping her usual lecture about how I shouldn't be single-handedly bankrolling that money-sponge of an antique store—on top of supporting Mom and Granabelle.

Serena doesn't get it; I owe them.

She'll never understand.

"Here it is." She sends it over. "I hate to say it, but a new rubber roof on a building that large and old is going to cost you well into the five figures."

"*Well* into the five figures?"

"I hope I'm wrong, but I know I'm not," she says.

"Gulp," I whisper.

"I'm sorry," she says. "I'm guessing there was nothing from your father?"

I tell her about the demand that I turn up in Karsovia if I want further details.

"Well... obviously you should go," she says.

"I can't drop everything and jet off. We're so busy here!"

Serena sniffs. "We're talking... what? A long weekend? You never use your vacation days, and we're swimming in frequent flier miles."

"Fly to Eastern Europe on the chance that my father left me something? Seriously, if he left me anything, it's probably a scary horsehair trinket soaked in bug juice or a cursed doily or something."

"I can't imagine any kind of legit law firm requesting your in-person presence for a trinket."

"But the launch..."

"We can survive a couple of days without our brain trust. The team can text you and loop you in if needed," she says. "And hey, what if it's your lucky break?"

I roll my eyes. I'm not a lucky-break girl. I'm not a fly-halfway-off-across-the-world-on-a-whim girl.

But what if there's money there?

I'm so tired of fighting. Tired of calculating what groceries I can skip this week. This roof is going to sink us. If it's money, it would make all the difference in the world.

"You can't go to Romania!" Mom says, shocked, over dinner the following evening.

"It's not Romania, it's Karsovia," I say. "And it'll just be a long weekend away. One day over, two days there, and one day back."

"And Serena is allowing this?"

"I have a zillion vacation days, and I'll be a click away. For Serena, and for you."

Mom furrows her brow. "How the hell did they even find you? It doesn't matter. Your sperm donor dad sucked, and his relatives will be worse."

"I'm going. And hey, obviously he didn't completely suck because he left something for me. Maybe it's some money that would help the store! I doubt they'd have me fly halfway across the world for nothing."

Or at least Serena doubts it.

I tear off a piece of dinner roll.

"Whatever that man's got for you, I don't think you want it," Mom says.

"Even if it's money to fix the roof?"

"We do need to fix that roof," Granabelle interjects.

Mom lodges a few more protests, all of which I've anticipated and prepared answers for.

It's unlike me to leap into the unknown like this. I'm a look-really-hard-and-calculate-the-prevailing-winds-before-you-leap kind of gal.

But what if?

I slather butter on another dinner roll. "It's just one of those things a person has to do, and I'm doing it."

Mom and Granabelle reluctantly let the subject drop.

TRACKING down my father a dozen years ago was an odyssey of searching through visa records, border crossings, and Slavic family records. I was like a data-mining silverfish, using every organizational trick I knew, and I did it.

He was impossible to contact directly, but somebody at the town post office directed me to a little café on a cobblestone street with a view of the Southern Carpathian Mountains. I spotted him instantly, hunched at a corner table: a male version of myself if I'd aged up and seen some shit.

His thick raven hair was shot through with silver, and his deep-set brown eyes were fixed on some sort of old-fashioned spiral-bound ledger that he held in his trembling hands.

"Mr. Renfield?" I stammered. "My name is Harriet Morgan. Do you mind if I sit?"

He mumbled something.

I took it as a yes and sat. "I believe you met my mother on a train from Braşov to Lviv thirty-two years ago."

He didn't look up.

Heart banging in my chest, I set a picture of Mom from when she was in her twenties on the cover of the ledger in front of him. "Do you remember her?"

He examined it briefly. "Goth girl in car seventeen, seat 42B," he recited with mechanical precision. "Purple Doc Martens with silver laces, fishnet stockings."

"Yes, yes!" I've seen enough old photos of Mom to know that's spot-on for her as a travelling twenty-year-old. "I have reason to believe that you're my father."

He didn't have much of a reaction to this; he just fussed with his ledgers and supplied more details. "Dried peaches in granola. Three spoon rings. Five Kurt Cobain opinions. Going on to Kraków."

"Okayyyy... she does like peaches."

"Transfer in Košice. Backpack with a pink ribbon."

"I remember weird things like that, too," I said to him, going for some bonding. "Little details like that."

He flipped a page on the ledger.

"And you guys had sex... and nine months later I was born."

At this, he looked up, eyes strangely piercing. "The master will be pleased." With that, he went back to his work.

What?

I pressed him about his own family, about where he was born, and if he had other kids or siblings. I tried for some semblance of a medical history, but he was evasive, uttering things like "really can't say" and "entirely immaterial." The only thing that seemed real to him was these ledgers.

Some of the ledgers were the traditional accounting kind, with neat columns for dates, numbers, and notes—plain old office-supply stuff. But others were tall and slender, their pages filled with columns headed by handwritten symbols or clusters of numbers and marks, like cryptic codes.

Something about these tall ledgers felt darkly compelling— the kind of thing you know you shouldn't touch but can't make yourself walk away from.

Finally, I pulled one to my side of the table and studied a page. His notations made sense in a strange, almost ethereal way that's hard to explain. I had the feeling he was trying to organize something vast and mysterious, driven by an internal logic I could sense but not quite name.

"No good, no good." He snatched it back.

"Okay," I said. "But look—see this column?" I suggested a cleaner way to arrange the symbols so they'd be easier to scan.

His eyes lit up with a desperate kind of joy, and for a moment, he seemed to really see me. He rumbled incoherently and pointed out various figures that clearly made a lot of sense to him.

"So what's it all mean?" I asked. "What are you tracking in these ledgers with the symbols? You're tracking something here, right?"

He shook his head vigorously.

I pointed to a circle with a squiggle. "This shows up a lot. What does it mean?"

Mutter, mutter.

He became increasingly agitated as dusk approached, constantly checking his watch. He started grumbling about "duties" and "punishments," which alarmed me.

"Are you in trouble?" I asked carefully. "If you need help, I could see about sponsoring you in the United States. I bet I could figure out how to get you back with me."

His face transformed into a mask of horror at this, like I'd suggested we go sacrifice a kitten. "Can't. Impossible!"

"Okay, okay!" I said reassuringly.

He went back to his work and once again seemed to forget I was there.

I asked him more about the ledgers, but he wouldn't reply. At one point, he snatched a fly out of the air and ate it. Just popped it in his mouth like a Chiclet and returned to his work.

I left soon after.

I've regretted a lot about that meeting in the years since.

I regretted not being more forceful with my questions about what was going on with him, his medical history, and what he meant by "the master."

But if I'm being perfectly honest, my biggest regret is paying so much attention to those ledgers, because now and then they show up in my dreams—or more like nightmares—and I'll wake up feeling like they're calling to me in a way that isn't right.

Sometimes I tell myself that I was only drawn in because I like data organization, and the nonsense structure of the ledgers got under my skin.

I can't stand messy information, that's all.

I've always been this way.

My mother doesn't get my intense relationship to data and the organization thereof, sometimes calling it my "Rain Man" stuff.

My grandmother thinks it's adorable.

Serena benefits from it, but even she treats it like a quirk.

No one else has ever seemed to feel the same passion for systems that I do.

Except my dear old dad, Mr. R.M. Renfield.

Chapter Four

Harriet

People in Transylvania really lean into the vampire tourism. Castle tours, themed Airbnbs, even a Dracula museum. I guess I can't blame them; it's probably a huge economic driver.

But it's when I cross from Transylvania into Karsovia, headed for "the castelul," that things get weird.

For one thing, my taxi driver keeps looking at me in his rearview mirror with this wary expression. Just ten minutes ago, at the bottom of a winding, serpentine road, he pointed out— very gravely—that his GPS had gone completely dark. Just a black screen.

I grin. "Okay, then!" Clearly, he's putting on a little show for me, a naive tourist from the U.S.

Though it seems a bit much here in this rural area, miles from the whole vampire tourism epicenter.

He gives me another dark and foreboding look.

"It's alright, I'm here on business. We don't need to do the vampire thing."

"This is Karsovia." He lowers his voice to a hushed whisper. "Where some never return."

Oh-kay.

I pull out my phone. No bars. I lean forward. "Is there some kind of cell service damper in this cab? If so, could you turn it off, please? I'd really love that."

He scowls at me in the rearview mirror. "No damper."

I sit back with a sigh.

It's a seamless experience, I'll grant that. We're following literal wooden signs with arrows carved into them, climbing higher and higher into the foggy Carpathian Mountains.

He pulls over at the base of a winding stone path. "Far as I go. Castelul Dracul is there." He gestures at a looming structure silhouetted against the darkening sky. He makes a sign of the cross, then taps his forehead twice.

"Okay, okay, if we both pretend that I'm super scared and I really think it's some Dracula castle and that Karsovia is even scarier than Transylvania, then can you drive me all the way?"

He furrows his big brow. "No further."

I dig around in my wallet and produce a couple of bills. "I promise I'll emphasize the spookiness in my review of your taxi company. Like, ten stars for the spookiness."

He twists around and fixes me with an intense stare. "Take heed," he grates out.

Apparently, you can't break character here in dark Disneyland. It's a bit frustrating, but one does what one must.

"I understand." I give him a nice tip anyway because he really did go all out.

I watch as his taillights disappear down the mountain, leaving me alone with my rolling suitcase. I make a mental note to find a non-vampire tourism cab for the ride back to my hotel.

Maybe I'll meet some relatives who will know of one.

I might have more relatives.

I gaze up at the castle, silhouetted now by the setting sun.

After my half brother, James, disappeared, it was always just Mom, Granabelle, and me. I love my tiny family, but the idea of aunts and uncles—or more half-siblings—makes my heart sing.

True, my father wasn't exactly a gem, what with the bug eating, the lack of interest in meeting his daughter, and the whole madness business, but every family has a weird relative, right?

I make my way up medieval cobblestones, which seem to be arranged for maximum trip-ability, thankful for my practical ankle boots and also grateful that the sun hasn't set entirely behind the mountains because I'm not seeing much in terms of walkway lighting. Good grief, if this were in the United States, the owners would have so many lawsuits, those craggy turrets would be spinning.

By the time I knock on a castle door the size of a minivan, my boots are scuffed beyond repair.

The enormous man who opens the door isn't wearing a uniform, exactly, but there's something... official about him. His coat is dark green, pressed within an inch of its life, and his shirt is buttoned all the way up to his throat. His hair is slicked back into a short ponytail, and his boots shine like polished onyx.

His expression is grim, like he stepped straight out of a Victorian period drama—stern, haunted, and entirely out of place in the modern world.

More vampire stuff?

"Okay. I mean, I guess," I mumble, feeling dismayed that they would hold my father's funeral or reading of the will or celebration of life or whatever this is in what seemed to be a Dracula-themed Airbnb. But maybe my father loved this place or something. Maybe this is what he wanted.

The butler, or whoever he is, takes my bag, and I follow him through one large, gloomy, torchlit room after another, until we finally end up in a cavernous room with stone walls that must be fifty feet high, the cobwebby corners illuminated by wall sconces like flaming torches. There are weapons hung on the walls and set into weird nooks. At the far end, bookshelves stretch up to the ceiling, creating a hellish chaos of books and papers strewn across the floor and piled willy-nilly among candles and papers.

I spot a few people sitting cross-legged in the middle of the mess.

One of them sees me and shoots up to her feet. "Hey!" She comes running toward us, brandishing a sword.

I jump back out of her way, and she streaks past me, only to slam into the door I've just entered through. She casts the sword aside with a loud clang and proceeds to bang on the door. "Let us out, goddamn you!"

It's now that I realize that the butler is gone... with my bag. And there's just a door—or actually, not even a door anymore. It's just a panel in the wall with no knob.

"What the hell?" I knock on the panel that used to be a door. "Hey! My stuff!"

The woman gives up and slumps against the door. "He took all of our stuff, too." Her accent is Slavic—Czechoslovakian or Yugoslavian, maybe.

I pull my phone from my purse. "At least I still have my..."

Gulp.

Not only are there no bars, but there's nothing on the screen whatsoever. "My brick."

She mutters angrily in her language. She's lovely, with short dark hair and beautiful tattoos on one arm. She also has the same squarish brown glasses as me.

"What's going on?" My mind is spinning. "Is this the Renfield memorial or whatever?"

Another voice. "This is no memorial; it's a prison." I look up to see a young man strolling toward us, also with brown curly hair and glasses. He sounds German. "We cannot get out. Thirty-four point three hours I've been here."

The woman who rushed the door pushes her glasses up her nose. "Twelve and three-quarters for me."

"Seriously? They won't let you out? What's going on? Did the butler guy say anything? What does he want?"

The young man shakes his head. "We have no idea, but we don't think they're going to hurt us."

"Or ransom us." Another woman, this one in a crisp maroon suit with a crisp English accent to match, strolls up. She, too, has similar hair and glasses. "They would've taken photos by now." She puts out her hand. "I'm Magda. This is Stefan and Irina."

"Harriet," I say, taking her hand and greeting the others. I look all around.

"So there's no way out? Could it be an elaborate memorial thing? Did he like escape rooms?"

"Thirty-four point three hours I have been here," Stefan says again. "This is no game."

I look up at the cathedral-like windows above the towering bookcases. "Have you tried stacking stuff and climbing up there?"

"Jah, of course we have. This is first thing we have tried," Stefan says. "And we tried everything."

Irina points at the far wall with her tattooed hand. "Somebody delivers food through that slot over there. We try to yell in, but there's never an answer."

Magda looks me over. "You're another one of his kids?"

My heart leaps. "Yes! I'm Mr. Renfield's daughter. You?"

She nods. They all nod.

In spite of the alarming circumstances, I can barely keep the smile off my face. "So we're... half-siblings? I mean, we do all look alike. And have similar taste in eyewear."

Irina smiles a little wistfully. "Oh, the similarities don't stop at unruly hair and glasses. All our mothers met Renfield once and only once on the Dacia Express, an overnight train through the Carpathians. They had sex once—using a mysteriously ineffective condom provided by him, naturally—and then he leapt from the train. Magda and I had stepfathers for a while, but both died in car crashes when we were five."

"Very suspicious ones," Magda adds, adjusting her suit jacket.

My jaw drops open. My mind reels. "This is... unbelievable."

"Oh, there is more." Irina crosses her arms. "We all worked in bakeries in high school. We all got scholarships from the Braydon Institute. And we all got pet rabbits at the age of ten after finding them in baskets on our doorstep."

"Same with me... including the rabbit!" I say. Bunster showed up on our doorstep in a little cage with a basket of rabbit supplies.

Irina raises one brow. "Four half-siblings, all born same month thirty-two years ago to different mothers who all had sex with the same man on the same train route? The rabbit, the scholarship, the bakery, the single parent, and who knows what else? It's a manufactured pattern."

"Agree," I whisper. The people on my true crime forum would lose their minds.

Stefan asks if I've ever seen the movie *Boys from Brazil*, which I haven't. He explains that it's a movie about a bunch of Nazis who clone Hitler and re-create the events of his life in order to help ensure he turns out really Hitlery.

"Somebody was grooming us in the same sick way," Magda says crisply. "Obviously, Renfield's involved, and I, for one, hope he's not dead so I can kill him."

"Only if you let me torture him first," Irina says.

"Wait, did any of you have a younger sibling who disappeared?" I ask.

No, as it turns out.

Stefan and Magda have little sisters, and Irina has a younger cousin who lived with their family.

"Losing your brother does not sound like part of the pattern," Irina says. "I'm sorry you lost him."

"I'm sorry your stepfathers were taken from you," I say. "I never had a stepfather."

Stefan never had a stepfather either. "It is important to the pattern that we were raised by a single mother, I think."

Magda glowers at the food slot. "Somebody needs to go down."

Stefan turns to me. "What is your profession?"

"Executive assistant to the CEO of InovaSpire. It's a tech company in Ohio."

Irina brightens up. "I know InovaSpire! Slices and dices unstructured data? I'm a mathematician and data mining engineer. Data is my world."

This would explain a few of her tattoos, including the Fibonacci spiral that curves into the sly shape of a fox mid-pounce, inked in fine black lines just visible beneath her sleeve.

Stephen gestures at Magda. "Magda's lead attorney at Interpol, and I am the youngest-ever head of Special Collections at the Austrian National Library. Very different professions, then."

"They are different," I say, raising a finger. "But when you think about it, we all create order out of chaos. My boss is brilliant but scattered, so I take her ideas and make them into coherent systems. Libraries catalogue information. Data mining sorts and creates order out of bits of information, and obviously, an attorney fits real-world circumstances into a legal framework."

Magda nods. "What's the point of this? Why go on a sick breeding spree and then arrange all these events to make our lives parallel?"

"Hard for me to believe Renfield had it in him," I say. "He didn't exactly strike me as the mastermind type."

Everybody turns to me here, shocked.

"You have met him?" Stefan asks. "You have met our *father*?"

"Only once. I tracked him down to a café in Ostra."

"What was he like?" Irina asks.

I try to think about how to answer that. "Very odd. Not well."

"In what way?" Stefan asks.

In the end, I tell them everything, because I'd want to know all of it. The good, the bad, and the buggy.

Magda makes a face. "A fly? Are you quite sure?"

"You don't mistake a thing like that."

"I'm impressed that you found him at all," she says. "I had a top private investigator in London on it. For three years!"

"He was not easy to find. Tracking him down was my hobby for a while, but I had some luck along the way." I shake my head. "An impregnation spree. That's not creepy at all."

Irina points to a door under a large oil portrait of a man with a ruffle collar and cascading dark curls—a real looker, if you can get past the Shakespearean prom outfit.

"There's a bathroom at the far corner. And most ominously, there are four bedrolls in another corner. He may want to keep us here. But the good news is that those knives and swords hanging all over the walls are real. All very sharp." She lowers her voice. "We've hidden them around the room, so if that guy comes back, we'll make mincemeat out of him." She takes a bejeweled scabbard off the wall and pulls out a small sword. "This is a good one."

"Oh. For me?"

"Yes." She helps me affix it to the belt under my jacket.

"What kind of captor gives their captives access to this much weaponry?" I muse, toying with the key around my neck.

Nobody has an answer.

Magda says, "I promise you, if our father turns out not to be dead?" She slashes the air with her sword and heads back across the expansive inlaid wood floor to the long table that's piled high with papers and books.

I trail behind. "Did you guys tear this place apart trying to get out?"

"Of course not, do we look like monsters?" Stefan says. "Once we realized there's no escape, we started sifting through all this chaos for some clues as to what's happening. And why not put things back in order? We may be here a while, and who can stand this?" He explains the categorization system they've decided to use.

Listening to him, I get the feeling the system was the result of a long and impassioned discussion.

A lot of people, when faced with this entrapment, would make battering rams out of the bookcases or fight amongst themselves, but my siblings are making order out of this mess, searching for clues and patterns. Being thoughtful and methodical.

I feel a jolt of love for them right then.

James disappearing devastated me on so many levels, but here are three more of my half-siblings. Wonderful, thoughtful siblings. One positive thing to come of this really awful situation.

They show me what they've been doing. Stefan's working on the nonfiction books.

Magda's organizing fiction.

Irina's been reading and sorting handwritten diaries. "Maybe there's some clue about the architecture. A secret door. Anything. So far, it's just business randomness—circa 1885 to last year."

Magda points at an unruly pile of papers, accounting ledgers, business folios, and what looks like... the tall ledgers with the mysterious symbols.

A pulse of dread blasts through my chest.

I go to them. I shouldn't, but I can't help it—I have to see if they're the ones my father was working on in that café.

Indeed, they are; I recognize the glyphs, the loops, the color-coding.

"Do you want to try and organize those? They're not all nonsense."

"I guess."

"Incoming." Stefan plops another stack of tall ledgers in my area.

I pick one up. It feels so strangely familiar in my hands. "The one and only time I met our father, he was working with these. He was obsessed. The news of me being his daughter meant less to him than these books."

"Piece of shit," Irina mutters.

"He seemed to have developed this whole system for tracking multiple variables using overlapping geometric patterns. I couldn't get him to say what it was for, but it was like he'd invented his own organizational language." I trace a loop on a page. There's a loop every thirteen entries. Sometimes twelve.

Stefan squints. "Tracking gibberish doesn't make it *not* gibberish."

"Like organizing a junk drawer inside a nightmare," Irina says.

"Could it just all be about... flies?" Magda says.

"I don't think so," I whisper.

"Arrange them however you like," Stefan says. "Take the bottom rows over on the end."

My siblings and I work together, organizing, chatting, and exchanging ideas for escape. I'm freaked out about our situation and tired from travelling, but I'm also a bit thrilled; it's as if I've discovered my people. Now and then, we take breaks and look for trapdoors or hidden ways out. We stash more weapons around the place but always go back to the work.

I tell myself that I should just group the tall ledgers in any random order, because who really cares?

But sadly, I do. I know there's an order.

I flip them open, one after another, comparing and contrasting. Soon, an idea takes shape—not based on content but on something else. An instinct.

I start with the symbols on the first pages—sharp little geometric spirals and interlocking shapes. I group them into families. Then I reorder within each group by vibe, which is a combination of margin notes, ink color, and the feeling I get from looking at the page with my eyes unfocused.

It's not like me to be so woo-woo, but it *feels* right. Like I'm singing along with a distant song.

At some point, a meatball noodle dish is delivered through the slot.

I don't notice at first.

"Hey! Earth to Harriet!" Magda says.

I look up.

"Sorry."

We eat dinner together at the little table under a tapestry depicting a disturbing hunt of some sort, and then we go back to work.

A few hours later, I'm standing in front of my part of the bookcases, admiring my handiwork. I don't know what the things mean, but they're organized. "Done!"

"You devised an order?" Magda asks.

"Yup!"

Stefan wanders over to the rows of tall ledgers. He pulls one out. Then another. "Help me understand. How did you decide which goes first? Can you walk me through it?"

I blink. "Umm... not really."

He puts the ledger back. "Well, as long as it's intentional."

Irina agrees quickly—too quickly.

Magda smiles brightly. "You did it!"

They're humoring me. Oh my god, I haven't even been here a full day—what is happening to me?

I assist Stefan with his more conventional task of book organization, eager to show him that I'm still a normal-thinking person. We work side by side, mostly in silence, though we do exchange horror stories about disorganized friends.

It's around nightfall that we hear the creak of ancient hinges.

I stiffen and turn toward a set of massive doors on the far wall. They swing open with theatrical slowness.

Chapter Five

Harriet

We're all on our feet, weapons in hand.

A massive figure stands silhouetted against flickering torchlight behind him—impossibly still, utterly dark. He strides toward us with the fluid grace of a predator. Well over six feet tall in an impeccably tailored suit that hugs the contours of his large form.

Every instinct in me screams to run. To hide. But somehow, I can't move.

We all watch, frozen, as he comes into the light, peering at us with coffee-colored eyes. Thick, dark hair tumbles over his right brow, lending him a wolfish asymmetry.

I feel mesmerized. Awestruck.

I shake my head as if I can shake the awe out of my mind, because clearly, this is the architect of our current travesty. He deserves no awe—none whatsoever!

And also, the slow door opening? Are we back to the Dracula-theme-park situation?

"I don't know what your game is, but you can't hold us here," I say.

"I'll do as I please, human," he says, voice like the notes on a cello, rich with vibration. His accent is British. Maybe he's from Britain, or maybe he learned English there.

I narrow my eyes. *"Human?"*

"Interpol knows where we are," Magda bites out. "They're going to come for us, and you'll be in much trouble."

"Yes," he says. "Very well."

Though we've taken up arms, none of us makes a move to attack him. I think it's a combination of his old-country gravitas and the fact that, let's face it, the four of us are bespectacled scholar types, not brawlers.

My breath catches as he strolls past me to the shelves. "All in order?" he asks.

"Depends on what you mean by order," Stefan says, which is as good an answer as any.

He continues to examine our work, large fingers moving with stunning grace.

And then he crouches in front of the row of tall ledgers and pulls out the first one.

Wildly, I wonder if he'll have comments on my decision-making. Will he see the sense behind why I put the triangle thingy with two dots in front of the circle symbol with the cross hatches?

I shake myself out of this line of thought and look over at my siblings. Are we going to attack now?

Magda speaks up. "Detaining individuals against their will constitutes false imprisonment under the European Convention on Human Rights, Article 5. Even Karsovia, despite its... unusual legal history regarding castle autonomy, ratified these protocols in 1994."

Attacking on the grounds of illegality wasn't what I was thinking, but...

The man pulls out another ledger.

"Was this some kind of twisted test?" I demand.

"Are you the one who killed Magda's and Irina's stepfathers?" Stefan asks. "Are you a Renfield?"

The man stands and regards Stefan with a dark look. "My name is Miramonte," he says in his clipped British accent. "Renfield was my servant for over a century."

I exchange glances with my siblings. Sounds like our father is dead. Even more notable: *for over a century?*

"Renfield's resourcefulness, his organizational systems, his sense of duty... were all second to none," the man continues. "Once his health and mind began to fail, I directed him to breed another like him. As my diligent servant, he produced the four of you, shaping your life events to mirror his own in hopes that one of you would be fit to take his place."

Stefan gasps. Magda swears. I grip Irina's arm.

"That's what this is all about?" Irina demands. "You did monstrous things to our families to shape us into servants?"

"Only one of you will serve," he says.

"How about none of us," I say, sliding my knife back into my belt scabbard. "Will that work out? None of us? Because that's what you're getting."

"You will release us this instant, and mark my words, you *will* pay for this," Magda says. "The hospital for the criminally insane is too good for you, though that's where you clearly belong."

He turns to me. "Harriet Renfield."

"Not my name," I snap. Like that's the main issue here.

He draws closer. "It is you who will serve me."

I straighten into my full height, which, being 5'3", is not that impressive. Nevertheless, I inhabit the whole 5'3" of me and look him square in the face. "I wouldn't even serve you a microwave pot pie. Congratulations—your deranged experiment failed. Now let us go."

He gestures toward the heavy door, which swings open with

a slow, groaning creak. Remote control? "The rest of you are not needed."

My siblings exchange wary glances.

"Screw that. Come on, Harriet!" Irina takes off toward the hall.

"Let's go!" Magda follows, then Stefan.

I follow.

A voice from behind me. "Harriet Renfield, don't you want to know about the ledgers? What purpose they truly serve?"

I slow.

"Their deep and inscrutable purpose," he adds.

Inscrutable. I generally find that word to be pretentious, but I need to know.

And fine, their purpose is inscrutable!

I turn and find myself caught in the gleam of his dark eyes. He's built like a predator made for long hunts, the kind of size that should belong to furs and chainmail—but the suit fits him just as easily. He's larger than life, or maybe it's only the intensity of his madness.

"Harriet!" Magda's voice is sharp now. "Hurry!"

What am I doing? I tear myself away with a shake.

I spin and head for my siblings, who are waiting at the door.

That's when the floor vanishes beneath them.

They're gone in an instant—except for the screaming that echoes into the dark below.

I run to them, but the floor seals up before I reach it.

"What the hell?" I drop to my knees, frantically feeling along the seams for a latch, a lever, *something.*

"Hey!" I yell, pounding on the floor. "Can you hear me?"

Another scream from way far below. God, how far did they fall?

I spin around. "What the hell? Let them out!"

"They are redundancies."

"You will let them out right now!"

"I will let them out, of course. I will choose one of them every month. Their blood will sustain me, and in that way, they'll live on."

"You are out of your mind!"

"Come, Ms. Renfield."

I pull my blade from my scabbard and fall to my knees, trying to use the thing to pry up the section of floor that seals them in. "They haven't done anything to you."

"They're Renfields," he grits out.

"You don't even know them!"

"I know they're Renfields."

I run the blade along the outline of the panel, but I can't get it in far enough to start prying. I work on one side and then another as he watches, cold and darkly luminous.

Will he really try and eat them or suck their blood or something? Is this his thing? I suppose the human body can ingest just about anything, and cannibals are apparently real. Why not vampire wannabes who drink blood? There's probably a subreddit.

I slide the small sword back into the scabbard and examine the floor panel with my fingertips. I can hear somebody crying down there—Irina, I think.

I look back over at Miramonte, who looks... bemused... as though he can't comprehend why I'd be upset about people in a hole. Not a good sign.

I'm thinking he must have a remote control in his pocket or something—the timing was too perfect with the floor swallowing up the three of them and sealing back up the second I got there.

I stand. I need to get the remote from him.

"It's not like we can help who our father is," I say, trying to cobble together a plan. "You couldn't help who your father is, right?"

He watches me with those deep brown eyes, not bothering to answer.

"I mean, come on. You need to end this. Look, I'll talk to Magda about the whole mental-institution-for-the-criminally-insane threat if you let us all go."

"It is not to be," he says. "Come, we have work to do."

"If you think I'm going to be your assistant—"

"Servant—you are to be my *servant*."

"Yeah, that's not happening, mister."

He comes near to me, now, his strange presence washing over me. "You will call me Alexandru."

My mind races. Alexandru will not be giving up the remote without a fight. I have a blade and the element of surprise, but he has his beastly size and his madness. They say seriously deranged people can sometimes lift cars.

"I have chosen you. It is done," he says sternly. "I have your desk prepared. Everything you'll need."

Because I'm the "chosen one."

I've watched enough true crime shows to know that being the chosen one is never a plus when you're dealing with a psycho.

I also know that the murder victim usually has one last chance to get the upper hand before the point of no return, and this is it. Right here. Right now.

Needless to say, I'm thinking about the small sword in the sheath at my belt.

Can I do it? I'm not a violent person, but those are my half-siblings down there, and I'm all they have. My legs tremble. My mouth feels dry.

I put my hands on my hips. "Why me?"

"I knew you were the one from the moment you set foot in the castle."

Discreetly as I can, I move one of my hands along my belt, feeling for the jewel-encrusted handle. "Uh-huh."

"Your connection to the ledgers and your impressive organizational skills only cemented that knowledge. You are far superior to the others."

I nod energetically, working the thing from the scabbard as he goes on about my mental tenaciousness and intellectual prowess.

Finally, it's free, hidden behind my back. It feels like a miracle that he didn't notice my machinations, but then again, the man is clearly not the picture of mental health.

I move nearer to him, rambling about my résumé, steeling myself. I'm five feet away. Three feet away.

I'll probably only get one blow in, and it's going to have to be a good one. A killing blow.

I picture myself plunging the blade into the side of his neck —the jugular, ideally.

I stop in front of him. Everything seems surreal as I whip out the blade and plunge it into the side of his neck, pushing past some faint resistance that has me thinking about words like tendons and gristle.

And he just... allows it.

Just stands there, amused.

I push it deeper into his neck. Why is he not stopping me? Doesn't it at least hurt?

Then he does something that truly surprises me. He wraps his hand around mine, cool fingers locking tightly over mine, and guides the blade deeper. Then he pushes it forward—slowly —pushing the blade out through the front part of his neck, ensuring that what might have been a stab is a slice.

Suddenly, the sword is free. Blood spills in steady ribbons across his white shirt, soaking the silk lapel of his dinner jacket.

"There we go," he says. "There's a proper stab."

I stagger back, letting the weapon clatter to the floor.

He fixes his cufflinks calmly as you please.

"W-what is this?"

He doesn't bother to reply, not that I would have been able

to process language at this point, because the gash is beginning to heal, right before my eyes. His skin is knitting itself together like real-life CGI.

Finally, his neck is smooth again. Whole. The blood from the wound darkens and dries, then seems to transform into dust.

He adjusts his sleeve with one final flick, then pulls out his pocket square and brushes off the blood dust. "If you want to kill me, you'll have to try harder. But personally, I don't recommend it," he says, voice clipped and elegant.

I blink, unable to make sense of what just happened. "I-I don't understand..." I look down at the blade. Was this some kind of trick? But I know what I saw. I know what I felt.

"Now, then." He straightens up to his full height. "Your father has been dead for ten days, and we have much work to do." He strolls off, expecting me to follow.

Which I do not.

He turns with a glare. "I am not asking, Ms. Renfield."

"A, not my name, and B, I'm not going anywhere until you let them out."

"The rebellion phase," he says wearily. "Your grandmother attempted to flee to America. Your father barricaded himself in a church for three days. Yet each one eventually recognized the inevitability of their position, as will you. I know you better than you know yourself. Your compulsions. Your obsessive need to systematize chaos. You were mine before you took your first breath, and you'll be mine as you take your last. Your place is at my feet, Ms. Renfield. You will come to see that and even crave it. And you will never, ever give me orders."

"Newsflash: I'd rather dive headfirst into that pit and die with my siblings than be a bug-eating foot servant to you."

A flash of something—shock? Alarm?—flits through his eyes before it's gone. His lips curve into a cold smile. "Nevertheless."

My eyes fall on a battle-axe mounted on the wall—medieval and heavy with a wickedly curved blade on one side and a spike on the other. I wrench it free and rush to the trapdoor. I manage to lift it over my head and bring it down with a mighty blow. The wood cracks. With a grunt and every ounce of strength I possess, I lever it upward again and bring it down. I then pry open a bit of the floor. Another bit comes up.

Brute force—that was the key!

Alexandru mutters something about somebody named Gregor having to fix the damage I'm causing, but for whatever reason, he isn't stopping me. I shove it aside and peer down through the hole.

Three faces peer up at me, barely visible in the gloom.

"Help us, Harriet! Magda's unconscious!" Irina calls, her voice echoing up from the depths. "She's breathing, but..."

"My leg might be broken," Stefan says, alarm in his voice. "There are bones down here, Harriet. Human skulls." He lowers his voice. "Hundreds."

"Okay. Hang in there." I wasn't there for my little brother, but I can be here for these three strangers who share my blood.

But how?

Alexandru is clearly supernatural. I saw what I saw, and being that he lives in Castle Dracul, I'm going with vampire.

Could I take Alexandru's head clean off? That's how you kill vampires, right? He seems to be giving me a lot of leeway now, maybe learning my ways, but I'm guessing if I did become a threat to him, he'd pull out the supernatural speed and strength.

I glare at him, and that's when I catch it again—the flicker in his eyes. Not anger or amusement.

It's alarm.

Does he think I'll fall in? Does he think I'll *jump*?

Does he need me, somehow? My forebears apparently served him for generations. Is there some symbiotic relationship happening here? A dependency?

I edge closer to the pit, feeling the cool draft rising from below. "Goodbye, Count Fangfiction. Headfirst ought to do it, right?"

"You *will not* jump." His voice resonates with centuries of authority.

"Live free or die."

He steps closer, voice dropping dangerously. "Do not be foolish."

I move close enough that the tips of my boots are over the edge. "I'll be as foolish as I wanna be."

Fear flashes across his face. Yes.

I bend my knees and make prayer hands over my head, like I might actually dive. I'm my own hostage—the one screaming *and* the one holding the detonator. "Clear the way below!"

"Stop!" he commands.

"If you want me to stop, you'll have to offer me something."

His eyes sharpen with interest. "What would that be? Money? Gowns?"

Gowns?

"You will let them out and help get them medical attention. The kind that doesn't involve fangs. Like regular human medical attention of their choice." I've dealt with enough tricky tech bros on Serena's behalf to know I need to close all loopholes.

"And you will agree to be my servant?"

I cross my arms, straining for sounds from below. "I might consider doing a few things to help you out if you let them free."

"I require more than a few things. You will be my servant. We will write a contract, and it will be binding."

He's definitely fixated on the servant thing, and his bargaining position—namely, my siblings trapped in a bone pit inside a murder castle—is quite strong.

"What exactly does servitude to Alexandru Miramonte involve?"

Something ancient and hungry sparks in his eyes. "Managing my business affairs and real estate holdings."

"That's what my father did?"

"Yes."

I'm thinking about his ledgers—not the tall, mystical ones, but the plain old office kind, crammed with numbers, addresses, and accounts. The non-weird ones. So that's what he'd been doing: running this guy's business the old-fashioned way.

An idea is starting to form in my mind here. "Would I have to use his whole ledger system? What if I had something superior?"

"You would be free to establish your own superior ledger system, as long as it is truly superior."

"What if I wanted to establish an entirely new system?"

He looks baffled. "Why would you want to do that?"

"Because it's the twenty-first century and they've invented more modern forms of ledgers. More effective and vastly superior. Doesn't that sound good to you?"

"As long as you manage my affairs effectively, I hardly care what manner of ledger you use."

"And efficiently, of course. You want efficiency, right?"

"Of course I want efficiency," he says, annoyed.

I could digitize everything and probably accomplish in twenty minutes what he did in a week. I could even hire it out to somebody on Fiverr.

I try to hide how worried I am about my newfound family. Men like Alexandru use that sort of thing. "Do I get paid for this servitude?" I ask.

"As my servant, you will have no need for money. You would have all you require right here."

"What if I didn't want to stay here? I have a home back in Ohio, and I could easily run your business empire from there."

He looks at me as if I've just proposed that penguins should drive taxis. "From Ohio? In the *Americas*?"

"Yes, in the *Americas.*"

"Your father made the journey to the post office in town once—sometimes twice—a day," he informs me, as if this is a cornerstone of modern logistics. "How exactly would you propose to manage that from across the ocean?"

I blink. Does he not know about computers?

He studies my eyes, all arrogance and ancient power. "Would you have bank correspondence and notarized contracts flown across continents in aeroplanes?" He pronounces the O in aeroplanes. "And what of truly important documents—would you entrust these to couriers whose names you do not know, whose loyalties have not been tested?"

"Uh..." I'm not quite sure how to answer this question. It's not the argument that's baffling me—it's the entire century he seems to be operating in.

His gaze deepens. He seems to think that he's winning this point. My god. He doesn't know... *so much.*

He lowers his voice to a hot whisper. "Or perhaps you would tie the scrolls to the throats of carrier pigeons? And what of the translators? The local scribes? The tenants in my vast real estate empires? Would you manage them from a parlor in Ohio, with a spyglass in one hand and a ledger balanced on your knees?"

"A spyglass..."

"You see my point, of course."

"Oh, I do." Though it's not the point he wants me to see.

He fixes me with a look, dark eyes dazzling as starlight. "And how, precisely, would you access the archives here in the castle? Reach for them through the mirror?"

Never did a man spout such utter nonsense in such a very compelling way. Is it possible my father managed a modern business empire with 1940s tools?

"Did my father ever try to modernize things like... do you have a computer here?"

"Your father had no need of a computer."

"Do you guys even have a phone? Did he ever get mail and look at files over a phone?"

"Your father was a bit addled toward the end, but he was not stupid," Alexandru bites out. "He knew the difference between a telephone and a crystal ball."

What the hell? "Can you describe your phone? Does it by any chance have a thing you put to your ear and a circle with numbers on the face of it?"

"I believe so. Have you not seen a phone?"

Yes, I think. *In museums and Instagram photos captioned "vintage vibes."*

"Fine. Here is the deal I'd like to make with you. I will manage your business affairs vastly better than my father ever did... once my brother and two sisters are safely on their way to the nearest city for medical attention."

"From here in my castle."

I smile. "I'll do you one better. I will position myself in such a way that communications are carried out even faster than my father could manage. I will work with your translators and scribes more closely than he ever did, checking in with them more frequently. There will be no carrier pigeons and no air-o-planes. I will make sure everything's at my fingertips—all the files. All the correspondence. I will hold your bankers to the highest standards, and I will use only the best modern tools. I will organize things so that I can find them right away."

"You shouldn't make promises you cannot deliver on, Ms. Renfield."

"Don't worry, Alexandru, I will deliver on my promises *so hard.*"

His eyes narrow. "Very well. We will draw up a contract establishing your duties. Then and only then will I allow your inferior kin to go free."

"I would be happy to sign a contract, and I would naturally

abide by my word and adhere faithfully to whatever is set forth in that contract down to the very letter, but how do I know you will?"

His lips curve in a cold smile. "A vampire is bound by his word."

So there it is. He's just saying it outright. *Hi, I'm a vampire.*

"You Renfields are bound by your word, too."

It's surprising that he would know this about me. The fact is, I'm meticulous about keeping promises and secrets and following terms I've signed on to. It's something of a compulsion.

I strain to hear any noise from the pit. I hope they can hear all this and understand that help is on the way. "Okay. Let's do this," I say.

"Come." He turns and strides across the floor.

I follow him down a candlelit corridor, talking myself into feeling positive about my chances of getting us all out of this alive.

He'll be good for his word—I have to believe that. And I draft contracts for Serena all the time, protecting her interests in a thousand little ways. I'm going to draw up a contract to end all contracts with this guy and get my siblings and me out of here.

"Your father demanded just such an agreement," he says.

"Interesting." I follow him up a winding stone staircase, each step worn in the middle from centuries of use. "So now that we're doing this, maybe you can tell me what those tall ledgers are all about."

"That is for you to divine."

"Why not just tell me? You said you'd tell me."

"Actually, I believe my words were, 'Don't you want to know what purpose they truly served?' I did not say I'd tell you."

"So you won't tell me?"

No answer.

"A hint?"

"In due time," he says breezily.

Chapter Six

Harriet

We reach the very top of the stairway—how high up are we? Maybe five stories?

He pushes open an ornate oak door inlaid with silver filigree, leading me into the most breathtaking library I've ever seen.

Thick Persian carpets cover the floor, and a roaring fire casts dancing shadows on walls lined with bookshelves filled with volumes of every shape and color that spiral up a hundred feet. Some of the spines glint with gold in the firelight. It's like one of those weirdly gorgeous libraries on Instagram that totally has to be fake.

Except this one is very real. I take a walk around, trailing my finger against ancient spines. The organization of the library is absolutely immaculate: books arranged not just chronologically but in concentric circles of knowledge—mathematics flowing into astronomy, mythology into religion, poetry into philosophy —a physical manifestation of how ideas connect across centuries.

"You act as though you've never seen a proper collection before," he says, watching me with those unnerving eyes. "Your father organized it for me, of course."

I feel a strange pull as I take it all in—not just to the majestic space, but to the kind of mind that would assemble such a collection.

I hate myself for it, but I guess even monsters have their charms.

"Let's just get this done," I snap.

Alexandru moves to a box and withdraws a parchment, handing it over with strong, elegant fingers. "This was the agreement between your father and me. You will copy it out onto a fresh scroll and modify it for our purposes. You will add a clause about setting your kin free in exchange for servitude. Their deaths en route to whatever medical facility they choose to visit, or deaths thereafter as a result of their wounds, will not alter the terms of this contract."

"How can this be my father's contract?" I point to the upper right corner of the aged paper. "The start date is 1921."

"As I said, your father served me for over a century. Your father was very long-lived."

"I met the man fifteen years ago. He didn't look a day over forty."

He shrugs. "He was born in 1893."

I stiffen. "Did you do something to him to make him... like you?"

He doesn't answer.

"What did you do to him?" I demand.

"It was your father's fondest wish to stay by my side as long as he possibly could."

"Not an answer."

He gives me a hard look. "What's more, he was respectful and deferential in his tone and manner, seeking always to please me. As you will learn to be."

Don't get your hopes up, I think.

Alexandru produces a blank scroll of bumpy, artisanal parchment paper that definitely belongs in a rustic farmhouse wedding. "You will copy the general framework, and we will make additions pertinent to our situation."

"Don't you think things would go better if you found somebody who actually wants this job? Why Renfields?"

"Renfields have a debt to pay."

"What kind of debt?"

"The kind that curses a despicable family to centuries of penance, and even that will never be enough."

There's clearly a story there, but wheedling it out of him won't free my siblings.

I sit at a sturdy old desk and smooth out the bumpy paper. "This was his desk?" I ask.

"Indeed."

I select the least freakishly ancient quill and start copying the old contract in my best cursive:

LET it be known that on this day, in full awareness and sound mind, the undersigned shall enter into a binding agreement, sworn in ink and intent...

"Do you ever run into problems working in the modern world?" I ask as I scribe. "If you have an actual modern business in this world, your things had to have been digitized at some point. Like, for instance, I would imagine Karsovian and Romanian tax documents have to be filed digitally. What if you have property in London or whatever?"

"Your father was not in the habit of bothering me with business minutiae."

I copy out the next line, wondering if these vast businesses of his are imaginary, somehow. But what does it matter? My siblings are in a pit.

"Did he ever say anything about PDFs?"

"Ah, yes, the PDF. It did seem to bedevil Renfield at times. He would sometimes have to go down to the village to meet a boy who would use some manner of contraption to transform papers into this PDF entity required by various tax professionals and certain associates in Bucharest."

"I'll be bypassing the boy. I will be handling PDFs on my own for you. How does that sound? Why trust some random boy with your business documents?"

He shrugs. "Anyone who dares to defy me will pay the price. This is something that is quite widely known. I'll have your father's old room remade for a female."

I nod, as if all this sounds reasonable. Years of managing Serena's executive whims have taught me well, though the stakes were never as high as this.

He makes me write out all of the duties he expects. I work as quickly as I can.

He has me add a somewhat bonkers clause stipulating that if I break this contract, he will hunt and kill my siblings, as well as everybody else in my life who is dear to me.

It all seems so surreal. This place. This man—a literal vampire.

And I'm agreeing to some pretty big things. But what choice do I have?

I make a theatrical production of negotiating my compensation, informing him that I have family members back home who I support, which is certainly true. I demand an allowance for Egyptian cotton sheets and Swedish furnishings. Each trivial demand serves its purpose: distractions that make him feel like he's winning while I quietly secure what actually matters—digitization of his holdings and the express stipulation that I work remotely.

I get to the tricky part. "I plan to use modern telecommunications to coordinate with your business partners—your bankers, vendors, renters, various regulatory and governmental entities. Do you have any objections to that?"

He settles himself into an elegant armchair. "As long as your methods are demonstrably superior to those that your father used."

"They are. It is my vision to upgrade your operations to rival those of the business centers of Zürich, Frankfurt, and Luxembourg."

Alexandru looks quite pleased at this. "If you're capable of doing such a thing, you will put that in."

I put it into the contract like a good little scribe.

"And of course this castle is very remote," I say to him. "I assume you'll insist that, since the castle is your center of operations, I shall also work remotely, as defined in modern business parlance."

Alexandru's perfect jawline tightens. Is he sensing a trick? He might be. Does he have some kind of vampiric lie detector ability? "Meaning what?" he asks.

"Remote work is an efficient way of using technology," I say, restricting myself to truthful statements. "You will agree this castle is quite remote."

His dark eyes flash with aristocratic disdain. He reminds me of a large, powerful jungle cat, annoyed by concerns he deems beneath him. "Of course, the castle is remote. A castle that's not remote is worth very little."

I nod, as if this is a perfectly coherent point. "So am I to understand that you'll demand that I work remotely? With the castle as your center of operations?"

"Yes, my castle is the center of operations. Did we not just settle matters regarding your bedroom? Your home here?!"

"So you insist I work remotely?"

"I will accept nothing less. You will put that in."

I school my features like he's just won a great concession. I make some demands about a view from my bedroom window, copy the rest of the language, and it's done.

He reads over the contract. "You forgot this last clause. The term of your service is your natural life or until you are unable to continue."

I swallow. I was hoping he wouldn't notice that I didn't add that in. "My natural life's a bit much. Could we start with ten years?"

"No, we will not start with ten years. You are my servant. You will handle my business and real estate holdings to the best of your abilities until you are no longer able. You will have seen to it by then that your line persists so that you will have a replacement ready for me, just as your father did."

"Wait a minute. Are you saying that part of servitude includes banging strange men on trains?"

"You will beget a new Renfield in whatever manner you deem expedient. But seeing to your own eventual replacement is non-negotiable, and failure to comply with this clause..."

"Yeah, yeah, tracking down and murdering me and everyone else and the horses they rode in on."

Annoyance clouds Alexandru's bold features. "There is no reason to kill the horses. The horses may live." He waves a hand in the air, signifying the generous reprieve of horses.

I don't love the idea of signing my name to a document containing this particular clause, which, let's face it, isn't too far off from promising my firstborn, but I'm keenly aware of my siblings in that pit while I sit here in library porn central. By the time I'm unable to serve him, maybe a nice little AI robot named Renfield will be the manner "most expedient." I imagine myself dressing the robot up in a little monocle and a top hat, just like Mr. Peanut.

I add a clause about letting my siblings out and immediately providing transportation and paying for said medical transport.

As soon as I deem them safe, I will prepare to start my "remote" work, which will definitely not take place in a remote castle.

I slide the contract over to Alexandru, who reads the thing with meticulous attention, still as a mountain, dark eyes scanning each clause.

I'll manage his holdings like a boss. I mean, sure, he's a deranged psychopath vampire, and all, but I don't sign a contract I don't mean to uphold.

"You will find that this modernization affords you greater leverage over your dominion," I say. "I have no doubt we can find ways to increase your wealth and power."

He seems to like the sound of this. "You truly are the worthiest of the batch."

And with that, the contract is done.

He signs his name and dates it the Euro way, with the day before the month, while I sign my name and date it the American way. He then produces an ornate silver seal from a desk drawer and presses it into a pool of melted red wax at the bottom of the document.

The imprint is some kind of serpentine creature. Medieval and extra, just like him.

"It is done," he says with finality.

Chapter Seven

Alexandru

I stand at an arched window battered by centuries of Carpathian winters, watching Ms. Renfield load the inferior Renfields into the waiting truck. There are tears and hugs. She kisses the cheek of the unconscious one, hair glowing in the moonlight.

This empathy is unusual for a Renfield. Their line has always been selfish, if not downright mercenary. Her father would've sold his own mother for a shiny new pen. I respected that about him.

Could this show of caring for these half-wits whom she has only just met be some sort of trick? I did sense deception earlier, but Renfields are exceedingly crafty. It makes them excellent assistants, but one has to take care with the tiresome process of bringing them under control.

This one will be far more trouble—I can see that now—but she'll come to heel just as they all do. It's the Renfields' lot in life to serve me.

I reach for the leather-bound tome on the side table—Evliya Çelebi's *Seyahatnâme*, the Ottoman traveler's complete collection of maps—and settle into my favorite chair. I withdraw a silk bookmark from between its pages, the garnet bead at the end glinting like a drop of blood in the firelight.

The book falls open to where Çelebi describes the Wallachian lands I once ruled. I've corrected his errors in the margins over the centuries. Humans perceive so little of the world around them, but what need is there, really? They are simply food. Annoying, tiresome, and often inconvenient, but food.

The truck clatters down the mountainside. I hear the creak of the outer door, and then the softer creak of the inner door. Footsteps proceed across the ballroom to the stairway that leads to the more inhabited portions of the castle.

She hesitates briefly, then begins to walk up. Her father was petrified at this stage. He never really got rid of his fear, and he carried an odor of nervous sweat about him all the time.

This one is indeed nervous—I can smell it beneath the lavender soap she uses. But deeper than that is the essence of her—spun sugar with a note of vanilla, bright and sharp like winter air.

Not entirely displeasing.

She makes her way up, one flight and then the next, pausing on the torch-lit landing one floor below, heartbeat quickening. She continues her climb toward where I sit in the main library.

This library occupies the great turret at the eastern corner of the castle—an architectural indulgence that rises three full stories into the sky. Books line the inner walls from floor to ceiling in a spiraling lattice of dark wood and ironwork.

Her father kept his desk on the east side where the morning light came in. I can see him now, hunched over his work, moving furtively from ledger to ledger, muttering and scribbling and tugging at his hair, sometimes crying out in anguish, which stopped being entertaining long ago.

I prefer the fireside reading room, a low alcove off to the side of the turret where the sun cannot reach. The chairs are overstuffed, the rug worn soft by time, and low shelves flank a small hearth.

The door creaks as she enters.

I observe her unnoticed from my shadowy nook. The rugs muffle her footsteps as she crosses the threshold.

Her eyes sweep from shelf to shelf, taking inventory of the layout and filing system. She is assessing the room, and I am assessing her, my new servant.

Her clothing is modern and functional: dark trousers and a dark knit jacket, like a man's suit jacket, but softer and smaller. Her raven hair is pulled back from her face in two clips, revealing the elegant line of her cheekbone, the subtle bow of her red lips. There's a quiet confidence to her movements.

Finally, she approaches her father's work area. Her fingers whisper across the pages.

"What the hell," she breathes.

Her father would never have uttered such crass words within these walls, even as his mind fractured. He was reverent with his speech, his posture always bent in submission.

As Ms. Renfield soon will be.

"What the ever-freaking hell?"

"You will mind your tongue in this castle," I say, not raising my voice.

She nearly leaps from her skin, whirling around. These creatures. So easily startled. There's a slight relaxation in her stance when she finally spots me in my chair, its wooden arms carved with serpents.

"You scared me!"

"Questions?"

"Honestly? This is a pretty twisted way to get help. There's this thing called job boards?"

"That wasn't a question."

She meets my gaze without flinching. "Where's your phone?"

"Gregor will show you when he gets back from town. For now, you will get to work updating my accounts and correspondence and such things."

"Is Gregor that butler guy?"

"He is indeed that butler guy." I return to my book.

"You don't know where the phone is?"

"You will consult Gregor."

"No idea, then? On the phone?"

I give her a hard look.

"What?" she protests. "You asked me if I had any questions, and that's a question."

"And I told you it is for Gregor to assist you with trivialities."

Her lips part in surprise. Outrage, even.

I sigh. "One of your primary duties as my servant is to make a distinction between bothersome trivialities and questions of import. The bothersome trivialities are for you and Gregor to work out. Questions of import you may bring to me."

"God, I thought the tech bros in Ashwood were entitled," she mumbles.

I raise an eyebrow.

"Also, this *is* a question of import. A question of import from my perspective."

"Your perspective does not matter."

"Good grief," she breathes.

"You will speak with decorum at all times. Know that I can hear even the quietest whisper."

She whispers, "Can you hear this?"

"I can."

Another whisper, light as a feather: "Can you hear this?"

"Do you know why you're alive?" I ask.

She straightens. "You mean in a theological sense? As in, why are we here?"

"I meant, do you know why I don't just kill you and drink every ounce of your blood before returning to my book?"

"I knew what you meant."

"You are alive because it's more convenient to me than killing you and training one of the others. Your affinity for your father's work showed me you would be up to speed faster than the others in managing my business empire. But you are not the only choice. Once the inconvenience of you outweighs the convenience of you, you'll take your place in the Renfield graveyard decades ahead of time."

Her plump lips form into a frown.

"As for the theological sense of it," I continue. "Your kind is here to provide food for my kind. The lucky ones provide servitude."

"So lucky," she says.

I study her for a moment. "Do not test me."

"As I told you, I'll pull your empire into shape like a boss."

I nod my head. This I do not doubt. "In his first years of servitude, your father kept a small notebook where he recorded my preferences and the best ways to serve me. You will do the same."

"Yeah, I won't be doing that."

My voice goes cold as a winter grave. "This is not a suggestion."

She crosses her arms. "It wasn't in the contract, was it?"

"Following my commands is implied by the word *servitude*."

"Not to me," she retorts.

"Servitude," I say, "means obedience without hesitation. Presence without question. Anticipation of needs without prompting. It means knowing what I require before I have to say it. It means you are mine to command in all things."

"To me, servitude means precision. It means making systems that don't fail. It means turning chaos into results. I do not fawn. I do not flatter. I do not wait on anyone's moods. I solve problems. Efficiently—way more efficiently than anybody else you could get for this job."

"This is truly what the word *servitude* means to you?"

Her pulse skitters, because of course, she knows that is not what the word means.

I rise from my chair, and she has the good sense to shrink back. "You will follow the commands I give you. You will complete the tasks that I give you."

Her gaze flares.

"You will sort through your father's systems and bring my accounts up to date, and you will not bother me with trivialities."

"Or you'll drain me and throw my dried-out body in the graveyard?"

We're standing face to face. "As a last resort. In the meantime, there is a dungeon in this castle made for disobedient Renfields. There is no light. You will count grains of rice from a bag in the pitch-black darkness with only the spiders and rats to keep you company. I must warn you, your father was not a fan of this task. But he successfully completed it several times. Would you like to try your hand at it?"

Her expression lights with disgust. This Renfield is more animated than past ones, though it could just be I've become used to her father in his more recent stage, broken and subdued.

"Your most stubborn forebear lasted a full fifty-nine hours before begging to be let out."

She watches me for a few moments, steeling herself, but I can hear her heartbeat. I can feel her fear.

But what is she thinking? Her father's thoughts were always visible—anxiety that he might displease me, that I might punish him, that he would cease to be of use.

"That Renfield's voice was hoarse for days afterward. The screaming, you see. The walls are thick enough, luckily, that even I can barely hear it over the crackling of a nice fire."

Her gaze flicks out the window. I know what she's thinking now.

"Don't even think of attempting escape, or you'll see the Renfield dungeon sooner than later." I pick up my book and settle back into my chair. "Gregor will assist you with the phone. Bother me again at your own peril."

With a huff, she spins on her heel and stomps from the room, presumably to look for the phone herself. "Whatever you say, magic-erase neck."

I track her footsteps through the labyrinthine stairways and ancient corridors. My mind holds a perfect map of all six stories of this castle, my hearing acute enough to discern her location at all times. Her mutterings reach my ears with perfect clarity: "What the hell!" "Oh, great." "That's nice." These last phrases are in a tone suggesting she's found nothing nice or great at all.

I see potential in her—once she settles into her role.

It comes to me that she is a bit like Elisabeta—more so than all the rest of them.

I brush away the thought. If anything, her reminding me of Elisabeta will make it more pleasurable to kill her if and when the time comes.

Some minutes pass, and then I hear her exclaim, "Aha!" from the castle's kitchen, nestled between stone walls blackened by centuries of cooking fires. She has found the phone.

She mutters to herself. I hear the distinctive *click-click-click* as she spins the dial, followed by a frustrated sigh.

"Operator? Yes, I need to place a collect call to the United States." A pause. "Ohio. InovaSpire Incorporated in Ashwood."

She chats with whoever is on the other line in a hushed manner. I catch phrases like, "This phone has seen nine popes and the entire big band era..." "... funeral is a bit more comprehensive than I imagined..." "middle of the night here" "A ton of estate duties, let's just say..." "need a powerful satellite Internet connection sent... fast as humanly possible... small generator...guess an Amazon locker was too much to hope for, huh?"

She rustles around the kitchen, looking for food, I suppose. Then, "Thank you, Jesus!" followed by a period of silence.

She makes another call to somebody named Josie, who peppers her with questions about an inheritance. "I got something all right, yeah, a big freaking obligation. I know. I know. It's bananas." A pause. "No, I wouldn't say 'bad,' just... a shit show." Another pause. "No, I'm fine. I'll explain everything when I see you. Love you."

She'll explain things when she sees her? Does she think she can host tea parties here? The next call is different.

"Mom! Yeah? Great! Things are fine here—it's just taking a little longer to manage the affairs than I expected." Her voice is steady and bright with effort. "How's the store? Did the fridge keep humming? Any news on Granabelle's thing? Tell me, was it today or tomorrow?"

Another pause. Then, lightly: "Do you need me to arrange someone to help? One of Josie's cousins?"

She's soothing them.

Gregor returns at some point, and she ends the call, peppering him with questions about her newfound siblings and demanding the name of the hospital and the doctors' credentials. She asks him for her suitcase and a place to sleep, explaining that she's been awake for "a million hours at this point."

"I will ask the master," Gregor says.

"Why are you calling him that? You shouldn't call him that," she whispers sharply.

Their voices grow louder as they make their way toward the library. She seems obsessed with coffee—if we have it, where it's kept, and the process for making it, all of which Gregor explains patiently.

"Over the fire? You mean in the fireplace?" Her tone is

incredulous. "Wow. Okay." Then, "How long have you worked for Alexandru?"

"Five hundred and thirty-seven years," he says.

She gasps. "Are you a vampire?"

"No."

"But how can you live so long? Are you some kind of other thing?"

"Some things do not concern you," he hisses, voice tight and grim.

"Sorry."

They continue to the library in silence. Ms. Renfield comes right in and sets her hands on her hips.

Gregor hesitates at the threshold because, unlike Ms. Renfield, he has decorum. "Where shall the lady sleep?" he asks.

I set the book aside and rise from my chair. There will be little reading done before this one is settled. "Bring her bag to her father's bedroom. Come, Ms. Renfield."

"Not my name." Even so, she follows me through the corridors past portraits of forgotten nobles.

I push open a heavy oak door to reveal a sparse bedroom. A single bed with crisp linens sits against one wall. The rest of the space is dominated by a large writing desk positioned for optimal light from the narrow window.

"Your father's room, milady," Gregor says.

"Seriously, call me Harriet." She touches the desk and gazes out the window onto the mountainside, where the first fingers of dawn stretch over the valley. The forest below is still dark as ink.

She goes to the wardrobe—tall, dark, paneled in carved walnut. "So this was his life. All those years. This room. The ledgers. These..." She runs her hand over the sleeves of the suit.

Whereas her father was gaunt and haunted, always presenting himself with his trembling hands clasped together and his eyes downcast, she stands with a straight spine and a disconcertingly steady gaze. Her features are strong and solid, the set of her jaw hard, chin tipped up, and I find myself wondering if her chin-up stance is part of her pose of defiance, or if it's due to the way her glasses sometimes slide down her nose.

"Do you think he was... happy with this life? I mean, is this what he wanted?"

"The inner lives of Renfields are not my concern," I inform her.

Her outrage is evident even before she turns her hot glare to me.

"Question?" I ask, stepping into the room.

"How did he die?"

"He died as he lived, milady," Gregor says. "In service."

"What does that mean?"

"I mentioned needing a particular document from the archives in the village below—records of a property deed dating back to the seventeenth century." I run my fingers along the edge of his desk. "Your father insisted on retrieving it himself, despite the approaching storm. The village archivist warned him to wait until morning, but he knew that it would please me to receive it before dawn. The storm worsened on his return, and the mountain road collapsed in a landslide."

"Oh no," she whispers.

"Gregor and I found him half a mile from the castle gates, hanging on to life by a thread. His leg had been crushed, yet he had stubbornly dragged himself toward the castle, eager to fulfill his duty to his master."

"Oh my god," she whispers.

I pause, remembering the scent of Renfield's blood mingling with the rain, his breathing pathetically labored.

"Before his arms gave out, he had apparently crawled to a low, hollowed-out tree trunk. With the last of his strength, he fashioned a waterproof covering from his own clothing and positioned the document inside to keep it elevated from the mud. He used his final moments not to call for help, but to craft an arrow in the dirt beside him—made from twigs and stones—pointing toward the hiding place, in case he lost consciousness."

Her heartbeat quickens. I can feel her horror rise.

"His final words were an apology for a small bloodstain on the corner of the top page. Even as he bled to death on the mountainside, his concern was for the precision of his service."

"Wait—he was still alive? Did you call him a medical helicopter or something?"

"He would not have wanted that. What use would he have been to me with a crushed leg?"

"What *use*?"

"He begged to kiss my hand, which I allowed. And that was that. Gregor buried him in the Renfield cemetery behind the castle."

She adjusts her glasses, all the better to goggle at me with maximum disgust.

"He was exemplary," I say. "An excellent model for you to follow."

She hisses out a breath and turns from me, continuing with her exploration. She eventually reaches the far wall. She draws the curtain aside to reveal a large, dark glass pane. "He had a TV in here?" she asks, incredulous.

"It is not a television, Ms. Renfield."

She gasps. "This is full of ants!"

"Your late father's formicarium. It connects to a larger colony beneath the castle foundations," I explain. "He required sustenance during his midnight labors. He found flies and ants particularly nourishing. A family trait, I believe."

"You would believe wrong," she says. "Like, so wrong."

Gregor goes to her, ponytail clasped neatly at his nape, jacket buttoned all the way to his collar. "Milady." He bends to show her the intricately carved silver door set into the upper corner, complete with a tiny arched entryway and flying buttresses. A delicate filigree handle no larger than her pinky nail allows it to swing open on hinges that haven't tarnished in centuries. He points out how the air holes are punched in patterns resembling the castle's own windows.

"He was very proud of his formicarium," I inform her. "And now it's yours."

"Excited as I am about my very own insect buffet, is there maybe another bedroom available?"

"I tire of your obstinacy. This is your new room. This is your new life. The consequences of further resistance will be educational."

"As in, the dungeon?"

"Gregor will see to anything more that you need."

Chapter Eight

Alexandru

Ms. Renfield and Gregor busy themselves over the next couple of days, making constant trips to the town below and returning with boxes upon boxes, as well as bags of foodstuffs from the bakery and the local cheesemonger.

Contrary to modern myth, I do not sleep during the day, and sunlight won't kill me, though it does burn my skin quite painfully if I do not cover up. A suit, gloves, and a wide-brimmed hat typically do the job, though I prefer to pass the daylight hours indoors reading or contemplating.

This is not easy under the siege of Ms. Renfield's modernization campaign.

She comes to me occasionally to get my opinion on changes to my holdings.

"If I make recommendations—properties to sell, systems to consolidate—do I have your blessing?"

"If it results in increased wealth and power, then yes, you have my blessing. Tread carefully. I'll know if you make mistakes."

She tilts her head. "Do you... have some kind of mystical

connection to your assets? Like, how will you know if I screw up something? Not that I plan to. Just curious."

"I have a network of bankers and solicitors across the world, all eager to curry my favor. They'll point out your blunders."

"And then it's to the dungeon with me? For a heaping helping of screams and some rice counting?"

"You won't joke about it once you've spent time down there."

"I don't plan on ending up down there."

"No Renfield plans to end up down there," I reply, needling her.

She snorts, and an unexpected lightness ripples through my chest.

"So what are your powers, exactly?" she asks. "You can't read minds, I'm guessing."

I study the way the line of her cheekbone disappears beneath the frame of her glasses. "Is there something I should know?"

She smiles to cover a sudden jump of fear. "No."

So she's planning something. They always are. "What are you not telling me?"

"So you can tell *when* someone's hiding something, but not *what* it is?"

"I can smell fear. Deception. Lust. Jealousy. Joy. Rage. I know when someone lies. I know when someone's withholding, as you are right now."

"So, emotion but not content. You get the *vibe*. Could be anything. Maybe I forgot a scone in the kitchen and rats got it."

I shrug. The less she knows, the better.

"Do you sleep during the day?"

"These questions are tedious."

"As your manager of affairs, I need to know how to work with you."

"I am nocturnal. I do doze during daylight hours, but it's not a necessity, and no coffins are involved. What is noon to you is the middle of the night to me. Let's say it's not my preferred working time."

"You feel a little crabbins?"

I do not answer. I neither know nor care what crabbins means.

"What's up with Gregor?"

I turn a page. "You'd do well not to ask about Gregor."

"Are there others of your kind?" she asks.

Others of my kind.

I grip my book tightly. "That is not for you to bother yourself with."

"And you drink blood from people. That's your sustenance."

"Yes, people are my food. I have superior strength. I have superior eyesight. I was human once, a soldier. The sun will not kill me. Holy water will not kill me. I have no use for a coffin. Garlic will not ward me off."

"And can you turn into a bat?"

I simply gaze upon her, letting her feel the heat of my annoyance. "Truly? This is what you ask."

"I guess not."

I can feel something under the surface. A question she wants to ask. Maybe she wants to know what will kill me. I can feel her thinking about it... thinking about it... and letting it go.

She crosses her arms. "Okay, so, when you drink from someone... does it always kill them? Or can you stop and let them live?"

"Why would I have half a meal?"

"So... can you stop or not?"

"Why would I?"

"To spare a life?"

I laugh—low, sharp. "I am a hunter, Ms. Renfield. Humans are my prey. Can you imagine a lion taking dainty bites and

walking away? A wolf unhooking its teeth because the deer
begged?"

"Well, no—"

I step closer. The heat of her pulse blooms in the air
between us. "Does the crocodile, having gone through the
bother of dragging a child into the water, pause mid-bite to ask
the child's preference?"

Her face tightens. "But you're killing humans. It's
different."

"Not to me."

"You yourself were a human once, right? So it's a little bit
different. Why not spare them if you could?"

"Again, why would I have half a meal?"

She stares at me, disbelieving.

"It is called the circle of life, Ms. Renfield."

Chapter Nine

Harriet

That'll teach me to ask questions about his abilities.

Even though I have so many more. Does he appear in mirrors? Why does he seem to hate Renfields so much? What is this debt we are supposedly cursed with? And how good is his hearing? More specifically, can he hear my phone conversations? I've taken to scraping a spoon on the tiles while I speak on the phone, just in case.

I didn't train in finance, but I've backed InovaSpire's CFO through enough quarterly panics that he owes me—and I've collected. I've also pulled in a few outside resources. Irina even contributed some research.

A business empire is just another data set. You tame it, then you bend it to your will.

I just have to finish getting this set up and then get the hell out of here, for all the obvious reasons, but also because people at InovaSpire are starting to freak out.

Alexandru *has* to let me work remotely.

He signed the contract, after all. And from what I can gather, he's bound by it, somehow.

But I don't have to be a psychic to predict that he's not going to be happy when he finds out what he's signed.

I'm going to need a way out of here right after I tell him—a taxi that actually drives all the way up to the door and takes me right to the Suceava International Airport for a flight to Heathrow, and then a connecting flight home.

I thought about asking Gregor for a ride out of here, even if just to the train station, but I can't figure him out, honestly. He seems to be some sort of prisoner here, but he won't talk about it, and he doesn't want to leave—I asked him.

"Like, even if Alexandru said you could leave? You wouldn't want to leave even then?" I'd pressed him at one point. This line of questioning only seemed to upset him. All he'd divulge was that he was once the gatekeeper in some sort of village.

So he's preternaturally old, yet he eats food. But he doesn't like good food. He makes himself this weird gruel. When we went down to the village to get supplies, I stopped at a bakery and bought us some amazing scones, and he refused to even try one. Even though, when pressed, he admits he *could* eat such a thing.

Maybe it's some sort of Stockholm syndrome... I don't know. I've seen Alexandru having him do terrible, backbreaking chores. I'd love to be able to break him out of here, but I'm not going to do it against his will.

The tales of the special Renfield dungeon and the special Renfield cemetery did have me thinking about just making a run for it, but there is that pesky clause in the contract about him going after all of my relatives if I don't fulfill my part of it, and I could see him carrying it out.

As much as he seems like a fixture of this castle, I don't believe he's confined here. It's obvious he's traveled; there are objects and artifacts throughout the rooms from all over Europe, even parts of Asia.

His accent tells me he spent real time in England. Who

knows what he was doing there. Or maybe it was Saxony back then. How old *is* he, anyway?

I had always pictured vampires as cool, beautiful dolls with fangs, but there's a raw heat to Alexandru.

I can picture him in battle, chain mail stretched over sweaty arms, muscles coiled as he swings some wicked, black-iron sword.

And whatever you do, best not ask the man if he snacks, because he eats the whole person in one meal like a lion.

Anyway, he could easily travel around Europe, killing Irina, Magda, and Stefan.

I don't think he's been to North America, or as he calls it, "the Americas," which says everything I need to know. But I have no doubt he's fully capable of plane travel, especially considering he won't have to endure the embarrassment of pulling a coffin off a baggage carousel.

No, my plan can work. We signed a contract so I can manage his empire remotely.

It'll be fine.

Chapter Ten

Alexandru

An exceedingly unpleasant racket erupts just outside my chamber window one afternoon. I fling the shutters open to the blinding sunshine, fully prepared to demand silence, only to see Ms. Renfield perched on the east turret, dark hair whipping in the wind, barking orders at Gregor.

She balances on the narrow battlement—absurdly close to the drop—as the two of them attempt to secure some ungainly metal disc into the ancient stone. Likely another piece of her infernal "infrastructure."

A rope is tied around her waist, but it is not adequate. The knot is careless. Gregor should know better.

She leans out, tightening a bolt with a wrench, her voice brisk, her movements fast. No hesitation. No sense of scale or consequence.

She could fall.

I remain at the window longer than I intend, intensely annoyed.

Why should I care? There are other Renfields.

She glances up suddenly, as if she can feel my gaze. And

then—God help me—she waves. A flick of the hand. Utterly casual. Utterly unbothered.

I let the shutters fall shut with more force than necessary and return to my chair, but I find I can't settle. The clink of tools continues. Boots scrape against stone. Voices rise and fall. And that ridiculous rope.

Eventually, they retreat to the basement to install a generator—some humming, gasoline-reeking contraption.

The next day, she bursts into the library, cheeks flushed, a whirlwind of energy. "We're in business, baby!" she announces, waving a glowing rectangle above her head like a victorious general hoisting a captured banner.

"Am I to be impressed?"

"Oh yes," she says, grinning ear to ear. "I am going to blow your mind."

"Unlikely," I say.

Cheerfully, she presses on. With Gregor's help and several "Fiverr freelancers"—whatever that means—she begins what she calls "the great digitization" of my empire.

I stand in the doorway of the library, arms folded, watching her fingers move like spiders over the strange device.

"You expect me to entrust centuries of records—holdings, accounts, acquisitions—to this insignificant contraption?"

She doesn't look up. "Yup."

"What happens when it fails?"

"That's the beauty of it. Everything is backed up to the cloud."

I sigh. "You wish me to believe my affairs can be stored in vapor and mist?"

She pushes her glasses up her nose. "It's a network of secure servers. Multiple redundancies. If this laptop were destroyed right now, we'd lose nothing."

"I've seen empires rise and crumble, Ms. Renfield. Each believed their systems infallible."

"Well, what happens if a fire sweeps through the castle and burns all your paper records? What's your big plan for that?"

I smile faintly. "This castle is made of stone. It has withstood centuries of war and petty arson attempts from superstitious villagers."

"Yeah, well, you said I could modernize. It's in the contract."

"You are free to modernize as much as you like," I say. "I would only ask that you retain your father's ledgers, should your vapor and mist decide to vanish."

"Fine by me. But check this out." She turns the glowing square toward me. "Look at this spreadsheet of your European holdings."

"What is this? An electric ledger?"

"Yes! That's exactly what it is. An electronic ledger. It's called a spreadsheet. Everybody uses them now. The Bank of Romania, the London Stock Exchange—it's all spreadsheets. Electronic data."

She begins to click and tap.

"This whole sheet is just your London properties. But check this out—when I bring the rents up to market parity, which they are very much not at, this restructuring alone increases your annual revenue by thirty percent."

Numbers flash across the screen—columns shifting, totals recalculating. It happens so quickly, it's difficult to make sense of it all.

"See? Old rent." *Tap tap.* "New rent." *Tap tap tap.* "Old income. New income."

"It calculates the numbers *simultaneously*?"

"Yes! It's like having a hundred scribes—really good ones."

I frown. I do not sense deception from her, but it all seems outlandish.

"Tiny little scribes. Always there when you need them. They never sleep, never complain, never make mistakes. Guaranteed."

I narrow my eyes, intrigued. "Like scribes kept in a dungeon. And they know that anything less than precision means death."

Her smile falters. "Well... okay."

"And they are chained to the wall. Each one scratching ink across parchment with fingers worn to the bone. They write ceaselessly through the night."

"Yeah, sure!" she says, brightening. "Except the scribes are made of energy. Kind of."

I contemplate this. I've seen enough technological change in the ten-plus centuries I've walked this earth to know that progress can seem outlandish at first. And this Renfield is not delusional, that much I have gathered.

I ask to see the numbers once more. "Thirty percent is impressive."

Her pretty cheeks harden as though she's suppressing a smile.

"And they are willing to pay it."

She nods. "It's market rent."

"How did you divine market rent so quickly?"

"My... electronic ledger allows me to communicate with experts all over the world."

Such an increase in profit across all of my holdings would be nothing short of stunning. I nod my approval. "Carry on."

She and Gregor toil away at this digitization process, whatever that is.

On her fifth night at the castle, she appears at my study door clutching her electronic ledger, practically vibrating with excitement over some discovery among the American holdings—investments that have apparently sat untouched since the nineteen seventies. "Dormant!" she announces, as if this single word explains everything.

She should not have approached me without invitation. I should correct this breach immediately, but her eager expression and sparkling eyes suggest she knows something I need to hear.

"Just... dormant!" What I see gleaming in her eyes isn't simple joy—it's the predatory satisfaction of a hunter who has spotted fresh tracks. I find this pleasing.

"You will address this matter," I command.

"I will," she says. "I've already reached out to a new property management company. Your old one... I don't even know what to say. Your income is going to go through the roof, Alexandru!"

She should be proud of having served me well... so what is this nervousness I detect?

"And?" Her father had a habit of offering good news before presenting something I would not like.

"I've created a twelve-month projection, and I'm not even done getting everything shipshape, but..." She makes a mark on the glowing screen with the strange white pencil she sometimes uses and turns it to me. "Look who's going to pass the billionaire threshold. And that's in euros, Alexandru!"

I blink, surprised. "That is indeed impressive," I say.

"I'll say. And I have something else for you."

Again, I sense nervousness. Fear, even. Here is the bad news, then.

She reaches into her satchel and produces an electronic ledger much like her own and places it in front of me. "This is for you and Gregor. I've already shown Gregor how to use it. It's very simple." She opens the cover, and it emits a chime. Images arrange themselves on the screen. "Do you see this picture of an envelope? This is how I send messages to you and Gregor." She taps the screen, and the words *Hello, Alexandru Miramonte!* appear.

"Unsuitable. You will speak to me directly if you have a message."

"Okay, well, I'm super glad you said that because I have the perfect device for us to speak directly." She pulls a small block from her bag and lifts a cover. A glowing grid of numbers appears. "This is a Jitterbug phone. It's made to be super simple and will allow us to talk at any time, day or night."

"I will speak with you directly or not at all."

"But this *is* for speaking directly. Check it out—I'm going to go into the hallway and call you. When it makes a sound, I want you to lift the lid and press the green button. See what happens."

Before I can object, she vanishes.

Moments later, the infernal device begins to shriek. I crush it in my hand and toss it into the fire.

She returns seconds later. "Uh, there are toxic metals in that phone. You can't burn it!"

I raise an eyebrow.

"Never mind. I bought extras." Her heartbeat accelerates in full-on fear. "You're going to have to learn to use it."

"I will do no such thing."

"I suppose we could stick with the rotary phone for direct communication, but eventually you're going to have to learn this."

"Again, you will speak to me in person or not at all."

Her pulse spikes now. She sets down her electronic ledger and adjusts her glasses. "Actually, you *will* need to use it because I won't be in the castle." She shifts her posture, making herself as upright as possible. Armoring herself. "I'm going back to Ohio tomorrow."

I frown. "Is this a joke?"

She swallows, fear ratcheting higher. "Here's the thing—I'll be working remotely from now on. Per our contract."

"Here in the castle."

She pulls out the contract and unrolls it. "The contract stipulates here that I shall be doing remote work for you as defined by modern business parlance. Remember?"

"Because this castle is quite remote, as we established."

"But actually, remote work means I'll be working from my home in Ashwood, Ohio. I'll be telecommuting. As specified here."

"That is wrong," I say, pointing to the text of the contract. "You will work remotely, *with the castle as the center of operations.*"

"Yes, but remote means I will not be onsite. It means I will not be at the castle for my work." She wears a mask of outward calm, but her pulse bangs so hard I'm surprised the oil paintings haven't rattled right off the walls.

My voice drops to a deep register, deeper than the dungeon. "You will remain here, as specified in our agreement."

"Don't you see? Remote work means *working from a location other than* the center of operations. Which would be somewhere other than the castle."

I look down at the contract. A strange feeling flickers to life. Shock.

I stare at her in wonder.

"You dare to deceive me?"

She bites her lip.

When was the last time anyone had the audacity? The Renfields were too cowed. My enemies were too afraid. And yet this slip of a woman...

"There was no deception. It was a contractual negotiation," she says quickly. "It's not my fault you didn't look up the terms."

I surge to my feet, sending the baroque chair clattering across stone. "You deceived me."

She points at the document. "I wrote exactly what you dictated."

"You should have clarified," I snarl. "That is your duty as my servant."

"I wasn't your servant when I signed that contract. You should, you know, never sign a contract you don't understand."

My sense of shock deepens as the reality of the situation unfolds before me.

A Renfield has tricked me.

It's been centuries since anyone has gotten the best of me.

But a Renfield?

I could kill her now. Should. But the binding contract prevents me from harming her or her siblings as long as she upholds the terms.

"Do not think you will not pay for this," I say, my voice barely above a whisper. "And know this: if you fall short of what you have agreed to in our contract, the death of you and every one of your family members will be exceedingly slow and unimaginably unpleasant. And you, of course, will be last, because I will make you watch as I torture and kill them. I will be looking and waiting for you to fall short."

She does not flinch. She straightens up, in fact. "And now I'm going to perform my duties to the absolute best of my abilities—from Ohio. You're getting the highest quality help possible. Help that would not, on any level, be possible if I had to stay here. You're making out like a bandit."

I move toward her, unable to stop myself. The scent of her fills my lungs—lavender, vanilla, and the crisp bite of winter air. "Know this: you are alive because I am bound by a law older than the wind."

I can feel something rise up in her at this last part. Good god, is she going to argue about the age of the wind?

She backs away, but not as far as she should. "I will give you the best service possible," she says, voice quivering. "Isn't that what you want? I'll make you a rich man. You've never seen a Renfield like me."

She backs toward the door with measured steps, never breaking eye contact. Only when her hand finds the handle does she turn and stride away—purposeful, not panicked.

Chapter Eleven

Harriet

Josie Galindo swirls her champagne cocktail, processing my news. "My best friend has two new half sisters and a half brother?"

"Crazy, right?"

"Amazing," she says.

We're at Tres Hermanas, the wonderfully retro steak and seafood restaurant founded by Josie's great-grandparents in the 1930s.

The Galindos own half of downtown Ashwood, and Josie got elected as a councilperson last year. She'll be mayor someday, of that I have no doubt, cementing the Galindo power.

"And here you worried it would be a horsehair trinket or something," she says. "That is far better than money, don't you think?"

"For sure."

"Also? Data mining, a lawyer for Interpol, and the youngest-ever head of Special Collections at the Austrian National Library? You guys are like mutant high achievers."

Mutant *something*, I think, scooping up a blob of artichoke dip with a bit of French bread, remembering how the four of us attacked the chaos of that library like our lives depended on it.

I look up and find her staring at me. "Are you sure you're okay?"

"Just tired. It's been hard to catch up on everything."

This is not exactly true. I've barely slept in the week since I've been back. Running Alexandru's empire while working at InovaSpire is almost too much even for me. It doesn't help that I'm completely paranoid about not fulfilling the terms of the contract. I can feel him out there, just waiting for me to slip up.

Josie's mother, Rita, comes by, and I give her a hug. Rita has been like a second mother to me for as long as I can remember. I practically lived at their house for the months after James vanished.

"I'm so very sorry about your father," Rita says.

"I didn't really know him."

"Even so."

Josie urges me to tell her mother about Karsovia and meeting my half-siblings, and she's genuinely excited for me. "You should keep up with them. Family is everything."

"I plan to," I say. The truth.

Josie leans in once her mother's gone. "Did you learn anything about your dad? Or, you know, his condition?"

"You mean the bug eating?"

She winces. I'd told her about that after my first trip all those years ago. She immediately texted me three possible diagnoses and reassured me it probably wasn't genetic.

I take a long sip of my cocktail. "He was... older than he looked."

"Huh."

"And he had a boss," I add. "Someone he was very dedicated to."

She tilts her head. "His boss was at the memorial gathering?"

"Basically, yeah." I don't elaborate. I don't even know how I would.

Naturally, she senses I'm holding back something big.

"Like... a hot boss?"

"No! I mean, yes, technically he's hot, but he's not somebody you'd want to know."

Josie watches me too closely. "How come?"

I draw a deep breath. What am I supposed to say? Because he dropped my siblings into a pit of bones? Because I stabbed him clean through the neck with a sword, and he healed in real time because he's a *literal vampire?*

"Cone zone," she adds, because we dubbed this booth the "sacred cone of silence" booth, though somewhere along the way it got shortened to "cone zone."

I sigh. This booth has held so many of our big life moments, it might as well have a plaque. She told me about her engagement here. I told her about Serena's job offer here. We've fought, cried, made up, and made plans.

I want to tell her everything, but it all feels too dangerous. And would she even believe me?

I say, "He's kind of a jerk, is all."

She waits. Doesn't push.

"Okay, and don't be mad, but I agreed to help him manage his business affairs."

"What? You took on another job? To help out a jerk? Serena already runs you ragged."

"It won't be much. And I couldn't resist. I mean, my father had the man operating like it was 1949. You wouldn't believe it."

She watches me carefully. "You have no responsibility to your father's boss."

"Well, I agreed, so," I say. "I know what it sounds like, but it's under control. It was unavoidable."

"Was it, though? What kind of a jackass makes his employ-ee's grieving daughter take over her dead father's duties?"

"I'm not really grieving."

"He doesn't know that, does he?" She grabs a piece of bread and tears it in half.

❧

BACK AT HOME, Granabelle is standing on a stepladder under the chandelier display, striking a pose in an ankle-length velvet coat and feathered turban.

As usual, Mom is serving as her reluctant photographer.

"Oh, thank heavens," Granabelle says. "Lorna, give the girl the phone."

I put down my bag and take up photography duty. "The angle is a problem," I tell Granabelle. "You're not gonna like anything shot from this low an angle."

"But my head needs to be in the chandeliers," Granabelle says.

"Okay, okay." I snap the photos as she works it.

"Laverne DeRue can suck it," she says.

Laverne is her new over-seventy influencer enemy. "Laverne is like a fast-food chain," she opines. "Her success comes from being everywhere, not from having the juiciest burgers in town."

"Work it, Juicy!" I say. "Three more shots."

Granabelle makes it count; she opens her mouth wide and crinkles her eyes like she's having fun. She still has a huge scar on her forearm from where the runaway dirty dishes cart smashed into her during that suspicious wedding accident.

It pisses me off every time I see it. Who goes around deliber-ately causing accidents at weddings and hurting innocent people like that?

I get a couple of amazing shots and help her down.

Mom catches me up on how the roofing crew is progressing on the roof. They should be finished in a few days.

My phone pings, and I check it.

It's a text, a picture from Magda. We have a Renfield sibling group chat now, and I'm pleased to see that Magda's up in the Alps, beaming at the camera. When we were imprisoned, climbing this peak was something she promised herself to do if we ever got free.

I heart it and write, **Niiiiiiiice!**

Stefan writes words of encouragement. Irina is probably asleep by now. I told them most of what happened at the castle once I was safely back home. They were extremely relieved and kind of shocked at what I pulled off, and they all pledged their help.

"Did you hear?" Mom says. "Somebody's actually rehabbing Kingston Manor!"

"No. What? Really?"

"Really," Granabelle says. "Candace told me at mahjong."

I push my glasses up my nose. "Kingston Manor? How is that possible? And what is there even left to rehab? It's like a rotting playground for woodland creatures, and the backyard is a cliff."

Granabelle holds up her hands in surrender. "Someone's doing it. They've already rebuilt the entire foundation. Crews are there day and night."

I blink. I *have* been seeing a lot of cement trucks. "Did they actually look at it before purchasing it?"

"No shit," Mom says. "Some people have too much money."

"No clue who it is?" I say.

"You should try and find out from Josie," Mom says.

I give Mom a sly smile. She's in a decent mood today, which makes me happy. "I will find out and you'll be the first to know," I assure her.

We leave Granabelle in charge of the store and trudge

upstairs to the kitchen. I grab a bag of Bugles and pour some into a bowl for us. Mom takes one and leans on the counter. You can see the silver strands in her brown bob, which she parts severely to the side, a style I've always thought of as vaguely French.

"I live in fear of the day she gets in a real rumble with one of these online foes of hers," she says. "You don't know what these people are made of."

I pop a Bugle into my mouth. "Here's hoping they all stay behind their screens."

I update her on a situation with some rabbit tea towels she wanted me to order, and she updates me on sales. The first groups of tourists have been trickling into town, and our store sales numbers are starting to reflect that.

Mom catches me up on the latest gossip about the Jansons, the family that lives two doors down in one of the few Victorian houses that haven't yet been rehabbed.

Sally Janson wrecked Mom's book club some years back. It started with their scorched-earth disagreement about *Life of Pi*, which Sally constantly came back to month after month, no matter what book was under discussion. Mom finally stormed out.

Now Sally Janson serves as Mom's main source of schadenfreude, thanks to Sally's two adult sons: one living in Bangkok doing something sketchy involving webcams and cryptocurrency, and the other who has joined the local motorcycle club, the Snag Tooth Riders.

I listen to her, shaking my head, but I'm really thinking about Kingston Manor.

It's very Alexandru to buy a place like that, but I can't imagine him undertaking such a massive project without my knowing. I've got my fingers everywhere in his financials, and I'm in contact with the point people for all of his operations.

No way can it be him.

I text Josie to see if she knows. As an Ashwood councilperson, she sometimes gets insider info on building activities.

She has no idea.

Later that night, I do a deep and somewhat invasive scan of Alexandru's financial activity and poke around in his personal accounts.

Nothing.

There's just no way he could secretly pull this off.

It has to be some family I'll never know. They'll send their kids to one of the private schools in Creighton or all the way to Cleveland and run in circles with the town muckety-mucks.

Kingston Manor is one of the five original mansions that overlook Ashwood from the heights of Summit Place—a once-grand road carved into the bluff above Ashwood. The houses were built in the mid-1800s by river tycoons and timber barons. For a time, Summit Place was the pinnacle of the area.

Eventually, the river trade dried up. The families left, and the money left. The houses stayed.

By the 1970s, the area was all graffiti and squatters.

Then, in the late 1990s, Ashwood started a revitalization process. Boutique shops sprang up. Tourists started coming around. The mansions got snapped up and restored.

All except Kingston Manor.

In its day, Kingston Manor was the largest of the Summit Place mansions, perched highest on the bluff where the wind hit hardest, a grand Gothic residence with a wonderful spire.

Back in grade school, James, Josie, and I—and a rotating cast of equally brave or foolish town kids—used to sneak up to Kingston Manor. We'd slip through broken windows, climb rotting staircases, and scavenge for treasure. Once, I found a crystal the size of a plum from a long-gone chandelier. James pocketed a doll's hand. He said it was part of a haunted doll and tried to get Josie to trade it for her Snack Pack.

But then our friend Kenny fell through a floor and had to be rescued. A chainlink fence went up a week later.

None of us ever went back.

Kenny's accident happened the summer before James disappeared. They included Kingston Manor as one of the prime search areas, but he wasn't there.

He wasn't anywhere.

My mind goes back to Kingston Manor repeatedly in the following weeks, always with a sense of dread.

Really, is it so impossible that some normal person could look at that ruin and see beauty and want to pour money into it? I should be excited about this new stage in our little town's evolution.

Chapter Twelve

Alexandru

The man wanders along the river path, face lit from below by the glow of his phone. Mid-thirties. Soft body, soft hoodie emblazoned with some form of insignia, things stuffed in his ears making him more defenseless than he already is.

I follow from a distance. He would not hear me even if I clapped. The path he follows winds past benches and plaques.

A breeze comes off the river, wet and metallic. The man veers off the main path onto a smaller, gravel-cut spur, toward a thicket where the river bulges inward. He's done this before, I think.

He doesn't notice me until I am too close. He spins around. "Why are you following me?"

I do not answer. The answer is in my face. He turns and takes off at a run, dropping his phone.

There's a rhythm in the chase that reminds me of another life. Hooves pounding. Wolves howling.

I reach him without much effort.

"Wait—"

I press two fingers to his lips, and he shivers. Not from the cold; from the knowing.

I sink my fangs into his warm neck and drink, draining him completely, relishing the sense of calm and weight and something like gravity anchoring me again. I drink until there's nothing left in his veins.

Fifteen minutes, maybe twenty, and I cast his body into the river and watch it get carried off in the rushing waters, fierce from the northern snowmelt.

I step back onto the path and walk toward the town square, the lights from old-fashioned lampposts blooming like low stars between the trees.

Chapter Thirteen

Harriet

I settle into my new life as a ridiculously busy and under-duress person. It's April now, two months since I left Karsovia. The trees are budding, and the days are getting longer. Summer will be here soon.

I wake before sunrise on weekday mornings to bike the dark path along the Silverton River to the InovaSpire offices.

Mom hates that I bike there. A tourist went missing last week. He was staying at one of the Airbnbs and went out for a vape and never came back.

The going theory is that he fell into the Silverton River and drowned. The current's so high this time of year, he'd be swept out to Lake Erie by now. But Mom worries that there could be a more sinister explanation.

InovaSpire occupies the coveted top floor of The Foundry, a high-end refurbished warehouse in Creighton, the town just up the river from Ashwood.

The building is generally dark when I get there, aside from whatever lower-floor startup is pulling an overnighter. Serena would never make us do that. She says if your team has to work all night, you're under-resourced.

It's a gorgeous space to work in, all exposed brick, glass walls, and floor-to-ceiling views of the Silverton River.

Photographs from Serena's travels are displayed all along the walls because, of course, she's an accomplished photographer on top of everything else—a true Renaissance woman. Up top, there's a pretty rooftop patio where she and I love to eat lunch and brainstorm.

It's an obnoxious time to be at work, but pre-dawn in Ohio is midday in the EU, which makes it the perfect time to manage the bonkers amount of red tape involved in taking over and running Alexandru's empire.

And by bonkers, I mean bonkers.

The process of establishing myself as the decision-maker across five banking systems, rewriting medieval power-of-attorney forms, and digitizing Alexandru's minor holdings has been outrageous.

And I'm paranoid about slipping up, so it all takes extra long because I'm double-checking almost everything. I can just feel him back there in that castle, monitoring my progress. Every banker and broker I'm dealing with right now could be reporting back to him.

He was so angry at being bested.

Sometimes, when I'm lying awake in the middle of the night, I wonder if it was selfish to have tricked him like I did just to get out of there. If I'd stayed and followed his rules, the entire world of people I loved wouldn't be at risk.

Though Alexandru is nocturnal and therefore *does* share waking hours with me, he refuses to use the phone or tablet I gave him, let alone Zoom. So Gregor becomes our intermediary, getting Alexandru's signature when needed, though I suspect he DocuSigns for Alexandru here and there.

Gregor has become pretty good at technology. He's even able to use Microsoft Word's annoying track changes update.

The master is displeased with the wording of Section 4.7.

The master wishes to know why the Holland property is flagged orange.

The master requests clarification on the term "favorable easement."

Little by little, I get things under control.

I hope.

Sometimes things seem very much out of control, and I have to remind myself that I'm doing the job perfectly. I'm fulfilling the contract perfectly. He can't hurt me or my people as long as I keep my end up.

So I continue coming in early. I work both jobs.

It's not like Serena would mind me using company Wi-Fi and other resources for a side project. She's all about surrounding herself with high achievers, and a lot of us have side projects.

But one day, she calls me on it.

It's lunchtime, and I'm spending mine juggling three client calls and a missing order of register tape for the antique store when she stops by my office. "Soooo... the access log has you coming in at 3:30 a.m. for the last few weeks."

"Yeah," I say. "It's EU stuff."

She gives me a strange look. "You running an EU startup I don't know about?"

"No, I would never!" I laugh. "No, it's just... helping out my late father's boss. His systems were from the Stone Age. You wouldn't believe it." She literally wouldn't, so I don't bother going into the details.

"That's really thoughtful of you," she says. "Just don't overdo it."

"For sure! Once I get this guy's EU systems settled, I'm gonna help him delegate it."

Serena nods her approval. She's big on delegation. "By the way, that app contract? Legal had zero changes, and it was so perfectly strategic. Very 3D chess."

"Thanks, boss," I say.

She sticks a pen in her bun. "I mean it about overdoing it. You could tip into burnout at this pace."

Too late for that.

Chapter Fourteen

Harriet

I can't stop staring at Kingston Manor. I can just make out the spire from my bedroom window. It looks intact. Like they've rebuilt it.

I grab my phone and text Josie to see what she knows.

Any word yet who bought Kingston Manor?
Like WTF they're REHABBING IT????

sooooo weird. I think they're doing a pretty good job tho they have some really high-end woodworkers re-creating some of the original parlor off-site. They redid the entire foundation. Owners are an LLC out of Delaware.

ME: A company? What are they using it for?

Permits are residential. Apparently, they plan to live in it??

Have they seen the place? Are they aware that their backyard is a literal cliff?

LOL no idea. Dave Skelly's doing some consulting—you know he's all up in the historical society and he says they're going all out right down to getting window casements handcrafted to match old photos. Crews around the clock. Electricians out of Creighton getting overtime up the wazoo. Unlimited funds, elite crews. $$$$$

They could've torn it down and rebuilt for so much less money.

It's a good thing for the town to preserve the history

History of squalor

LOLOLOL

I take a deep breath. Of course, it's good for the town. I don't know why I have such a negative feeling about it.

The owners... just nothing?

No. Nobody has ever seen them

What's the trust name? Just curious........

A SERIES OF DOTS APPEARS, disappears, and then reappears. Finally, a text comes through.

They haven't filed with town hall yet so...

NM!! I was just curious. It's no big thing. I totally respect your councilperson cone of silence.

&

Work on Kingston Manor continues at an impressive pace. The new thing now is tradespeople smuggling out pictures—hasty shots of chandeliers, carved ceiling roses, ancient stone basins restored to showroom perfection.

The pictures get sent around on group chats. The money being poured into the project is just shocking.

Granabelle thinks I should turn my true crime forum friends loose on the mysterious building project.

Not likely.

I'm still stinging from their smackdown over my wedding sabotage theory, which, for the record, I still a hundred percent believe.

I'm not stupid. I know that people think I'm obsessed with spreadsheets and with tracking crimes on spreadsheets because of what happened to James. Because of the trauma and the guilt that I hold from it.

Yes, I feel guilty. If I hadn't selfishly run across the street to see a boy at the ice cream shop, leaving James to play by himself, he might still be around today.

But it doesn't make the patterns that I see less obvious.

And I'm *not*, as a therapist once speculated, using spreadsheets as an attempt to control an uncontrollable world.

And yes, I also understand why people side-eye my wedding serial killer theory, especially when they find out my grandmother was injured in one of the less serious accidents.

I get how it looks.

But I can't help it. I can't unsee it!

One of the few good things to come out of my time at that castle was meeting siblings who are all about bringing order to chaos, just like me. I felt seen.

The only other person who ever really appreciated it is Serena.

And maybe Alexandru, but he doesn't count.

Chapter Fifteen

Harriet

I forget about the Kingston Manor mystery until that weekend, when I stop by Aster Press to restock our vintage-style recipe cards. The bell over the door gives its usual chime.

Sloane is boxing up an order for a customer, nestling it in brown tissue. There's a silver tray on the counter holding her business cards, printed with her basement offset press:

Aster Press

*Letterpress * Archival * No pixels.*

I study the front of the *Ashwood Gazette*. There's an article about the gazebo roof repair, and the tourist who went missing on the riverwalk earlier this month.

They still haven't found his body.

Sloane drifts over. Her lipstick is matte plum, and her hair is pinned in an elegant, slightly menacing updo.

"How are you, Harriet?" Her voice drips with theatrical concern.

"I'm well," I reply with sweetness. "But how are *you*? Hanging in there?"

The corner of her mouth ticks up in that familiar half-smile that acknowledges our game.

We were good friends before the great Ashwood High newspaper fallout. Now we just do this weird thing where we pretend we don't hate each other. A cold war is better than a hot war.

"We need more of those recipe cards printed," I say. "Granabelle wants a new size added, and she'd like to do some more of those cherub postcard packs on consignment if you've got extras." I slide the list across the counter. Sloane has a website, but people who order the analog way get a discount.

"Postcards are selling like hotcakes," she says, moving to the register. "People are really moving back to the good old U.S. Postal Service. Who knew texts and emails would turn out to be so soulless? Right?"

This dig is aimed at me, Ms. Digital everything.

"All in the eye of the beholder, I guess." I slide a fifty across the scratched glass counter.

"Or not." She grabs the fifty and looks up our tax number in the little notebook she keeps by the cash register.

I examine a postcard from the display—an illustration of a paddleboat with a woman in a hoop skirt watching from shore. "These'll sell to the river-walkers."

"Yup," Sloane says. "Can't believe Easter's next week."

Easter is the unofficial start of tourist season. People in Ashwood tend to be divided on the subject of tourists. The boosters—like Mom, Granabelle, Sloane, and Josie's family— love them for the retail and restaurant traffic. But if you're just trying to live and work, you start to dread the summers.

"So," Sloane says, boxing up a set of cherub postcards with surgical precision, "the new owner of Kingston Manor stopped in yesterday evening to place an order."

"Really," I say too quickly.

"Very interesting." She doesn't elaborate, of course. She wants me to ask. She wants me to beg.

I try not to look interested. I try not to *be* interested. I want to ignore her dangling bait and leave, but Mom and Granabelle would be delighted with some news of our mysterious new Richie Rich family, and Sloane knows it. And I need to know, too.

"Interesting, huh?" I say.

"Very." She folds the top of the bag and smiles.

"Okay, come on. What were they like? Is it a family or something? I understand they're from the East Coast."

"It was the man of the house, and he loved the store. Ordered custom calling cards in a heavy cotton stock. His taste is exquisite."

This is so evil of her. Who cares what he ordered?

"And?" I prod.

"He appreciated the samples I showed him from the offset press and was very pleased to hear I could do his entire order like that. He went with the Claude Garamond version of Garamond. Just his name."

"Sooo... what was he like? What does he do? Is there a whole family moving in? Will they live in Ohio year-round? Does he own some massive corporation or what?"

She drifts a finger along the silver edge of the business card tray. "I can't reveal a customer's private details or the contents of a printing order."

"You just told me he ordered calling cards with his name. Also, why would somebody do that?"

"He's clearly a history buff restoring the house to its original grandeur, and he no doubt understands that a calling card with just a name is the way it was done at the time the house was built. People would call on a house offering their card to the butler, and the butler would inquire whether the occupant was home, meaning whether the occupant wanted to see that person."

"Oh, I get it," I say. "I see why that kind of card would come in handy... if we lived in an Edith Wharton novel."

"We're done here." She hands me the order.

I text Josie about these latest developments.

New owner of Kingston spotted. You will NOT believe where...

Sloane's shop. Last night.

He ordered calling cards with just his name, but she won't tell me what it is.

Three dots appear. Disappear. Reappear.

Calling Cards WTF.

I send her the steam-from-nose emoji and tuck my phone away, already planning how to drop this into conversation with Mom and Granabelle later.

I don't love this new information. Alexandru is living in the past. Would he order calling cards? But then again, who would he visit? He despises humans.

For socialization purposes, anyway.

Chapter Sixteen

Harriet

I tell Mom and Granabelle about the rich history buff who bought Kingston Manor.

"This calls for breaking out the Wharton whites," Granabelle declares.

Before I can protest, she's clambering downstairs. She reappears a few minutes later in a full-length Edwardian walking suit—complete with gloves, a veiled hat, and a ridiculous feathered muff.

"My calling card, if you please," she announces, extending a napkin out between two fingers.

"Okay," I say, taking it.

Mom shakes her head darkly. "You look ridiculous."

"It's a great theme," Granabelle protests. "I'm gonna get a lot of mileage out of it. I wonder if the new owner will let me do a shoot at the place."

I grab the potatoes. "That would be quite the get, Granabelle!"

Mom spears a cherry tomato. "For Christ's sake. They're rehabbing a historic mansion. You'd think they'd at least stop into the local antique store for a few pieces to match the period. But he gets useless calling cards instead?"

Granabelle sets aside her giant hat. "We've got half a dozen Eastlake chairs that would be perfect in there. And the Hepplewhite sideboard in the back room. That thing belongs in a house like that. I wouldn't be surprised if it came from that house."

"No kidding," Mom says. "Maybe try interacting with the community that you're moving into. The one thing he gets is calling cards? With just his name? What the hell is that?"

Granabelle laughs. "Some people really are ridiculous."

The next bit of news about our mysterious new resident comes as I'm leaving work that Friday afternoon. A text from Josie lights up my screen:

> Got it on good authority: Kingston Manor guy reserved a table for two tonight at the Stag. Soooo… I reserved us a table too. Same time. 😈

I laugh. The restaurant mafia strikes again.

> You're shameless.

> That's why you love me.

We get there fifteen minutes early and settle into a comfy booth. The Golden Stag Supper Club's interior is all polished wood and old chandeliers, leather booths and historic photos of Ashwood's glory days on the walls. Luckily, in spite of the name, there are no animal heads on the walls.

We order drinks, and Josie promptly informs me of another piece of gossip: Sloane has been telling everybody that the new owner of Kingston Manor is a prince.

Something twists in my gut. A prince means a European.

"What's wrong? Something against princes?"

"Not all of them." I've already got my phone out. I'm

looking for the place where I stored Alexandru's giant, long freaking title, aka his full dynastic name.

I finally find it. His Serene Highness Alexandru Ilie of the House Dracul, Princeps of the Ancient Line of Vânători, Sovereign Heir to the Principality of Karsovia, Lord Protector of the Eastern Vale.

I don't see the word prince in there. Though there is princeps. I look it up and confirm that it doesn't mean prince—it means "leading figure."

Nevertheless, I have a really bad feeling. The waiter brings us our wine and I down half my glass.

That's when I feel the tiny hairs at the back of my neck prickling to attention.

The place falls silent. No more chatter. No more clinking silverware.

Josie leans in, eyes wide. She nods over my shoulder.

I turn.

It's him.

Alexandru.

He's following the host across the floor, moving with the grace of an apex predator. His dark hair gleams under the soft overhead lights.

His black three-piece suit fits him like a second skin, and his tie is the color of blood.

Every eye in the place is on him. Alexandru Miramonte, Kingston Manor's new owner, with Gregor following dutifully in his wake.

My heart falls through the floor.

He sits and takes a menu. Then and only then does he turn and meet my gaze. He inclines his head in a nod.

No. This can't be happening.

He's here.

In my town.

In my life.

The man who kills without compunction. The man who smiled when I drove a knife into his neck.

Josie whistles low. "That is some definite princely action over there. If I weren't happily married..."

"No," I say under my breath. "He's... bad news, Josie."

She blinks at me. "You know him?"

"He's my late father's boss."

"The boss stuck in the Stone Age?"

I nod.

She slides a glance over to where a waiter is chatting with the two of them. "More like stuck in the stone-cold-fox age."

I stare down at my shiny white plate. This is not happening.

"Are you going to say hi?"

"I don't know."

"Who's his sad sack friend?" she asks. "Do you know him, too?"

How to explain...

"He's coming!" she whispers. "Red alert."

No, I think. No, no, no.

And then he's there at our table, his presence unmistakable as a thunderstorm. "Ms. Renfield," he says, voice low and resonant.

"Alexandru." I look up, praying my voice doesn't shake. "What a surprise."

"And this must be Josie."

Panic skitters under my skin. How does he know? I don't want Alexandru anywhere near Josie. I don't want him near *anybody*.

But she's waiting. No way can I get out of this.

I straighten. Glare at him. "Josie, this is Alexandru. My late father's boss."

Somehow, he has her hand in his and gives a regal nod over it before letting it go.

"I've heard all about you and your whole..." She trails off, clearly remembering the string of unprintable words I used to describe his archaic record-keeping. "...system update project."

"It's quite the thing," he says charmingly.

"Quite the thing," I say, heart pounding so violently in my chest, it's a wonder my rib cage doesn't crack. And of course, he hears it.

But he doesn't look at me. Instead, he's smiling at Josie. And she's charmed.

Nooooo! I think. *Don't be taken in. He sees you as food. He would eat your face given half a chance.*

"Ms. Renfield has been extremely helpful to me," he says.

"Ms. Renfield is amazing," she says with a mischievous glance that tells me I'll be explaining why the hell he calls me Ms. Renfield later.

"I am amazing," I mumble.

Josie somehow tears her gaze away from Alexandru in order to put it on me, and she has a brand-new look now, one that could be described as: HOW COULD YOU NOT TELL ME HE IS A HOT PRINCE?

I swallow. "Alexandru, I don't understand. Kingston Manor? That's you? You love Karsovia."

"I do love Karsovia," he says, with a touch of theatrical sadness. "And the people there are wonderful. But you spoke so fondly of this town, and now I see why. It is... beautiful. And the people have been wonderful so far. Absolutely wonderful."

Ice rakes down my spine.

He's still talking—something about modernization and bringing his business interests into the twenty-first century—but all I can think about is the missing tourist.

I shove back my chair. "Excuse us for a second," I say to Josie. I don't wait for a response.

I seize Alexandru's arm and pull him from the table. He allows it, smirking, as though my distress amuses him for the moment. I try to stay focused on what I'm going to say, and how

I'm going to manage this new horror, and not the heat where my hand wraps around muscle, hard and immovable, like something forged for battle.

We end up in a shadowed alcove near the coat racks.

"Did you take that tourist?" I whisper.

A smile curls at the edges of his mouth. "Define *take*."

My throat tightens. "Did you drain him? Are his body parts in your basement?"

"Oh, no," he says. "The rest of him is long gone down the river."

My stomach turns. "You killed him."

He tilts his head slightly, like I'm asking a math problem that's beneath him. "I believe I explained the process to you once before."

"You can't kill people!" I whisper-yell.

"Can't I?" he says, voice low and cool.

"You have to leave. You can't stay here. You can't... hunt here."

He steps closer. The air seems to condense around him. "I don't recall anything in the contract that prohibits me from residing—or feeding—wherever I please. You chose Ashwood. And now, so have I."

"Look, I can't let you kill people. You can't."

He tips his head. "And how precisely will you stop me, I wonder?"

"Alexandru, these are my friends, my neighbors. They aren't livestock!"

"Livestock is in the eye of the beholder, wouldn't you agree?"

"Hell, no, I wouldn't agree!" I put my hands over my face, totally smearing my glasses. "Oh my god."

He leans in, his voice dropping to a whisper. "You cannot stop me. I have chosen to come here. And it will be here that you will serve me. It will be here that I will take my meals." His gaze drifts toward the dining room—toward the warm, laughing humans. "I find the people of Ashwood to be delightfully unwary," he continues. "Back home, they were paranoid. Always walking in pairs. Slinking away from me the moment I set foot in the village. Do you know that I had to travel a hundred miles to get a good tailor?"

I grab his jacket front and shove him, but of course, he doesn't move. He's like a wall of muscle under my hands.

And now we're close. Way too close.

His eyes sparkle down at me, bright and cruel, the color of rich coffee.

"You can't be killing people in my backyard."

"But it's such a lovely backyard. If I'd known about it before, I would've relocated years ago."

"You will not touch any of these people."

His voice drops to a level that makes my blood run cold. "You'd be wise to make that the very last command you ever give me."

"Or what? Do you have a Renfield rice-counting pit in your new house?"

His words are a feather on my lips. "You should be thankful that I'm not slaughtering everybody in sight after your trickery."

I swallow hard and step back.

"Okay, look, what if I got you blood? Like... pig's blood? I've heard that's close to human blood."

He blinks once, lip curled with disgust.

"Okay, how about blood bank blood? Blood from a hospital or something."

"No."

"Can't you just try it?"

"There is no substitute for the living," he says. "I'll need another meal in just under two weeks, and we'll see who I pick."

"I'm going to stop you."

"How? Will you call the police?"

"Maybe I will. I know the police in this town. I'll tell everyone what you are and make it impossible for you to live here."

"Would they listen? Would they search Kingston Manor on your word? And what, really, would they find?"

I can already hear Maverick Cooper explaining probable cause to me. He thought I'd lost my mind when I came to him with the wedding killer theory. He'd never believe this.

Alexandru adjusts his beautiful jacket. "People have tried such things before. It never ends well. I understand they no longer favor insane asylums here, but people still know how to whisper." He leans in a fraction closer, and I back up, hitting the wall. "They know how to smile and pretend nothing's wrong. But every time you walk into a room, the conversation will cease. Every polite nod will carry a question. *Has she always been like this? How did we not see it sooner?*"

I drag in a breath, thick and unsteady. *How is this happening?*

"Screw it," I say under my breath. "I'll happily blow my life up to save somebody else's."

"Then do it," Alexandru murmurs. "Go. Tell them what I am."

I grit my teeth. He's right about what would happen if I raised the alarm. It would come to nothing, and he'd have more control over me than ever, because people would think I lost my mind.

"Speaking of friends, your Josie seemed sweet."

"I swear," I say, fists clenching, "you go near Josie, and I will stake you myself."

He raises his brows. "That I'd like to see."

"What? That's not how to kill you? What exactly *would* I have to do to kill you? Inquiring minds want to know."

"You? There is nothing you can do to kill me. Nothing whatsoever. I will hunt here in your Ohio, and you will serve me to the end of your days." He plants his hands on the wall on either side of me, boxing me in. "Your instructions are to bring your things to Kingston Manor. You will serve me there. I have prepared a bedroom for you."

"I have a room already. In my home."

"What's more, my agents inform me that you hold another job at a place known as InovaSpire. That is unacceptable. You are my servant. I do not share."

"I'm doing both jobs just fine. I'm managing your empire way better than my father ever did."

He straightens, casually adjusting his cuffs, the gesture so maddeningly civilized... it's not right. "I look forward to seeing you tomorrow. Seven sharp." With that, he turns and leaves.

Chapter Seventeen

Alexandru

The bell at the gate rings.

She has arrived at the appointed time, as I knew she would.

I don't need to be downstairs to know precisely how the scene unfolds: Gregor greets her with his slight, practiced bow, then ushers her into the great room. I track each footfall across marble, then wood, then marble again.

The pages whisper against each other as I close my book. Her steps falter below, and there's a quiet intake of breath.

Which detail has captured my crafty servant?

Maybe it's the banister, carved with writhing serpents.

Or the ancient tapestries depicting fantastical hunting scenes, lurid in their savagery.

Or the chandelier of wrought iron and crystal.

A whisper: "What the hell?"

I smile.

"This way, milady," Gregor says.

Two sets of footsteps ascend the curved staircase and then pause.

The door opens, and there she is at the threshold in her practical clothes, chin tilted up. A warrior's stance.

"Leave us, Gregor," I say.

Gregor recedes and closes the door.

I wait for Ms. Renfield to make sense of what she's seeing. "You've recreated your library."

I set aside my book. "It always was my favorite room."

She walks around, touching the books as she did last time. "I mean, exactly."

I stand. "Did Gregor take your luggage?"

"Nope."

"What was that?"

"That was a nope," she says. "Aka a *nope-a-reeno*."

"You were told to move in," I say.

"Okay, look. Here's the thing." She drags in a breath, gathering herself. Bracing.

I watch with mild curiosity. What desperate card will she play now?

"I understand you want me to live here," she says.

I lower my voice. "And live here you shall."

"Well... I don't know about that because the contract stipulates that my work shall be remote. Remote means anywhere that's not the center of operations. Thus, wherever you reside is the one place I contractually cannot work."

"Tread carefully, Ms. Renfield. I met a great many interesting people last night. I'm already hungry."

Her fury sparks, all righteous fire. This urge to champion her little villagers is so quaint, so hopelessly human.

I smile. "Have you given any more thought to how you would kill me?"

"Another day, perhaps. For now, I want to propose a deal. I will agree to an addendum in the contract, removing the remote work stipulation. Meaning, I will move in. I will be your most diligent onsite servant, living here and completing every task you require. No quiet quitting. No shenanigans. No complaints.

And I'll give notice at my other job and help my boss find my replacement."

I narrow my eyes. This feels a bit too easy. "And in return?"

She meets my eyes without flinching. "We hunt," she says. "Together."

Her request catches me off guard. Of all things— "Hunt?"

"Yes. Together."

"How would that work? Would you lure the villagers to me? Hold their arms while I tear open their throats?"

"No, I don't mean like that! I would help in the selection process, ensuring you wouldn't hunt and kill innocent people."

"You would choose my prey for me?"

"Sort of."

I nod. "I see. You want me to slay your enemies and your rivals."

"No! We would choose together. We would identify murderers and serial killers. They would be your prey."

"Murderers and serial killers..."

"Humans who prey on the weak for pleasure. We'd hunt them down using our wits. And you would be able to kill with the confidence that the person deserved it."

"That is hardly a concern of mine."

"You've been hunting the same way for years. Why not shake it up a little? You have this insight into people—super senses. You can smell fear and deception, right?"

"I can smell a lot of things," I tell her.

"And you have all kinds of other traits that make you an excellent sleuth."

"I am not a Swiss Army knife, Ms. Renfield. This sounds like a great deal of trouble for a meal."

"Have you ever heard the phrase 'like shooting fish in a barrel'? It refers to a form of hunting that requires no skill. This form of hunting requires skill."

"You believe this is something I'd prefer?"

She steps closer. I breathe in the scent of her—vanilla with that wintry bite. "You were a soldier once, weren't you? I'm thinking you were, and soldiers protect. They fight to save their people. Their homes. Their farms. What if you could do that again? Deep down, I bet that was important to you once."

"My life as a soldier is not a tale you would enjoy hearing."

"Fine, but think about what I'm proposing. You'd prey on predators who prey on the weak."

"You would have me cull the wolves," I say.

"Exactly," she breathes.

I tilt my head, studying her. "Preying on the weak makes the wolf pack stronger."

She lets out a frustrated breath. "Well, either way, this is my proposal. I'm offering to amend the contract in a way that you would like, and in exchange, I would direct your killing. You mentioned that you need to feed every month, which is about thirty days. You killed that tourist on April second. May second is ten days away. I believe we could find a murderer in that time."

I stroll to the hearth and gaze at the low flames there. "One month is the maximum time between kills."

"What happens after that?" she asks.

The flames dance and lick at the air above. "We reach the edge of my restraint."

"Let's just try it. Because I already have somebody in mind. Somebody who's been killing in this area. We'll unmask them together. Doesn't that sound like a fun challenge?"

I turn. "And then you will take your place here."

Her heart beats fast, but her gaze never wavers. "Upon the completion of the hunt."

"Whether or not we succeed in unmasking this killer of yours, somebody dies by May second, and then you will come here to work for me and only for me."

She crosses her arms. "Yeah. But you'd have to pay me extra.

If I quit my job with Serena—after training my replacement—I'd need to replace that income. People count on me."

"I will admit," I say, "the stalking of prey was once quite pleasurable to me. But it has lost some of its challenge over time. It's become ..." I pause, searching.

When did it start to dull?

"Too much like the snack aisle at 7-Eleven?" she offers.

I give her a hard look. "We hunt," I say, voice low and certain. "Together."

Chapter Eighteen

Alexandru

Friday evening.

I stand near the fire in the eastern dining hall. Not warming myself. Just remembering.

Or more like immersing myself in moments from the past, the way animals do.

I'm riding Hunter, a black stallion with a white blaze on his nose. Algernon, Duke of Densmere, is on Margrave. The air is sharp and fresh, the sky white and wide. We're pursuing a well-fed tax collector across muddy lanes somewhere in Normandy.

We thunder over frost-covered fields and past thatched cottages. A family of peasants runs into the woods to hide, but it's not them we're coming for.

Our friendship spanned centuries of hunting, traveling, and endless conversation. There were years and sometimes decades that we'd spend apart, attending to our various affairs, but even then, we'd correspond, exchanging updates and ideas.

Algernon was my greatest friend.

Until he became my most dangerous enemy.

And I his.

But for now, I'm on that hunt, and there's the smell of smoke and winter. And the thrill of the chase.

We wouldn't actually feed on the same prey. I'd taken the last one; I was warm, flush with energy. This one would be his.

I haven't hunted with another since Algernon. I hadn't intended to.

I didn't have to agree to this one's terms. I could've drained the friend called Josie and put Ms. Renfield in the pit here. She would've amended the contract after a few days of that.

Then a more discomfiting thought comes to me: maybe she would kill herself as she almost did in Karsovia. Would she do that just to spite me? She is very different from other Renfields —bull-headed and idealistic.

Her death would be an enormous inconvenience—and an expensive one, too, given how she's grown my empire.

In any case, it pleases me for now to try this new thing. And I'll have what I want.

Gregor moves behind me, laying settings on the dark, oil-rubbed table that stretches the length of the room. The chairs around it are hard and high-backed, not made for comfort.

"How goes the preparation?" I ask without turning.

"Well, Master," Gregor replies. "I have prepared roasted chicken with rosemary. Lemon. Wild rice. A pastry in the shape of a bugle for dessert."

"That seems... strange."

"She was constantly asking the shopkeepers in Karsovia if they had bugles. When one brought her an actual bugle from the back, she informed him she would have a bugle to eat. It is some manner of corn-based delicacy."

Renfields, I think darkly.

I catch the sense of something. "You are displeased."

A pause. "Not at all."

Gregor's lying, but it's no concern of mine. The bell rings, and he disappears to answer it.

Ms. Renfield strolls in a moment later, shoulders squared, jacket open over a white shirt, curls secured with those small clips of hers, then left to spring free to brush her shoulders. She is not displeasing to look at. I might even say she has a classic sort of beauty if I didn't know she was a Renfield.

She carries a long, rolled sheet like a declaration.

She looks around, pretending nonchalance, but she is curious. Scared. Hopeful.

And then she sees the chandelier.

From a distance, it's a massive sphere of twisted iron, like a brutalist sculpture suspended from the ceiling by a heavy chain.

As one looks closer, the true nature of the piece reveals itself: not abstract metal at all, but an intricate fusion of swords and daggers, their blades permanently welded together like a violent cage for the glowing orb within. Some still bear the dried blood of their owners.

Ancient firearms spiral throughout the composition, some bent by my own hand. I do not love getting shot.

"Is that from the Room & Board outlet?"

"It is every weapon used to try to end my existence between 1552 and 1961. I commissioned Emil Van Horn, the mid-century sculptor, to create it."

"That will be a hit on the *Ashwood Gazette* parade of homes. I can totally see it on a photo spread alongside Sally Janson's breakfast nook curtains."

"The requests for tours have been relentless." I move to the table. "You have brought me something?"

"I present to you, my spreadsheet!" She says it with humorous pride, but her nervousness spikes as she unrolls the oversized sheet across the long table. It looks like a grid with words written all over it. "I thought you'd appreciate it printed out on actual paper. We don't want any more tech thrown in the fire."

"What do I want with paper? Let's begin the hunt."

"This is the hunt," she says. "Gregor, can you find something to weigh down the corners?"

Gregor crosses to the mantel and returns with four iron candleholders. He sets one at each corner.

"The killer is hiding here," she declares.

"In the paper?" I ask, dismayed.

Ms. Renfield grins. "Think of this as a giant ledger where I track things. The killer is hiding in the data. Or actually, more like in the noise that obscures the data—the random, irrelevant information that hides what's important. Like a fog," she adds. "But if you know how to read it..." She plants both hands flat on the page, a hunter bending over a map.

The posture. The intent. Again, I think about my old friend, Algernon. Brilliant, cruel, tireless.

"You think you're clever," she says softlyto whatever she sees there, "but you can't hide from me. 'Cause I'm coming for you."

Chapter Nineteen

Harriet

I look up from the giant printout courtesy of the Creighton FedEx and find Alexandru watching me with that unsettling calm of his.

A familiar heat creeps up the back of my neck, and I start feeling nervous. Does he think this whole thing is stupid already?

"I know there's a killer in here," I say, trying to sound confident instead of pleading. "Someone's been staging accidents at weddings. The last two resulted in deaths."

"Your giant ledger tells you this."

"Yes. At first, the accidents weren't fatal. But over the past year, they've escalated. And three months ago, when the first fatality happened—that's when the smaller stuff stopped."

"So you see a pattern," he says.

I explain the columns and show him the progression. I drag my finger across the printed cells, the colors forming a visual pulse.

Your most pathetic theory yet. Cry for help.

I try to put the forum criticisms out of my mind as Alexandru studies the chart. His gaze moves over the data.

What if he doesn't see what I see?

He gestures at the top of the red column. "Cake toppling. This is the first suspicious accident?"

"That I know of. The woman who baked it is one of the most highly trained pastry chefs in the region, and an honest woman. She felt it was deliberately ruined by an outside force. People don't believe her, but I do."

"Hmmm."

"I was personally at another wedding soon after that, where a confetti cannon went off at the worst possible time. The woman in charge of the cannon was mystified at how it could've happened. There was a wedding after that where a cart full of dirty dishes careened down a hill and smashed into a group of wedding guests, including my grandmother. She fell and fractured her arm and was all bruised up. It was awful. The caterers insisted somebody pushed it."

"Humans do hate to take the blame for things."

"I wasn't sure who to believe myself, but the accidents keep piling up. There have been seven this year, including two deadly ones, and I believe there are more I simply don't know about." I point to the list at the top right.

1. Cake topple
2. Confetti cannon malfunction
3. Runaway dirty dishes cart
4. Champagne tower collapse
5. Creighton Arms dance floor cave-in
6. Deadly balcony fall
7. Grand staircase collapse

"And you believe it is the work of a saboteur."

"Yes, because if you plot the accidents on a spreadsheet, the pattern is obvious—the way they are spaced, the way they escalate in severity. Why did the small ones stop once the medium

120

ones started? Why did the medium ones stop once people began to die?"

Do I sound too hopeful? Too desperate for him to believe me? I remind myself for the umpteenth time that it's enough that I believe.

Alexandru has this habit of going super still, and right now, I hate it.

"I feel like the little accidents are where the killer honed their craft."

He points to the deadly balcony fall column. "What happened here?"

"A groom fell off a balcony. Supposedly, when a rusted-out railing gave way. But the venue's handyman had recently inspected it, and there was no rust."

"And you believe him."

"I do, but with you here, we can interview these people and get extra information."

He points to the last column. "Stairway collapse?"

"A lot of local bigwigs were lined up on a curving staircase for pictures during a fancy wedding. The stairway collapsed out of the blue, killing the deputy mayor and injuring the mayor. The police found a remote-control device in the debris—a small hydraulic jack. They concluded it was an assassination attempt on the mayor, but I believe the wedding killer was there and simply didn't have time to retrieve the thing."

"You believe it was part of your pattern."

"Yes. I'd been expecting a larger accident around that time."

Alexandru studies the sheet some more.

I wait.

After the deputy mayor's death, I brought my spreadsheet down to the police station to show Maverick, and he told me that it made me look insane. He threatened to throw me in jail if I interfered with his investigation.

Alexandru seems to be turning things over in his mind. "You

think the stairway collapse was the last in a long line of staged accidents."

"Yes!" I say.

The fire crackles softly behind us.

"You are all so accident-prone, you humans. Disorderly. Oblivious. Often drunk. Bumbling through your short years," he says. "It's a wonder to me sometimes how any of you reach advanced ages."

My heart sinks.

"Yet you see a killer hiding in these papers of yours. Somebody causing these accidents."

"Yes," I whisper, throat dry.

He waves dismissively at the sheet. "If you see a killer there, then a killer is there."

"Wait, what? You believe me?"

"Of course I do."

He believes me!

I'm trying really hard not to smile like a weirdo, but my heart is doing a happy dance.

"I do not hunt on paper. But your kind does," he continues. "You see across the passage of time and numbers. You see the surface and discern when something lurks. You are like little ferrets in this way—snuffling and organizing, rooting through shadows until you corner something."

"Okay, um, thanks?"

He shrugs. "It's in your nature."

"So, you don't see it yourself, but you totally believe that I see it?"

"Don't be tedious. I have said I believe you. You are a Renfield, are you not? Lowly creatures that you all are, you do have certain abilities."

"Maybe we could go back to the ferret analogy?"

"Whoever did this—whoever is still doing this—is escalating," he says.

"Exactly! They're escalating."

His eyes linger on the red column, darkening with a predator's focus. "They've crossed into hunger."

"That's what I'm thinking."

A dark lock of hair falls low over his right brow as he lifts his gaze to mine, and I see the calculating stillness of a predator there. "Tell me who this killer is. Show them to me. I'll gladly take their blood. I'll drain them so completely that death will be a mercy. And then you will come here to live."

"Okay, well... yeah, that's a good plan," I say. "But we're not at that step yet. It's not as if I know their name. We have to investigate. I mean, I have a couple of suspects—a wedding planner and an event bartender. They were at both deadly accidents. I need more information to confirm if they were at the others."

"You've narrowed it down to two. I could simply kill them both."

"But one or both of them might be innocent!"

Alexandru sighs.

"You told me you can sense people's emotions. And if they are being deceptive."

"Are you suggesting that we go to these two suspects of yours and ask outright if they caused these accidents?"

"Oh. Interesting. Would that *work*?" I ask hopefully.

"No. I've known killers who, if I were to ask them directly about their crimes, the most I would feel from them is pleasure and excitement, even as they lie about the crime. The deception would be comparatively faint."

"So if a person is like a perfume, you get the top notes."

"Exactly. And I can't tell why those notes are there. I may sense fear in a person, but is it fear of being exposed? Or do they fear that somebody suspects them wrongly? Maybe it's guilt, but is it guilt for the crime or for not stopping the crime?"

"I see," I say.

"That said, the ability to discern emotions and deception does have its advantages in interrogation."

"I can imagine. Because little things show you the big things. It's all data, and the more data, the better. Between you and me, we can nail this, Alexandru!"

He just watches me with those dark, fathomless eyes. He's so hard to read sometimes.

I stroll toward the fireplace, feeling his gaze on me. "Kip the bartender and Whitney the wedding planner are obvious. But this is a small town with a small pool of vendors, so it could be that everybody uses Kip's mixology service, and everybody uses Whitney's wedding planner services. Their presence at these weddings over the months might be circumstantial."

"So it might not be them at all."

"We don't know. And we need to think about their motives. My motive column is completely blank."

"Your motive column," he says.

"Yes. But the first thing we need to do is to get all the guest lists for the accident weddings. Maybe there is some guest out there who attended all of them. And I know just who to ask for those guest lists."

Alexandru homes in on me with interest. "And who might that be?"

"Why do you say it like that?"

"This person has your adrenaline spiking. Your heart rate. You have intense feelings about them."

"Are you reading me right now? You can't do that."

He shrugs.

"And it's not like I have any kind of feelings about her. It's Sloane—the woman who runs the stationery shop. She's a difficult person, that's all. But she made the invitations and place cards for all of the weddings with suspicious accidents. We need to get her to give us those lists."

"The village stationer. I ordered calling cards there."

124

"Yeah. I didn't realize you were a prince. She's very excited about that fact. Did you actually put Prince on your calling cards?"

"Of course not. They bear only my courtesy name—Alexandru Miramonte—and the word princeps."

"Does that mean prince?"

"No, princeps means I am first among equals."

"That seems like an oxymoron. If you're first, how can you say everyone is equal?"

He adjusts his shirt cuffs. "I am not one of the equals. I am first, the rest are equals."

Groan.

"I wonder why Sloane thinks you're a prince, then. She loves history, and she's a good researcher—she wouldn't make a mistake like that. And she told everybody, so they all think you're royalty."

"Well. Prince is one of my legacy titles. I don't use it, though. She would've had to dig deep."

"So you *are* a prince? How did I not know this?"

"It's an ancient title. No land or kingdom. Just the name."

"Well, Sloane loved that you were a prince, so maybe you can turn on the charm."

"I can certainly do that, but contrary to lore, I cannot mesmerize people."

"Oh, I know. Or you would've done it to me by now, I'm sure." I grab my phone. "Let's go talk to her."

Gregor, who has been standing in the corner all this time, mumbles something about dinner.

"I'm sorry, Gregor, there's no time," I say. "We have an hour before her shop closes."

I lead Alexandru to my car, still reeling.

I can't believe I promised to quit my job and move in with him.

But what choice did I have? He's here because of me. That tourist's death—that's on me.

Offering up my servitude was the only card I had to play.

I'm already dreading telling Mom and Granabelle I'm moving out. Josie's been pushing me to move out of my old bedroom for years, but not like this.

And Serena—she'll be disappointed when I quit. She believed in me when no one else did, championing my obsession with collecting and organizing information instead of treating it like some troubled girl's attempt to control the uncontrollable.

Alexandru settles himself into the passenger seat of my old Volvo like a king enduring a sub-standard throne.

Chapter Twenty

Alexandru

Ms. Renfield's car is a boxy thing, its door groaning like an aged hound. Yet she guides it down to the village with ruthless precision, sliding into a space so carefully that I have no doubt the gaps on either side are identical to the inch. Her father was the same. The green truck. The obsessive symmetry. The refusal to leave anything to chance.

It's not far from our parking place to the stationer, but no fewer than a dozen villagers gawk at us as we make our way down the sidewalk.

"People here in America are not as shy as the ones around my castle," I say. "They stare openly."

"Dude, you bought Kingston Manor in secret, rehabbed it in secret, and then Sloane told everyone that you're a prince, and here you are walking around town looking like David Gandy and a Bond villain had a lovechild. Of course, they're staring."

"I do not know who that is. But if this Gandy resembles me, he must be quite impressive."

She sighs. "They're probably wondering why *I'm* with you, too."

"Have you not told villagers that you are my servant?"

"Yeah, 'servant' isn't exactly in vogue anymore. FYI."

"Why not?"

"It's disrespectful, that's why."

"You are a servant. You are not to be respected; you are to be commanded. That is the place of the servant."

"It's just wrong. And it has baggage and implies you are superior to me."

"But I *am* superior to you. In all measurable ways."

She gives me a look that I have come to call her "WTF" look, being that she often utters the letters "W.T.F." after displaying this expression, wherein she widens her eyes.

"It is true," I say.

"Bet I could beat you in a hot dog eating contest."

"Insignificant."

"Cartwheels?" she tries.

I give her a dark look. "What's more, my station is superior in that I am your master."

"Yeah, and master is definitely out. You might inform Gregor of this as well. He can't go around calling you master. Not cool."

"I care nothing for your human rules."

"Well, you should. You need to act normal because I promise you, the Ashwood *villagers* may prove far more trouble-some than the villagers in your old country, if they start suspecting you're not human."

"The Ashwood villagers will not be a problem to one such as myself."

"Midwesterners can make a salad out of Jell-O, canned fruit, and mayonnaise. You think they can't take down a vampire?"

"I think they can't."

We proceed on.

"*Not to be respected,*" she repeats my words with disdain. "Whatever. I'm just a tool for you, aren't I?"

"Yes. You are a Renfield."

"What's up with you and Renfields?"

I turn to her. "Do not think just because we hunt together that you may question me like a barrister."

"Fine. Then don't think you get to know things about me."

"I know you're a Renfield. It's all I need to know."

"How could I forget? My inner life is of no concern." She adjusts her black cardigan as we near the stationer's shop, as if steeling herself for a duel. "I'm serious about the master-and-servant thing. You need to not be an offensive freak. Or at least not offensive."

I sigh. I've found through a long trial-and-error effort that it is sometimes worthwhile to appease a Renfield, and indeed, the villagers around the castle back in Karsovia were tiresome in the way that they would rush off when I appeared. "Very well. What would you both call me?"

"Gregor can call you 'boss.' I'll call you 'my client.'"

"Ludicrous. Unacceptable."

"Pick something better, then."

"You will both refer to me as your overlord."

She blinks. "Seriously?"

"Does that have baggage? Will it offend?"

She considers. "I guess not. Unless people hate medieval tyranny. Or the 'Immigrant Song' by Led Zeppelin."

"So it shall be. And you are my underlings."

"That's not a word people use."

"Now it is."

We reach Aster Press, which occupies the bottom floor of a narrow brick building. Its display window shows a set of cream-colored invitations arranged on dark green velvet.

She turns to me before we go in. "You'll be polite, right? No beast mode stuff."

I smile and open the door for her. It's a small gesture, one I've done a thousand times in a thousand lifetimes, but she startles. Like she hadn't expected manners from me.

"Oh. Thanks," she mutters, and steps through—tense, wary, the way a rabbit might edge past a wolf who hasn't yet lunged.

"Prince Miramonte, hello!" Ms. Cunningham calls out from behind the counter. Her eyes are set wide, and there's an elegance to her bone structure.

I incline my head. "Please, Ms. Cunningham. Call me Alexandru."

"Alexandru, then," she says, overcome with a mixture of awe and just a whiff of fear, a natural human reaction to one such as me. "And you may call me Sloane."

Her gaze flicks to Ms. Renfield, and her smile cools. "And our Harriet!" she exclaims in the tone one might use for a bothersome pet.

I find I do not like it. My gaze falls to her neck, where her blood flows sure and strong.

Harriet follows the line of my gaze and stiffens beside me. "Just a quick question," she says, but it's as if Sloane hasn't heard.

Sloane says, "Your cards will be ready Monday, as discussed. They're coming out so beautifully."

"Of that I have no doubt." I step closer, lifting a delicate sheet of ivory stock from a nearby tray. My fingers trace the grain. "French linen?"

She flushes, visibly pleased. "It is. I'm impressed."

Her scent is sweet. She would be easy to run down.

Ms. Renfield steps forward. "Not to ruin the 'French linen Burning Man festival' here, but we have an important request, Sloane."

Sloane sighs wearily. "What?"

"We'd be really grateful if you could get us the guest lists from the following weddings." She steps up to the counter and slides a piece of paper across it. It's her list of seven accidents. "I wouldn't ask if it weren't a matter of life and death."

Sloane examines the paper and then looks up at me. "We?"

Ms. Renfield flicks a glance my way. "Alexandru and I."

Sloane frowns. "How is this a matter of life or death, Alexandru, if you don't mind my asking?"

"The list will aid us in hunting a killer, who we very much want to end."

"End their career," Ms. Renfield puts in. "Their career of killing."

"Thus, we require the list."

Sloane slides the paper back across the table. "Alexandru, I know you've probably heard America is crawling with killers, and no doubt Harriet's encouraged that view. And yes, she has every reason to see a murderer behind every potted plant, given what she's been through—but I'd strongly advise against getting dragged into one of her sleuthing sprees."

I gaze at her, unmoved. "Nevertheless, I require the list."

She turns to Ms. Renfield, alight with gleeful defiance. "I'm truly sorry, but I can't hand out information like that. People trust me with their privacy."

"There are pictures of these weddings all over the internet," Ms. Renfield says.

"Then go look at the pictures."

Ms. Renfield's jaw tightens. "Do you keep the guest lists?"

"That's proprietary."

"How is that proprietary?"

Sloane crosses her arms, brightening with amusement. "Because I say it is."

"That's like saying the temperature outside is proprietary."

"Then go outside and take the temperature. No one's stopping you."

Ms. Renfield draws in a breath, fighting to hide her frustration. "Look, if we're right, somebody's out there killing people, and they could kill again. Your help could save lives."

"In your imagination," Sloane says, but I can tell that she's intrigued. Curious.

I lower my voice. "We require your help."

"I'm sorry," Sloane says. "I cannot divulge private lists."

I stare at her, confused. "*You* are denying a request from one such as me?"

"I'm sorry, Alexandru," Sloane says. Her eyes flick to Ms. Renfield. "I simply can't. Even for a prince such as yourself."

"Come on, we have to go." Ms. Renfield seizes my arm and attempts to drag me from the shop.

I blink, unable to process this. A mere shopkeeper would deny me? She seems to get pleasure from denying Ms. Renfield, but who is she to deny me? What's more, there's a part of her that seems to *want* to divulge the list. It's positively maddening.

"Please," Ms. Renfield whispers under her breath for only me to hear. "There are things you don't understand... critical to the hunt."

I slide my gaze to where she has grabbed my arm. The heat of her frail little hand sparks a strange shiver through me. She lets go.

I turn to the insolent shopkeeper. "Good day, Sloane."

"Good day, Alexandru."

I stroll out.

Ms. Renfield comes up alongside me.

"This peasant thinks to deny me?" I grumble.

"Alexandru, I get that people bowed and scraped before you in terror back in ye old country, but you have to play it cool here. You can't pull rank on people."

"A mere shopkeeper!"

"Yes, a mere *shopkeeper*, because this is America and a *mere shopkeeper* gets to deny whoever she wants. But here's the important thing... how can I explain it..." She ponders intently as we stroll past the bright little shops. "As a soldier, were you ever forced to kind of camouflage yourself in order to blend in with the enemy?"

"Do not insult me. I fully understand the utility of camouflage."

The fussily ornamental streetlamps cast a dainty glow upon the wide, clean sidewalks.

"Right. That's why I'm saying not to pull rank. And also, when you're trying to get information from people, wouldn't you agree it's always better to stay on their good side? Have you ever heard the expression, 'You catch more flies with honey'? It means people are more cooperative when you're nice to them."

"I find people are more cooperative when I hang them upside down, bound hand and foot, and allow the rats to nibble their faces for an hour."

"Yeah, but we're not doing that, remember? You said you would do this my way. You want me to move into your place, right?"

I sigh wearily. "There is a limit to my patience, Ms. Renfield."

I wait for her to say it. *Not my name.*

For once, she doesn't. "Trust me, our hunt will go better if you're nice to people and don't pull rank."

"Your methods are shockingly cumbersome."

"But you said you would do it my way. This is my way, shockingly cumbersome as it is."

"This shopkeeper enjoys saying no to you. It was... impressive."

"It wasn't impressive to me," Ms. Renfield grumbles. "And what's up with staring at her neck? I'm surprised you didn't just come out and ask for her blood type."

"I knew her blood type the moment I walked in the door." I adjust my right shirt cuff. "What happened between you two?"

"I'm a Renfield. I thought that's all you needed to know about me."

"True enough." I adjust my other cuff. "I'll have you know that your friend Sloane *wants* a reason to comply. She would very much like to hand over the list. She needs to get something for her trouble. A bribe would probably do it."

"A bribe? You think so?"

"Absolutely. She enjoys being the bearer of knowledge."

Ms. Renfield's lips part. "You're right! Wow." She's quiet for a moment. "You think she needs a bribe."

"She's curious about the mystery, too."

"You think she believes I'm onto something?" Ms. Renfield asks, brimming with hope.

She is so invested in being believed. Does she not comprehend her own abilities? The thought stirs a flicker of consternation.

No matter. As long as those abilities serve my ends, that is all that matters.

I say, "A bribe would enable her to comply without seeming to give in."

I feel a bright satisfaction spark within her as the idea takes shape. She turns to me, eyes alight with triumph, red lips formed into a small smile. "And I know exactly what to offer. I know what Sloane collects."

Ms. Renfield's certainty is oddly pleasing.

Of course, progress in a hunt is always pleasing.

"It'll take a little doing to hunt it down," she says. "*If* I can hunt it down. And it will cost something."

She unlocks her car and gets in.

"Cost is not a concern of mine," I say, settling into the passenger side.

"Yeah, we know your beastly concerns."

I fix her with a hard gaze, still unused to Renfields speaking to me in such a manner. "It would be prudent of you to bear my beastly concerns in mind."

Heat steals up her neck, and she looks away, focusing on starting the car. "It's something I'll have to do real research to find. I'll pay for it through your cash account and have it sent to your place. Tell Gregor to keep a lookout for it."

"That would be your job, Ms. Renfield."

"Fine. I'll tell him. Now, next steps: we need to talk to wedding industry people. I especially want you to interview Berky the cake baker. And I have the perfect place to gather intel."

"What would that be?"

A twinkle appears in her warm brown eyes. "You'll see." She turns the corner, maneuvering her car expertly.

"When your father desired intelligence from the villagers, he would take coffee at a place in Ostra. Very humble. Small."

"With a healthy supply of flies? Perchance a dung beetle nestled prettily in the sugar bowl?"

"He ate what he felt kept him at peak function. His mind was... compromised. But his diligence never wavered."

Her jaw tightens slightly.

We pass the gazebo, lit by spotlights in all its pink painted glory. The hill slants upward toward the homes that overlook Ashwood, everything bright and cheerful, even at night, so unlike the misty mountains I'm used to. The dogs here are fluffy rather than sleek. The flowers are planted in rows. Even the trees flutter cheerfully in the darkness, nothing like the solemn, secretive pines of my homeland.

"What did she mean when she said you have good reason to suspect killers around every corner? Why do you have good reason?"

"Who knows?" she says breezily.

"You know."

She stares at the road. "What does it matter, though, right?"

She would deflect my question? Deny me this information I have requested?

But she is right. What does it matter?

She is a Renfield.

Chapter Twenty-One

Harriet

I wake before my alarm. A faint light glows through my curtains.

I swing my legs out from under the quilt and start my morning routine, which I've honed like clockwork. Stretching, bathing, and a quick check of the news.

The cool spring breeze drifts through the window as I tame my curls with dark brown barrettes that match the color of my hair.

Is this investigation even going to work? Alexandru is so much a fish out of water. He sees people as peasants. Will he be able to contain his princely disdain?

On the plus side, his charm is a formidable weapon. He's the kind of predator that draws people to him, though the villagers around his old castle were clearly wise to his bloody ways.

And he believes me.

If you see a killer there, then a killer is there.

After all the pitying glances, the tight smiles and polite nods, this cold-blooded killer believes me.

The way he read Sloane back there was impressive, too. It's very Sloane to desperately want to refuse me the information I need, while at the same time wanting to deliver that information.

So Sloane.

And the idea to let her save face with a bribe? Genius.

My clothes are laid out on my dresser: white shirt, black pants, ankle boots, and a women's light knit jacket—soft with excellent pockets, one of six identical such jackets that I rotate through. Today's jacket is walnut brown. I put on the one piece of jewelry I always wear: a long gold chain with a single pendant—a gold key that belonged to James. It fits in a box currently on my shelf and still holds the rocks, marbles, and other little treasures he collected.

I put on my favorite red lipstick with the precision of a surgeon, and then the perfect amount of black eyeliner. I go through my bag like a pilot doing a pre-flight checklist. Phone, wallet, backup lipstick, compact, mints, pen, tiny notebook, Tide stick. Check, check, check. My bag makes a satisfying *click* when it shuts.

I grab some coffee in the kitchen. I was up late last night working on Sloane's bribe to track down the 1971 Sears exclusive "Enchanted Evening" edition of *Mystery Date*, printed in a very limited quantity and only sold through holiday catalogs. It has an alternate "mystery suitor," a woodsman instead of a prom date. It also has gold-edged cards, better artwork, and a glittery mystery door with a metal hinge instead of the usual cardboard.

Sloane and I were close friends in high school. We spent hours in her bedroom doing homework, mooning over boys, and hatching plans for the next cool feature in the *Ashwood High Gazette*. It was there that I first encountered her extensive vintage board game collection. We played some, but many were strictly off-limits—especially the various editions of *Mystery Date*.

Sloane once told me that the "Enchanted Evening" edition

was the holy grail: the one she wanted most, and the one that was impossible to find.

I was a show-off when it came to research back then. Naturally, I took it as a challenge. When I finally tracked it down, I was thrilled. Her research skills were fine, but nothing like mine. Nobody's were like mine.

But that was right around the time of the Great Newspaper Blowup—the fight that torched our friendship. I deleted the link in a fit of anger. It didn't matter, I told myself. The game costs as much as a used car.

I'm amazed there's still one out there to find, but I found it buried in a hidden listing on a Swedish forum for vintage game obsessives. It's even more outrageously priced fifteen years later.

But what does a centuries-old vampire care?

I paid for it and arranged to have it shipped to Alexandru's house. I alerted Gregor that a package was coming from Sweden and to treat it like the Crown Jewels.

Downstairs, the scent of lemon oil and rosewood hits me. I move through the antique store slowly, part of me cataloging what's out of place. Someone's shifted the Georgian sideboard. A tiny smudge on the mirror above the Victorian fainting couch. Granabelle must've opened up the curio cabinet again—its lock sits crooked.

Mom is doing the books. Granabelle, however, stands like a sentry near the register near the door, arms crossed.

"Good morning," I offer brightly, pausing to give them each a kiss on the cheek. Granabelle stays stiff.

I straighten. "Something wrong?"

"What could possibly be wrong?" Granabelle says. "Except the fact that you brought your new employer to meet Sloane and show off Sloane's store, but you couldn't be bothered to bring him down the street to say hello to your own family? Are you asking if that's what's wrong? You barely get along with that girl, but hers is the shop you visit together?"

"Jesus Christ," Mom says. "We don't care."

"Of course we care!" Granabelle says.

"Look," I say, "I know he's this illustrious new citizen of the realm and all of that, but he's not somebody you want to know—not at all. Like, he's not a good person."

To say the least.

The idea of him meeting these two women I love with all of my heart has me quaking in my boots.

"Not a good person? What does that mean?" Mom's suspicious now. Maybe I went too far.

I want to tell them he's a dangerous monster, and that they should stay away from him, but they wouldn't believe me. They both think I see crimes and patterns where they don't exist, and they certainly don't go in for the supernatural. Mom hates it when I suggest James might be alive. I think she survives in part by assuring herself that he's dead and buried and no more harm can come to him.

I wouldn't say she's overprotective of me, exactly, but if she did somehow become convinced I was in danger from Alexandru, I could see her going after him—I really could. She's got a switchblade and a shotgun right behind the counter.

I hate myself for leading him here.

"This is a fine store—nothing to be embarrassed about," Granabelle says.

"It is amazing!" I go to her and give her a hug. "I'm proud of this store, and I'm proud of you. I love you guys."

"Oh, god, sugar rush alert," Mom says.

Granabelle makes me promise to bring him next time.

"We'll see," I say.

I can feel them watch me as I leave.

They're not in danger as long as I find a killer for Alexandru to eat. Drain. Hoover up like a Slurpee.

Chapter Twenty-Two

Harriet

The Glassworks Galleria in neighboring Creighton is a massive old-timey warehouse that used to be a glass factory.

Now it's Grand Central Station for all things artful and tasteful. The first floor hosts yoga studios and boutique designer shops. The top two floors form an event complex for concerts, small conventions, and weddings.

Today it's a bridal expo, and it's packed.

Rows of booths stretch down the length of the venue. There are florists, photographers, calligraphers, bakers, and more. There's a stage at the far end for a bridal fashion show tonight, but right now it's all dramatically lit florals.

A harpist plays somewhere in the distance, and cake and signature drink samples are set out like bait to lure passersby.

But all eyes are on us.

Okay, not us.

Him.

Alexandru strolls along in his three-piece suit like someone who just stepped off the pages of *Evil Incarnate Menswear Daily,* all majestic bearing and weaponized cool.

Since it's daytime, he wore a hat, gloves, and dark sunglasses on the way here. On any other man, the ensemble would have been fussy, but he makes it work, what with his whole beastly prowling thing.

I nearly lost my balance when he removed his gloves—one slow, crisp finger tug at a time like a man at ease in his power. And then he pulled the gloves free, revealing those large, strong hands, fingers flexing.

"This event serves several towns," I say. "Plus, there are probably a few Cleveland brides going for a small-town vibe."

He doesn't answer. His eyes track movement—waitstaff, caterers, planners. Is he watching the herd for signs of weakness? Looking for a spot to settle in for a nice heaping helping of human?

Eight days left. We can catch a killer in eight days.

Right?

I grab a program from the info table and study the names. "Check it out!" I point to the corner area on the map. "This is Kip's business. I bet he's here. Kip is the bartender who was at every single wedding where there was a suspicious accident."

Alexandru's eyes gleam. "Excellent," he says. "Point me to him."

"But we're just here for context," I remind him. "Still in the information gathering phase. The motive column of my spreadsheet needs to be filled out before we do anything like outright accosting a suspect, okay?"

"The motive column? Good god."

"I know what you're thinking. Cumbersome though my methods are, you're going to let me take the lead, right?"

"For now."

A baby bursts into tears as we pass. Does it sense Alexandru? Is that possible?

I study his patrician profile. He appears oblivious to the

attention that he's getting, but appearances can be deceiving. He probably takes it as his due.

I return to the map. My heart sinks when I discover neither Whitney nor Berky is listed as vendors. "Dang," I say. "I wanted you to hear Berky's cake story and meet Whitney, the wedding planner. Never mind. There's still a lot of sleuthing to do here."

"Mmmm," Alexandru says.

"Weddings are probably boring to you," I say.

"Not at all. Weddings and marriages are an important part of the supply chain for my kind."

Somebody takes a not-that-discreet picture of him. I'd be a little bit worried if I hadn't seen those pictures in the castle of him during his travels.

I go back to studying the guide. "I should've come to one of these events when I was first starting to research this killer."

"Why didn't you?"

"I don't know. I'm much more of an online researcher."

"I prefer the direct approach." He's looking around at the people. Maybe cataloging everybody's blood types.

"It's possible we could even identify a new and unexpected suspect."

"A new suspect? That would elongate our process."

"But the goal here is to find the guilty party, not rush to judgment and... etcetera."

Alexandru's eyes sparkle. "Etcetera?"

"Check it out!" I point to booth thirty-nine. "DJ Sassy Sadie! She was the DJ at one of the early accident weddings. She had the confetti cannon I told you about. She was sure it wasn't her fault."

"A *cannon* of confetti." His voice drips with disdain.

I lower my voice as we walk. "She was supposed to shoot it off the moment the bride and groom kissed after the ceremony, but the thing went off way too early. While the preacher was asking for objections. The mother of the bride thought she set

142

it off on purpose because the timing was so outrageous, but DJ Sassy Sadie was really insistent that she didn't activate the remote and that the cannon was in perfect working order. I'm going to get her to talk about it, and you see what you pick up."

Alexandru sighs.

DJ Sassy Sadie's booth is strung with neon lights and metallic garlands. A banner above her reads "DJ Sassy Sadie" in glittering pink cursive. Sadie is fiddling with a soundboard. Her hair is teased upwards, and her hoop earrings sparkle in the light.

"Hey, hey," she calls when she sees us. "How's it going?" She glances at Alexandru nervously. He really seems to make people nervous.

"Good," I say, trying to project a friendly vibe. "Just checking things out."

"Let me know if you have any questions." Behind her, a banner reading "Big Fun for Your Big Day" flaps gently in the HVAC breeze.

I take a card, a slick black number with a holographic QR code. I hand it to Alexandru, and he scowls at it.

"All my packages are online now—updated weekly," Sadie says. "Everything from bare bones to total extravaganza."

"I was actually just at a wedding you did. It was a few months back, out at Gazebo Park in Ashwood? The confetti cannon went off right in the middle of the 'Any objections' part. I felt so bad on your behalf."

Her entire demeanor shifts. Even her hair seems to deflate. I feel like a jerk bringing it up. "That... should not have happened."

"Did you ever figure out what went wrong?"

She squares her stand. "Yes, I did. Somebody set it off purposely. I know that might sound paranoid to you."

"Not at all!" I say. "How'd you find out?"

She glances nervously at Alexandru. "It's a long story, and I've ensured it won't happen again."

"I want to know," I say.

Sadie sighs. "So, like, those confetti cannons operate by remote control. The buttons are super touchy, so I've always made it a practice to keep the batteries out of the remote until the very last minute. They were still in my pocket when the cannon went off."

"Could it have been a malfunction?"

"I wondered it myself, but I couldn't see how. They're not complex machines, you know? I use them constantly, and it makes no sense. I felt so bad when it happened. I'm telling you, I spent hours trying to get the manufacturer on the phone. They were zero help, so I loaded that thing in the back of my truck and drove down three hours to the U.S. headquarters. I need to know I can rely on my tools, and people love the confetti cannon."

I nod.

"They called the overseas factory and ended up taking my cannon apart to check the circuitry. It was perfectly operational. They assured me that the only way it could have happened is if somebody else had a remote."

"How would somebody else get the remote to your cannon?" I look at Alexandru. He's listening intently.

"Turns out these cannons all use universal remotes. Anyone with the same model could have set it off."

"Did you ask for a list of other buyers? Like of the model you have?"

"That would've been nice, but they claimed they couldn't provide one—sales go through Amazon, party store chains, middlemen. Clearly, it would take a lot of doing."

Alexandru leans in slightly. "Do you think they could be... persuaded?"

She stiffens. "Persuaded? Like... how?"

144

He lowers his voice to a tone that's a little scarier than the situation requires, let's just say. "*Persuaded.*"

"He's just joking," I say quickly. "But what do you make of it in hindsight? Do you have other theories about who did it? A rival DJ? A mischief maker?"

She gives me a strange look. "The DJ community is pretty cooperative. But a mischief maker? Somebody who hates the couple enough to purchase a confetti cannon just to get the remote and deliberately set it off at the wrong time?" She pauses here. "Is there... some reason you have a specific interest in this? I mean, if you're worried about your own wedding..."

"Oh, that's not why we're asking," I say quickly, drawing Alexandru's attention, probably with my spiking heart rate. "We're not engaged or anything like that."

"Her kind serves me," he clarifies unhelpfully.

"Oh!! Got it. Totally cool!" DJ Sassy Sadie says. "I love it!"

"He just means he's my boss."

"Yeah, yeah, say no more!" she insists. "And I want you to know I am down with all sorts of ceremonies and the entire spectrum of potential relationships! Really down with whatever you've got going."

"Okay, thanks."

"And I want to put your minds at rest right now," she continues. "I personally reprogrammed the remotes. I'm obsessed with making your day unforgettable."

Alexandru hands her back the card, slow and elegant. "You've given us much to consider."

"Please, keep it," she says.

I snatch it from his outstretched fingers. "We will!"

"Seriously, Alexandru!" I say as we walk away from her booth. "You one hundred percent need to drop the servant thing."

"She imagined we were betrothed. I cannot think of anything more preposterous. I would not marry a Renfield even if the alternative were to be chained to the bottom of the sea and consumed by eels. Slowly."

"If you act cool today, maybe I'll get you a T-shirt with that on it." I run my hand over a hanging display of silky ribbons at the wedding present wrapping booth.

He gives me an imperious look, and for just a moment, it's weirdly hot.

I look away, ignoring his dark lord beauty, reminding myself that he's an inhuman killing machine, and whatever hotness he has is probably some vampire mesmerizing trick.

And his English accent is not helping.

"Though we are at a wedding expo," I say. "It could serve us to let people think we are in a relationship. And that was pretty interesting with DJ Sassy Sadie, right? Did it seem like she was telling the truth?"

"She was being honest," he says.

"The culprit would've had to know the model of cannon she uses and where to order it. And how did they know the remotes were universal? This is somebody who's been around the wedding game."

"Not a guest, then? Perhaps we don't need the guest lists from Sloane anymore."

"I still think we need them. More information is better than less." I go back to my map.

"This place is an assault on my senses. The brightness, the scents, the chaos of emotions."

I look up at his glowering face, like something Michelangelo might've sculpted to represent the concepts of beauty and majesty, except then it got possessed by a demon. "I didn't even think of that. It just comes at you? All the emotions around this place? Like a soup of emotions?"

"Like competing orchestras."

"You need to leave?"

He gives me a dark look. "I have been through worse."

There is an edge to the way he says this. Almost an accusatory edge, as though I put him through something worse.

A small display with an elegant gold bird logo catches my eye. Golden Goose Catering. "The runaway dish cart!" I say. "It was their dirty dish cart that careened into my grandmother and a bunch of other people at a wedding reception in Gazebo Park. We should question them."

Chapter Twenty-Three

Alexandru

Ms. Renfield hesitates, pressing her white pencil to her red lips, seeming to collect herself.

It is not a real pencil, as I discovered recently. It has no lead. It only writes on her electronic ledger.

"Let's not tell them my grandmother was hit. I don't want them to think I'm being accusatory."

"What do you care?"

"It's an empathy thing."

I sigh wearily.

"You were human once. You understand empathy. Surely you have some shred of empathy in there."

"A bit of advice, Ms. Renfield," I say coolly. "Do not hunt where there is no game."

Another baby bursts into tears.

Tedious.

"Are you going to question these peasants, or shall I?"

"I will. You just stand there and see if you can get a sense of their emotions. Do they know deep down they didn't put the brake on the cart? Or did they park it wrong?"

The Golden Goose owners seem to be a married couple.

The man has a short beard and a piece of paper affixed to his chest that says "Hi, I'm Isaac!" The woman has rosy cheeks and a similar chest paper that says, "Hi, I'm Amanda!"

Both wear matching black aprons with a gold bird embroidered on the pocket.

Amanda smiles uncertainly as we approach. "Looking for wedding catering?"

"Fact-finding," Ms. Renfield replies, nerves spinning. "Your menu looks amazing."

They talk for an interminably long time. Amanda gives her a menu. Isaac offers a sample of a pastry. It's as if Ms. Renfield has forgotten why she's here.

"We have heard about the runaway cart incident," I say. "We require an explanation."

Ms. Renfield turns to me, eyes wide.

Isaac's expression darkens. "You *require* an explanation?"

Ms. Renfield takes my arm. "He… uh… heard about the story. He wants everything to be perfect, that's all, and he's the direct sort. I'm sure it wasn't your fault."

"It wasn't," Amanda says. "My heart goes out to those people and the newlyweds. It was an absolute disaster, but it couldn't have been something that our team caused."

"How can you be sure?" I ask.

"We have protocols to prevent things like that," Amanda says nervously. "Especially when we're doing events at Gazebo Park. We have a specific way of collecting and staging dishes to be loaded, and our team follows that protocol strictly."

"Very strictly," Isaac agrees. "Or they wouldn't be on our team. When we make mistakes, we own them. This wasn't us."

"We think it was some neighborhood kids…" Amanda says.

Ms. Renfield nods. "So some kids… snuck up and pushed the cart down the hill?"

"Yes, they released the brake, aimed it toward the crowd, and pushed," Amanda says with a glance in my direction.

Isaac thrums with righteous anger. "When we left the top of the hill, the cart was secure. The footbrake was on. I did it myself. And that thing sure as hell wasn't pointed downhill. You can even tell from the pictures."

Amanda sets her hand on his arm. "We examined the pictures afterwards."

Ms. Renfield tips her head thoughtfully. "Did you notice who was around the cart before it was pushed? Can you think of anyone else who might've done such a thing aside from kids?"

Isaac rolls his eyes. "People said it was a ghost, but nobody really believes that."

Ms. Renfield puts her hand on her chest. "We really appreciate this comprehensive explanation. I believe you've put our fears at rest." She looks up at me. "Wouldn't you agree?"

"Such as they were," I growl.

Amanda smiles uncertainly. "I'm going to go out on a limb here and guess that you're thinking of holding your event at Gazebo Park? Do you have a date?"

"Not at this time, but you've come highly recommended. Your Tuscan menu looks incredible!"

Once we're safely beyond earshot, she turns to me. "You require an explanation? Did I not say that I should be the one to ask the questions?"

"But you weren't asking the questions."

"I was getting around to it."

"You'll be happy to know that they believe completely in their innocence. They harbor genuine anger about the incident. Isaac, in particular, could not be more confident."

She turns her attention to her electronic ledger. "I would love to get a look at the pictures from that wedding. I say we hit up the photographer next."

She's telling me about some local photographer, but my attention is focused on a man who is walking briskly toward us.

He's roughly Ms. Renfield's age with a face full of copper freckles. He is chewing gum. Loudly.

"Harriet," he says.

She spins around, surprised. "Maverick!" Her pulse hitches up in a way that I don't like.

Maverick eyes me up and down, sensing a threat. He chews busily. The gum is a crutch. I've seen it before. I've broken men like this.

Ms. Renfield touches my arm. "Alexandru, this is Maverick Cooper. We went to high school together, and he's a policeman now. Alexandru is a friend of my father's. He's the one who rehabbed Kingston Manor."

"So I've heard." Maverick shakes my hand with a solid grip. He's wary of me, but he hides it well. "The prince."

He turns a suspicious gaze to Ms. Renfield. "Interesting to see you two here."

"Alexandru is interested in American customs. And I was just telling him about the stairway collapse. Have you figured out who purchased the parts for the hydraulic device yet?"

"Now, you wouldn't be conducting an *investigation* when I told you not to, would you?"

"We are indeed conducting an investigation," I inform him, voice calm and final.

Maverick turns to me, still chewing gum—faster now. "Don't tell me she's got you wrapped up in her wild wedding theory."

I lower my voice, letting it slip into something colder. "Are you disparaging my underling's theories?"

"Underling?"

"Oh my god! What?" Ms. Renfield interjects, too brightly. "I already know your Christmas present, Alexandru, a 'Kookiest boss ever' mug."

Maverick doesn't laugh. He just keeps chewing that gum. "They say you're not from this country, so I'm going to take this moment to make a few things clear, just in case Harriet hasn't:

interference in an ongoing police investigation is against the law. Could be grounds for deportation."

It takes me a few moments to register this as a threat. It's so very unexpected and... entertaining.

"Is that funny?" Maverick asks. "You look like you think it's funny."

Ms. Renfield's nervousness spins wild. "Of course he doesn't think it's funny!" She gives me a pleading look.

"No, it was very fierce," I assure him. "I thank you for that information."

His expression doesn't change, but he's full of uncertainty now. "You're welcome."

She claps a hand on my arm. "Look, Alexandru! There's my friend Josie. Remember her?" She waves desperately. It is indeed her friend Josie.

Josie waves back and heads over.

Maverick gives me one last look and then stalks off.

Josie looks amused. "So... bringing your father's Karsovian friend to a wedding expo. Either you secretly hate him, or you're about to marry him."

"We are not betrothed; we are stalking and hunting a killer," I say.

Chapter Twenty-Four

Harriet

I nearly swallow my own tongue. "Well... kind of!"

Josie narrows her eyes. "No wonder Maverick seemed pissed. You're back on your wedding saboteur thing?"

I snort. "I never left it."

Josie shakes her head. "I really think the stairway collapse was a warning from the Snag Tooth Riders. Everyone thinks it. It's the whole 'fight nights' thing."

"So I've heard."

Naturally, Alexandru perks up at this. "Fight nights?"

Josie studies his face. "Our local motorcycle gang, the Snag Tooth Riders, used to have these barn fight nights that were a massive income-generating situation for them. They'd sell alcohol and everything. But the mayor of Ashwood shut it all down. Cue the threats flying back and forth, and the next thing you know, the mayor and the deputy mayor are lying in a pile of rubble."

"Did they get any proof that it was them yet?" I ask. "Did they make any arrests?"

"Maverick says it's just a matter of time. He's a good cop and you know it."

"I also know there's a pattern," I say, "and it's escalating."

"I mean, you're amazing at tracking things, but it seems like such a clear cause and effect."

I can feel Alexandru's gaze burning into my profile, oddly warming. "Her kind possesses an uncanny ability with patterns. If she senses something, it exists."

Josie's brow furrows. "Her... kind?"

"My father did his bookkeeping for him," I say. "Alexandru is super impressed with our family's spreadsheet skills."

"Harriet is brilliant," she agrees. "You were smart to hire her. But I'm not so sure about this theory. At least, I hope you're wrong because that would *not* be good. Wedding festivities are one of Ashwood's top tourism drivers."

I pull out my iPad. "We just confirmed two of them."

Josie peers at my list. "Wait. You don't have the curtain fire on here."

I stiffen. "What curtain fire?"

Josie winces, clearly regretting saying anything. "Never mind."

"Screw off, you have to tell me now."

She leans in. "It was here at Glassworks Galleria, but you can't let it slip that I told you."

"You knew I was looking into this and didn't mention a fire?"

"I didn't know it wasn't on your list!" Josie says. "It wasn't huge. No injuries, thankfully. Some decorative curtains on the third floor caught fire during a reception, and the sprinklers went off. It was not pretty. Chief Knox found traces of accelerant and concluded a photographer had spilled equipment cleaner near a candle."

"Accelerant?" I say, keenly aware of Alexandru tracking my rising interest or my pulse or skin temperature or who knows. He's like a predator on a scent trail. It's a bit unsettling.

"Accelerant can be a lot of things, though," she says.

"Was it Richardson Photography?" I ask.

"Who else? I think it was at Mandy and Jim Gordon's wedding. The Richardson crew might still have the photos. You should check. Not that I suggested it, okay? You didn't get it from me." Josie fixes me with a gaze that can be translated into *I'm really, really, really serious!* "Harlan Delmere has been aggressive about keeping it quiet. You cannot tell him I mentioned it."

"Harlan was trying to cover it up?"

"Who is Harlan?" Alexandru asks.

"Sort of a local developer and power player," Josie explains. "He owns the Galleria and a whole bunch of other places."

"We'll keep quiet about it," I say, shooting a look at Alexandru. The last thing I want is to get Josie in trouble.

I tuck away my tablet. "I can't believe I missed this one. Also, sprinklers went off during a wedding reception, and there's nothing online? That's a little scary."

Alexandru's eyes glitter with predatory focus. "Where would we find this Harlan?"

Josie looks panicked. "Absolute discretion."

"Alexandru won't say anything, I promise," I say.

"And that's my cue to go schmooze with potential voters. You two have fun with your... activities." She gives me a look that promises a detailed interrogation later.

"This is all very interesting," I say, making a note.

"If we don't unmask our killer, I'll simply pay a visit to this Harlan."

"What? You can't!"

"You and your friend dislike and fear him."

"Yeah, but that's not a reason to kill a man."

Alexandru gives me a mystified look. "Maverick, then?"

"Whoa, whoa, whoa! What? No!"

"He wants to bed you."

"Excuse me? Maverick is not into me." I broke it off with

him, but he definitely had a lot of complaints about me, including that I asked too many follow-up questions after sex. *"I don't appreciate undergoing an exit interview every time we bang,"* Maverick once said to me.

He didn't love my true crime hobby either, which at the time involved researching the big regional cases. Like everyone, he chalked it up to my unresolved trauma about James.

One of the nice things about Alexandru's arrogant disinterest in my life is that he doesn't know about James. He hasn't formed opinions about me based on my refusal to accept that James is dead.

Alexandru stares into the crowd milling about in the huge space, hopefully not tracking a 180-pound morsel of freckle-faced prey. "Maverick Cooper wishes to bed you, and I will not tolerate it. Renfields in my employ belong to me. They do not court and they do not mate, unless it is with the express intention of seeding future Renfields."

No comment.

"Where do we find this Harlan Delmere?"

"His usual habitat is a gross mansion on the river up in Creighton, though he could be here somewhere, considering he owns the place. But don't forget we're hunting with data right now."

Alexandru keeps his stare up. Somewhere off to the side, another baby bursts into tears.

Chapter Twenty-Five

Alexandru

The Richardson Photography area is staged like a drawing room, complete with tufted chairs and Persian rugs of abominable quality. Along the back wall hang photographic banners of laughing brides, their eyes shining with delusion.

Ms. Renfield flips through a book of photographs, photo after photo of weddings. Couple after couple, beaming out at the camera.

"Got it!" She stabs a photo. "This is the runaway cart wedding." She angles the book toward me. "Before it happened. See the cart up there? You can just see it at the top of that steep hill."

I examine the photograph. People in bright clothes are assembled around the gazebo at the base of the hill in the foreground, some frozen in laughter, raising glasses to their lips, and so forth. There's a path that curls up the side of the hill, turning into stairs at one point, leading up to the so-called bluff, which looms above the park.

She taps a figure up top. "That's Whitney Sternell, the wedding planner, with the dramatic white skunk streak in her hair. Interesting that she's up there."

I memorize this Whitney's face.

Ms. Renfield turns a page, and then another, scanning through the photos. "Most of these images are cropped so that you can't see the hilltop above, but look, there's another one with the cart. Amanda and Isaac were right: it's always parked parallel to the hill. At some point, somebody had to have turned it, released the brake, and pushed."

"Where is the bartender? Kip Kidderson? Show him to me."

She points out a man with artfully disheveled hair and a fashionable suit.

"A dandy," I say.

"Yeah, I guess he is."

"Hmmm."

We find a few photos where Kip and Whitney are in the service area up on the bluff. "This is suspicious, is it not?"

"Yeah, but it's also legit they'd be up there. Whitney would be overseeing everything, and it looks like Kip's getting bottles from the truck."

"Then who are these people down at the bar?"

"Those are his workers. Kip runs the alcohol operations—mixology, as he likes to call it."

"So he's more than a bartender. He's an owner," I observe.

"Yeah, I always think of him as a bartender because that's how he started, but he is also the owner. The boss."

"Why, then, would the boss be running up and down that hill, getting new bottles and so forth? Would he not send an underling?"

"I suppose that's a good point. Why not send one of the kids? Though maybe he wanted to steal away for a smoke or something. That's always possible. But, yeah, that is interesting."

I study the unsuspecting humans who will soon be covered with discarded food. Which is her grandmother?

She turns to another set of pictures. "This is the wedding

where the curtains got set on fire," she whispers. "I don't see Whitney. And no Kip."

"These photographs look like all the rest. I see no fire."

"Well, they're not going to have pictures of disasters in their book."

A woman with giant bright red glasses and a rectangular paper on her chest that says Valerie walks up and takes my measure, slow and suspicious.

"I love seeing these pictures of Mandy and Jim Gordon's wedding," Ms. Renfield says.

Valerie's pulse rate goes up. Defensive. Upset. "You know them? Were you there?"

"No, but I heard it was beautiful."

"It was a beautiful wedding. We got some wonderful pictures. There was a bit of an unfortunate accident at the reception, but it was lovely all the same. This shot's my favorite." She shows us an image of the couple in the corner of a large ballroom. The man sits on a bench with his back to the wall. The bride's head is in his lap.

"She has fainted," I observe. "Terrified, perhaps, of the marriage bed."

Valerie blinks.

"Such a joker!" Ms. Renfield says. "Actually, we did hear about the fire. And that Chief Knox found traces of accelerant and concluded a photographer had spilled equipment cleaner near a candle."

Valerie's anger burns hot and fast. "He may have *concluded* it, but it's complete bullshit, if you'll pardon my French."

"That is not French," I point out.

"Chief Knox doesn't know jack shit about how photographers operate," Valerie says. "For one thing, I can guarantee you that professional photographers do not clean their equipment during a wedding. That's not something that would ever happen. And then a guest randomly moved a candle near the curtain?" She makes a furious wiping motion. "Never mind, though."

Ms. Renfield nods sympathetically.

"And not only did nobody actually see us cleaning cameras by the curtain, but they have no idea what the accelerant was—it was too degraded to tell whether it was cleaner or rubbing alcohol or strong vodka. But hey! It was a long time ago, and I'm not going to worry about it," she says cheerfully, but it's a lie. She's boiling about it.

"Totally get it," Ms. Renfield says. "Do you remember who else worked that wedding? Did Whitney Sternell do the wedding planning?"

"Maybe. I don't know, why?"

"Research," Ms. Renfield says innocently. "If we were interested in seeing other photos from a specific past wedding, do you guys have some kind of archive? Like all the outtakes and discarded photos?"

"Nothing that we'd be able to show anyone." Valerie tries to act calm, but her alarm is spiking.

I find myself intrigued. Is she hiding something?

Ms. Renfield frowns exaggeratedly. "I'm sorry you were wrongly blamed."

"Thank you," Valerie says. "The idea that Manny or I would clean our cameras during an event and slosh cleaning fluid all over is ridiculous. That's like if you went to a gala and decided to wash your hair right in the middle of the dance floor."

"Did you explain that to Chief Knox or ask him for some sort of rationale?" Ms. Renfield asks.

Valerie huffs out a harsh breath. "I've forgotten all about it. Let me know if you have any other questions." She wanders off to talk to a pair of women sitting in the living room arrangement.

"Welp! Don't need predatory emotion-sensing abilities to figure out that she has *not* forgotten about it."

"She'd shout it from the hilltops if she could—but she can't. Her anger is as intense as it is throttled."

Ms. Renfield sharpens her gaze on me. "Throttled?"

"She wants badly to lash out, but something stops her."

"Harlan?"

"It could be that. Or it could be self-preservation. People who protest too loudly are often the first to burn."

Her dark brows knit. "Okay."

She goes back to paging through photographs. "I don't see Whitney or Kip in any of these pictures, but it doesn't mean they're not there." She closes the book, eyes gleaming with the thrill of a new lead. "We have to find out if they were there."

"Agreed."

"And I'd love to get you in a room with Chief Knox. Sounds like he rushed to judgment. And why wouldn't the fire marshal pursue the arson angle? Isn't that a central job duty? Did someone put the kibosh on the investigation?"

"There was something else interesting about our conversation with Valerie."

Ms. Renfield perks up at this. "What would that be?"

"There's something about the archives that makes Valerie very nervous."

"Really?"

"A sense of something hiding in there," I say. "And she wants to keep it hidden. It was very interesting. Could she be our culprit?"

"I don't see how. She wasn't present at a good half of the weddings. And not only was she not present, but she was likely working at other weddings at the time, some of them out of town. Richardson Photography has three employees and a bunch of assistants, and they work weddings in different combinations. Sometimes it's Valerie and Roy. Sometimes it's the owner, Bo, and Roy. Sometimes it's Roy and Manny, etc."

"Nevertheless, I think we should consider Valerie to be a suspect."

"But don't you see? The spreadsheet specifically rules her out."

"My gut rules her back in. There's something secret in the archives."

"Couldn't it be something as simple as her being embarrassed by her earlier efforts at photography?"

"It's more," I say.

Ms. Renfield relents and makes a note of it.

The bridal exposition grinds on, a relentless parade of pastels, florals, and sugary treats, all in service of love and the illusion of forever, for a species whose lifespan barely exceeds that of a gnat.

Villagers flit from booth to booth, weighing fabrics and florals. Some hold clipboards and notebooks. Others tap at electronic ledgers like Ms. Renfield's.

Ms. Renfield scans the room like a tactician—eyes sharp, posture efficient, so intent on this mystery of hers. I've never known a Renfield to be interested in anything other than securing their own comfort or doing things to gain my favor or avoid my wrath.

A woman selling paper garlands regards us approvingly.

"I suppose it is convenient that these people think we're betrothed," I observe. "Ridiculous as it may be. The human brain grows complacent at the sight of a mated pair."

"I was wondering..." She pauses here.

I look down at her, drawn by the spike of heat and curiosity, and what is this? Embarrassment?

"I was just wondering," she says. "Do vampires mate? Or you know..."

I smile. *Aha.* "Ask what you really want to ask, Ms. Renfield."

Her pulse quickens. "I think you know what I'm getting at."

"I think I do. Do I enjoy bedding a woman? Do I make a practice of it?"

She rolls her eyes. "Forget it, don't tell me." She sets off walking again. "If you want to alley cat around, that's your business. Also? No more telling people we're hunting a serial killer."

"So you don't want to know?"

"I'm good!"

"Little liar," I say.

She spins around. "Don't read me."

"How can I resist? You are so desperately curious."

She rolls her eyes.

I move closer. "Are you wondering if I'm as practiced a lover as I am a hunter? Am I just as devious? Am I just as dangerous? Am I able to use my superior senses to give a woman the most exquisite, most soul-shattering pleasure she's ever known?"

She goes beet red. "Maybe I'm wondering why you can't turn into a bat."

I grit my teeth. Of all the vampire lore, I dislike the bat nonsense the most. A small, squeaking flying creature? What imbecile would choose to transform himself into such a thing?

"The way you question people is needlessly circuitous."

"The way I question people is careful and thoughtful. This is a small town, Alexandru. Not a giant city where you can just be weirdly blunt and it doesn't matter because you won't see the people again. Or if they're a problem, you can just..."

"Just what?" I prod.

"Just kill them." She stabs a finger in the direction of my chest. "Ashwood is not your new buffet, mister."

I slow my steps and smile down at her. "Well, that seems to be largely in your hands now, doesn't it? At least for the moment. Though, of course, the clock is ticking."

She makes an exasperated sound that is so very her and once again takes her place by my side. "Look! Check it out—Twist Mixology, Kip Kidderson's operation."

"Let the buffet begin," I tease.

"Seriously, buzz off with the buffet talk. I'm going to ask him questions. See what you pick up." She leads me toward a booth decorated with twinkling lights shaped like tiny bottles. Young people in matching vests shake cocktail mixers with theatrical flair as a small crowd looks on.

The leader is easy to spot. Hair carefully shaped with some manner of wax, beard stubble shaved in a neat shape. Overpowering scent of chemical musk.

His face lights up with recognition. "Harriet Morgan! What's up?" He flicks his gaze to me and his pulse spikes, sensing, perhaps, that I may soon be the one to end him. "And you must be the mystery prince."

I put out my hand. "Alexandru Miramonte."

"Kip Kidderson, master mixologist." There's a microtremor beneath his charm. "And now you two are at the bridal show." He turns to Harriet. "Anything I should know?"

"Alexandru is a friend of my late father's," she says. "I'm doing some work for him, and I thought he'd enjoy getting to know the area."

"I'm sorry to hear about your father. Granabelle told me."

"Thanks. I didn't really know him."

He turns to me. "I still remember this one and her little friend Josie getting drunk as skunks on daiquiris at the Ashwood Tap."

Her cheeks darken. This one is so easily embarrassed. I do not dislike it.

"It was Josie's twenty-first," she says. "And then your blender broke, and we switched to Chablis. Big mistake."

"Yeah, it wasn't really broken. I got sick of making blender drinks."

"What?" Ms. Renfield plants her hands on her hips. "Just for that, I'm going to order blender drinks whenever I go into the Ashwood Tap and you're working."

"Sadly, the blender will be broken." Kip gives me an assessing look. "Sooooo, you wanted to see the town, and she brought you to a wedding expo? Are you in the wedding business?"

"Alexandru's into property holdings," she says.

"That explains it. Kingston Manor? That place was a pile of rubble. It's the last place anybody imagined fixing up. Are you making Ashwood your home?"

"I am."

Ms. Renfield stiffens next to me. "So you know what I just heard? There was a curtain fire here! During a wedding reception? It sounds wild. Did you see it?"

"Oh, yeah." Kip's pulse ratchets... with pleasure. "I had a front-row seat. Two floors of guests were evacuated onto the street. Sprinklers soaked the entire mezzanine. Bridesmaids screaming. Ruined hairdos gone wild."

Ms. Renfield draws closer. "I heard it might have been arson."

"It was ruled an accident," Kip says.

"Do you think it was an accident?" I ask.

Kip holds up his hands in mock surrender. "Hey, I'm just the bartender."

"Do you think it was arson?" I ask him pointedly.

His smile widens. "You know what I think? I think you should go ask Harlan."

Ms. Renfield snorts. "Yeah, right. Come on, spill."

"All I know is that something flammable got spilled or poured on the curtain. And at some point, there was a candle involved because wax was found in the debris. The fire marshal decided it wasn't worth looking into for whatever reason."

"Did you find that odd?" I ask him.

He shrugs. "Nah. It wasn't a huge fire. Unofficially, the conclusion was that Bo Richardson's people were responsible.

They were definitely pissed off because it makes them look like idiots."

"But you don't think it was them?"

"Nah. The Richardson Photography people are pros. I think Harlan wanted to make sure the blame went to someone other than his staffers. Valerie—she was the lead photographer on that wedding—was talking about suing Harlan for libel for a hot minute, but she got shut down. That can't be good for business, right? Having your employee bring a libel suit against the owner of the most popular wedding venue in the area? Not gonna happen."

"You know what's weird?" Ms. Renfield says casually. "There have been a lot of strange accidents at weddings lately. Like that runaway cart. Weren't you at that one?"

I sense another distinct flicker of delight from Kip. "Sure was." He half-sits on the table. "Lotta outfits ruined."

"What do you think happened?" I ask.

Kip eyes me, curious. "I think some people are assholes who shouldn't let their kids run all over the place."

Ms. Renfield waves at one of the employees on the other side of the booth, a young woman with thick, dark eye makeup and black hair. "You think it was kids," she observes casually.

"Don't tell me you think it was a ghost," Kip says.

"And remember the champagne tower collapse?" she asks.

"Oh, maaaaaan. Right?" Kip shakes his head. "Well, that accident was preventable. They should've hired me to build that thing instead of leaving it to the caterers. Big mistake. I was already doing the mixology, but they wanted to save a buck. And what did they get for their trouble? Glass crashing everywhere."

I smile. Kip's delight in glass crashing everywhere is quite strong—definitely something for Ms. Renfield to put in her motivation column.

I look over at her. Did she notice? This mystery solving is

oddly enjoyable, adding a quaint, game-like element to feeding that I had not expected.

The young woman with black hair has wandered over. She bumps shoulders with Ms. Renfield. "Hiya, Harriet."

"Hiya, Lisa!" Ms. Renfield turns her attention back to Kip. "It's amazing it doesn't happen more often with those towers. They never look stable."

"Champagne towers?" Lisa says. "Actually, they can be really stable if you build them right and if the couple is taught how to pour properly."

"The one that collapsed was poorly constructed," Kip adds. "The caterers didn't know what they were doing."

"Maybe," Lisa says. "Though it is possible they built it right but were just unlucky. It could have been a perfect storm of vibrations, like vibration resonance from the subfloor due to asymmetrical guest movement patterns and soundwave interference from the DJ booth placement. It was a very bass-heavy environment—"

"Okay, professor," Kip says, cutting her off. "Let's keep the physics lesson behind the bar. It was a hundred percent a case of poor construction."

Lisa makes a little squeak.

Kip gives her a look. "Also, this isn't social hour."

Lisa heads over to the other side of the booth.

"What she's trying to say is that no champagne tower of mine'll ever be toppling over," Kip says. "It doesn't cost much more to go first class." Right then, his eyes light up at something he sees across the room. "If you're interested in that champagne tower collapse, Bo got some photos that will blow your mind."

"We'd love that!" Ms. Renfield exclaims.

"Hey!" He waves at a man some distance away. He's slender with severe features and carefully styled blond hair.

The man ignores him.

"Bo was shooting the groomsmen doing some shenanigans.

The tower was in the background, starting to fall, and he caught the whole thing. The pictures were spectacular. Hold on." Kip steps out into the river of people wandering by and waves energetically. "Bo! Hey, Bo! Come 'ere a sec."

Bo doesn't want to *come 'ere*, but Kip won't relent. "Quick question!" He motions him over.

Finally, Bo comes. "What?"

"Dude, do you have those champagne tower collapse shots on your phone by any chance? Harriet and Alexandru want to see."

Bo's annoyance is intense. "Why would I have those on my phone?"

"Because they're amazing."

"It wasn't amazing to the bride as I recall. The collapse of that tower was a devastating event for her, so no, I don't carry them around on my phone so we can get our jollies."

"No one was hurt," Kip protests.

"One woman cut her foot so badly she had to go to the hospital and get stitches," Bo says.

Kip sighs. "We were all studying them right afterwards to see if anyone had bumped it. That's how we know the tower went down by itself. But the shots!"

"Hi, Bo." Ms. Renfield puts out her hand. "We met a long time ago when you were taking pictures of Mrs. Morgan's Curio Shop. That's my family's store."

"Oh, sure, back in my *Gazette* era. Your grandmother's really living her best life these days, isn't she?"

"She is," Ms. Renfield says.

"Granabelle's off the chain," Kip says.

Bo checks his phone. "Gotta jet." He mumbles a goodbye and heads off.

Kip snorts. "Bo Richardson. Too cool for school. I'm telling you, though, the champagne tower pictures were poetry. He should put them in a gallery."

Kip's expression shifts right then, and the sense of mischief I feel from him is intense.

"Hi, Harlan!" He waves over a man in a slate-gray suit, silver hair swept back like a crown.

"Don't call him over!" Ms. Renfield says.

"What? You wanted to know about the curtains that caught on fire, right?"

Ms. Renfield mutters a string of words under her breath.

This Kip loves trouble. It's fascinating.

Harlan approaches with a regal air, scanning the group for threats and maybe pecking order. His gaze lands on me and stays there. "Mr. Kidderson," he says, not bothering to turn to the one he addresses. "Is everything alright?"

"Awesome," Kip replies. "But my friend Harriet here was just—Harriet, tell him what you were asking about."

"Nothing," she says.

"Harriet and Alexandru wanted to know if the curtain fire at that wedding here was arson." Kip is practically glowing.

Chapter Twenty-Six

Harriet

Harlan's gaze goes dark as soon as Kip mentions the fire.

Kip could not suck more! And what's up with the staring match between Harlan and Alexandru?

"We weren't seriously asking about it," I stammer.

Alexandru sets a protective hand on my shoulder. "We'd heard some discussion about a fire. I'm interested in preservation."

"So I understand, Mr. Miramonte," Harlan says, making a big show that he knows who Alexandru is and all that goes on in the town.

They talk about the restoration, but my mind is short-circuiting from Alexandru's protective and possessive hand on my shoulder. It feels heavy and good and a little bit dangerous.

"Hands off, buddy," I whisper-breathe, so softly even my ears can't hear it.

"And what drew you to Kingston Manor?" Harlan asks.

Alexandru removes his hand from my shoulder, smiling broadly at Harlan. "The cliff."

Harlan blinks, uncertain if it's a joke or a threat, then barks out a fake-sounding laugh. But they don't stop looking at each other.

Awkward.

"And you're inquiring about an insignificant, months-ago fire because..."

"Alexandru's from Eastern Europe," I explain. "A place called Karsovia. He has a castle back home with actual torches on the walls, so naturally he's interested."

Kip makes a face. "He's interested in a small curtain fire because he's from a castle with torches?"

Kip, never missing a chance to shit-stir. I shoot him a look, the visual equivalent of kicking him in the shin.

Alexandru smiles at Harlan. It's a beautiful smile. A devastating smile.

Harlan turns to Kip. "You're carding everyone, I presume?"

"Absolutely," Kip says, grinning. "Go ahead. Try me. Order a drink."

"No, thank you." Harlan nods stiffly at the group of us and marches off.

I exhale sharply. "Seriously?" I say to Kip. "Are you trying to get me banned from the entire state of Ohio?"

Kip's grinning. "Harlan's so uptight about that fire. Hilarious." Then he turns to Alexandru and goes pale from whatever he sees on Alexandru's face. "I was just fooling around," Kip mutters.

Alexandru says nothing.

"A joke," Kip adds desperately.

"A joke isn't funny if you're the only one laughing," I put in, because honestly.

Kip mumbles something, managing to sound both offended and cowed.

"Let me ask you this," I say. "Was Whitney the wedding planner at the champagne tower collapse wedding?"

Kip furrows his brow. "Can't remember."

"Was she the wedding planner for the wedding with the curtain fire?"

"I don't know. They all kind of blend together. Why? You think Whitney had something to do with the accidents?" Kip lights up with glee. "Shit, are you thinking that because of the Schmidt chairs incident?"

I go still. "The what?"

Kip's face brightens. "You don't know about that?"

"No."

"There's a rumor that Whitney sabotaged some chairs at the Schmidt Mansion. Maybe six or seven months back?"

I exchange glances with Alexandru. *What?!?!!?*

"An elderly woman got hurt." He lowers his voice further. "You know Denny Cole, the handyman?"

I lean in. "Granabelle knows him."

"Denny the handyman was telling everybody who'd listen that Whitney loosened chair legs right before a wedding ceremony in the Schmidt Mansion's great hall. Total disaster. She had a beef of some sort with the owner. You should talk to Denny. He'll tell you. He'll tell you all day long."

Chapter Twenty-Seven

Harriet

"What's up with the He-Man hand on my shoulder?" I say once we're out of earshot. "I'm not territory for you to mark like some beast."

"That is precisely what you are," he says.

"I agreed to work for you. That doesn't make me yours."

Alexandru's eyes glitter like black ice. "You are very much mine, Ms. Renfield. If that man were to so much as breathe at you wrong, he would be made to regret it—slowly and without mercy."

"I mean, *breathe at me wrong?*"

Alexandru lowers his voice to an impossibly low register. "Deep down, he understands that now, though perhaps not the particulars."

I swallow against the dryness in my mouth. "Newsflash: I can take care of myself."

"Debatable, Ms. Renfield."

We climb to the second level of the Glassworks Galleria complex. Alexandru strolls like a country lord surveying his lands. Heads swivel in his wake.

"Mr. Kip Kidderson is chaos-kissed," he says. "The kind to

start a fire just to watch the people scatter. He delighted in those accidents."

"Really? Wow. Did you get any sense of guilt off of him?"

"No, but that doesn't mean much. Some people cause trouble without guilt, and some people kill without guilt."

"I suppose. And I didn't appreciate how he sent Lisa away. I, for one, wanted to hear her scientific explanation."

"Kip did not like that," Alexandru agrees. "As for Harlan Delmere. He could kill. He has it in him."

"You can tell that with a person?"

"I've known men like Harlan. I know what he is."

"Interesting. And he was definitely invested in burying the curtain incident. Wow, could he be doing all of this? Once we get those guest lists from Sloane, maybe we'll find that Harlan was at all of the accident weddings. He was definitely there when the deputy mayor died."

Alexandru nods thoughtfully, pausing near a harpist.

"And that's an interesting tidbit about Whitney, right?" I say. "I wish she were here. As a wedding planner, you'd think she'd want to keep her finger on the pulse." I wince. "So to speak. Not literally."

He flicks his gaze at me. "Don't worry, I won't go feral at the thought of blood," he says. "For several days at least."

I gaze up at him, so cool and composed. "I think you're messing with me. I don't think you'd go feral. I don't think that's your style."

"But then, you don't really know me, do you?"

It's true—I don't really know him. He's a monster. He doesn't think like a human. He might even see the world differently—on a visual level—like when you see a picture of how your cat perceives the world and it's a lot of gray blobs.

And there's also his sexytimes insinuations: *Am I able to use my superior senses to give a woman the most exquisite, most soul-shattering pleasure she's ever known?*

174

It's disturbingly easy to imagine those dark, liquid eyes locked on a lover's, hands skimming over skin, mapping each shiver, using his animal senses to know where to linger, where to press harder, how to push her over the edge...

I shake the picture from my mind as we pass a confectioner's display full of dessert samples.

If only they were offering brain bleach.

"This outing has been helpful. We learned of two new accidents to investigate!"

We turn a corner and find Sloane stationed behind a pale oak table lined with bespoke invitations and paper samples. Her hair is in a roll, like she just stepped off the set of *Downton Abbey*.

"Well, well," she says. "Hello, Alexandru. You're still humoring our poor Harriet and her theories, I see." Her gaze drifts to me, assessing and amused.

I smile, remembering what Alexandru said about Sloane being curious about our investigation. It's the high school reporter in her. "We've discovered some very important information, actually," I say with a glance up at Alexandru. "A few bombshells, in fact."

"That's nice." Sloane folds her hands on the table like a patient hostess. "But if you're still hoping for those guest lists, my answer hasn't changed."

A hand on my arm. Alexandru. "If you'll excuse us, Sloane," he says.

Sloane's eyes laser beam to where he touches me.

I look at her, innocently enough.

"What's up?" I ask as he guides me across the room.

"She's here."

"Who?" But then I see her. Whitney is teaching some kind of mini workshop about tying cloth bows around little boxes to a group of women sitting at a long table.

She comes over when she sees us. "You're Granabelle's

granddaughter, right? Would you like to try your hand at the fine art of bridesmaid giftwrap?"

"No, we're just wandering around," I say, introducing Alexandru.

"The prince!" she exclaims.

Inwardly, I roll my eyes. The Ashwood grapevine strikes again.

"Let me give you my card," Whitney says conspiratorially.

"We're not here planning a wedding or anything," I say.

"I understand." She winks and tucks her card into my hand. "I look forward to hearing from you."

A woman comes up to show her an elaborately tied bow.

"If you'll excuse me." She leads the woman back to the table, making delighted noises of admiration.

"You think she has it in her?" I ask Alexandru.

Alexandru looks thoughtful. "Not the way Harlan does, but all humans have it in them."

His gaze slides to mine, and I know he's thinking about the neck stab.

Chapter Twenty-Eight

Harriet

I ARRIVE at Chez Dracul to pick up Alexandru at eleven the next morning. Our mission today is Berky's Patisserie, but it's a Sunday, so we don't want to get there too early.

Gregor is in his usual long coat when he answers the door, the only man I know who can make a ponytail look severe and totally military.

"So, how are you liking your new home, Gregor?"

"Well enough."

"We're going to visit an amazing pastry chef today," I inform him. "Do you have a favorite kind of pastry? I'll send some back with Alexandru."

"As I have told you, I do not eat pastries."

"Do you like cookies? Berky makes some really outrageous cookies."

"I will alert our overlord that you are here." He exits the room. I listen to his receding footsteps. Is he a demon of some kind? Is that how he got to be over five hundred and thirty-seven? Or is he a human that Alexandru did something to, like whatever he did to my father?

At any rate, he got the memo on "overlord."

Alexandru appears in his day-walking attire—a fine three-piece brown suit, dark glasses, and wide-brimmed hat and gloves. He pulls off the look with his usual predatory elegance.

"Did I do something to offend Gregor, do you think?" I ask as we head to the car. "Is he mad about the overlord terminology change?"

"Gregor does not care about such things."

"He seems unhappy with me."

"Gregor is always unhappy."

"But he seems more unhappy. Like I did something to offend him. Are you sure you haven't picked something up with your Spidey senses?"

"Gregor churns with dark emotions at all times. You should not worry about him."

"Maybe he needs a day off. Does he ever get time off or anything nice from you?"

Alexandru doesn't deign to answer.

I think back to Gregor's room in the castle—it was a barren little garret, like something out of a medieval prison. "Did you at least make a better room for him here, since you had all this custom construction done?"

"That is not for him."

"I don't know if I accept that answer."

Alexandru turns to me with strange intensity. "It is not for you to decide."

"Did Gregor do something to make you want to punish him?"

"That is his confession to make, not mine."

I start the car. "What if he reaches out to me, like he wants something nice, or to have a friendly chat?"

"He won't."

"Maybe he would if he knew that sort of thing was available to him in life, or if he had your blessing. Five hundred and thirty-seven years of scrubbing castle floors and being at your beck and call, never eating anything more than gruel, and you can't give him a break?"

Alexandru turns to me with a cold smile. "I sometimes make him scrub blood from the dungeon walls with nothing but a small toothbrush."

I study his evil, beautiful features, trying to decide if he's messing with me.

But deep down—deep enough to chill my bones—I know he isn't.

I've been getting too cozy with him.

I've somehow forgotten he's a monster. What's the matter with me?

"Are you ever going to tell me what happened between you and the Renfields? Any clue on the mysterious debt that 'curses a despicable family to centuries of penance,' as you put it?"

"No."

"Why not?"

"I do not wish to."

"Maybe I wish you would."

He regards me coldly. "Be careful of what you wish for, Ms. Renfield," he says, voice so grave that it stops me from saying anything more. The rest of the ride is spent in tense silence.

The bell on the door rings as we enter Berky's Patisserie. Two exhausted employees slump behind the counter, barely looking up from their phones. The air smells like espresso and warm sugar, and the display cases are mostly empty, save for a few croissants and a lonely eclair.

Alexandru removes his hat, tucking it under his arm so he can give the gloves his full, unsettling attention. One finger at a time, he works them loose—slow, methodical tugs, each sharper than it needs to be. I can't look away. When all ten fingers are loosened, he slides the gloves off completely, strolling the room, him and those hands—broad, strong, unapologetically masculine. He flexes them once. Why is that hot? It shouldn't be. Those are killing-spree hands.

Berky opened this storefront twenty-two years ago as an upscale pastry shop. I was ten at the time, and I remember going there with James. I'd try to read the signs written in French, all delicate calligraphy and illustrations of macarons, and he'd eat the samples. But over the years, she was beaten down by Midwestern tastes, and now the place is a confusing hybrid— part coffee shop, part pastry shop, and part accidental cookie emporium.

She never meant to become a cookie queen. Berky Bombs started as a gag entry for the River Fair, the town's annual shrine to all things fried, battered, or outrageously sweet. Much to her dismay, her tray of giant cookies stuffed with caramel bits, chocolate chips, sprinkles, fudge, and everything else she could wedge in sold out instantly.

People came into the patisserie and requested them, so she started carrying them. She added a stuffed sugar cookie, all frosting and garish sprinkles, probably swearing in French the whole time, and people embraced that one, too, leaving her poor puff pastries in the dust.

"Is Berky around?" I ask.

The kids behind the counter regard Alexandru warily. The younger one peels himself off the wall and disappears through the swinging silver door.

Moments later, Berky emerges, wiping her hands on a striped dish towel. Her tight, dark curls are pulled back in a puff. Her name is actually Celeste Berquin, but somewhere along the line, somebody gave her the nickname Berky and it stuck.

"Bonjour, Harriet," she says with a slight lift of the chin. Addressing customers in French is one of the last things she's clung to.

"Bonjour, Berky! How's it going?"

"A very busy Sunday." She nods at her young charges. "Take a break, you two."

"This is Alexandru, a friend of my late father's."

"Yes, yes, the Karsovian prince who lives at Kingston Manor." She gives him a polite smile, but her eyes stay sharp. "*Enchanté.*"

"*Le plaisir est pour moi*," Alexandru replies, because, of course, he speaks French.

Berky brightens at this. "*Ah, enfin, quelqu'un avec un bon palais. Attendez.* I have something for you."

She disappears into the back in a swish of her flour-streaked apron and returns a moment later carrying a plate topped prettily with a small golden cake that has a tiny orange twist on top. She sets it down on the counter between them. "My latest *baba au rhum*. Wild yeast from my rooftop starter, Zacapa aged rum, and the citrus is mine too—kumquats, soaked and candied."

"Ohhh, it's one of your rum babas," I say. She's always trying to push these on people and put out samples. *Go ahead, try! It's more than soggy booze bread!*

"I made a small batch today," she says to him. "Try."

"I'm sorry, Berky!" I rub my belly, hoping to provide an excuse for Alexandru not eating. "Not sure if we have room for any more food right now."

Much to my surprise, Alexandru picks it up and smells it, then takes a small bite.

Excuse me, what?!?

His eyelids drift closed. "*Mon dieu*," he says. "Exquisite. Better than in Versailles."

Berky presses a hand to her heart. "Don't say that unless you mean it."

"I never say anything I don't mean," he replies.

I'm just standing there struggling to hide my surprise because, hello, Alexandru can eat food?

Berky claps her hands together. "Finally, someone who appreciates pastry that doesn't come with sprinkles."

"I'm sorry," I tease. "The chocolate-filled almond sprinkle Berky Bombs? You won't tear them from my cold, dead hands."

"Clown food!" Berky turns back to Alexandru. "Did you know the first ones were made for a Polish king who found his cake too dry?"

"I was there," Alexandru says absently. "In a manner of speaking." He asks for a box, explaining that he wants to bring it home and savor it later on.

Berky grabs a box flat and assembles it. "Now, then. To what do I owe this honor?"

"This might seem to be an odd question," I say, "but we're looking into certain events that have occurred at weddings over the last year or so. I wanted to ask you about that cake of yours that collapsed—the three-layer cake—"

"*Merde alors*," Berky mutters.

"Have you thought more about it? Come to any conclusions?"

"Conclusions? Oh yes. I have concluded what I will do to the person responsible if I ever get my hands on them."

"So you're sure it didn't collapse from natural causes? Like being too tall?"

"Too tall! Is the Eiffel Tower too tall? *Non*. There is no such thing as too tall, so long as a cake has the correct supports, the proper weight distribution and temperature management. I promise you this: That cake was perfect. The engineering of it was perfect, and it was, of course, delicious."

"So what do you think happened, exactly?"

"Somebody ruined it. Deliberately. A heat source was applied to one quadrant."

"Are you sure?"

"*Bien sur!* The caterer saved the remains for me to inspect, and from what I saw, you would've thought it was the work of a blow-dryer, but somebody would've noticed that. I do not know how they did it."

"So you weren't there when it collapsed?"

"Of course not. The pastry chef does not stay for the wedding. I deliver the cake a few hours before the event, and the wedding planner helps ensure the cake is stored safely. Whitney was the planner that day, and she is a consummate professional. She and her people have a very specific system for bringing out the cake and protecting it from children and curious guests. She would've noticed if anything was amiss."

I exchange a discreet glance with Alexandru. "So it looked like a blow-dryer was taken to it?"

Berky throws up her hands. "Do not ask me how they did it. One lower quadrant of the cake was melted. Maybe it was something underneath the table that was radiating heat, which was then discreetly removed. I have even wondered if it was a laser. I know how mad that sounds, but if you had seen the perfection of this cake!"

"Did you ask Whitney about it? It was in her custody, after all."

"We discussed it a great deal, of course. She was as mystified as I."

"So you're quite sure it couldn't have been her?" Alexandru inquires politely.

Berky rears back as if struck. "Whitney?! *Mais non!* Whitney was as shocked and horrified as I was, defending me to high heaven. She, too, believed it was sabotage. We have worked together for many years now. We are great supporters of each other. It was not her."

Alexandru leans in. "We heard a strange rumor about her

recently. This person believes she sabotaged chairs at the Schmidt Mansion."

"The chairs! Pfft! That was Schmidt Mansion mismanagement. They have a history of such things—chandelier bulbs burning, a refrigerator left unplugged. Thank goodness it did not contain a cake of mine, but a certain wine steward was livid. They have a history of negligence. I am sorry, Harriet, I know Denny Cole is a good friend of Granabelle, but he is a lazy oaf."

"The person who gave us this information told us that Whitney sabotaged the chairs because of a fight she had with the owner of the Schmidt Mansion."

"Reggie Schmidt." She practically growls the name out. "That man is a jackass to be sure. If you are not one to kiss his hairy ass, he goes out of his way to make things hard."

"So he made things hard for Whitney?" Alexandru asks, weirdly more polite to her than anybody else.

"*Oui, absolument.* But I cannot imagine her stooping to sabotage. And she would certainly have no cause to destroy my cake. I would trust her with even the most elaborate of cakes, whereas Denny? Again, such an oaf."

"Can you think of anybody else who could've done this?" I ask.

Her brow furrows. "I cannot."

"What is your relationship with Kip Kidderson like?" I ask.

"*Le playboy du bar à champagne,*" she says with a sniff. "Could he do such a thing? Kip is too busy fixing his hair and hitting on girls to do anything requiring ingenuity."

"What about Valerie Johnson?" Alexandru asks. "She works with Richardson Photography. Do you have any thoughts about her?"

"Valerie? With the brightly colored fashion glasses?" Berky frowns. "You do not imagine she would do it?"

I check my spreadsheet. "Valerie didn't even photograph that wedding," I say to Alexandru. "It was Roy LaRue and Bo

Richardson. Which means Valerie would've been at a different wedding with Manny or one of the other assistants."

"What is your interest in all this?" Berky asks.

I smile. "Just concerned citizens."

"Concerned about my cake?"

"It may be more than just your cake. Have you noticed there seem to be a lot of accidents at area weddings?"

Berky's eyes widen. "Like when that poor bridegroom went off the balcony?"

"Yes. And the champagne tower collapse, the confetti cannon, the dance floor cave-in at Creighton Arms..."

"*Mon dieu*," she says.

"If there's a connection, we want to figure it out. Let me know if you think of anything more."

I pick out some croissants for Mom and Granabelle, and Berky directs her young charges, who have returned to their posts, to pack them up.

We head down the sidewalk past Sloane Cunningham's fussypants emporium, that is the Aster Press.

"Dude, I didn't know you could eat things! I thought you couldn't. Aside from... you know."

"I can taste," he says, glancing at the box with the rum baba. "But food turns to ash in my mouth, so I prefer not to."

"Actual ash?"

"It feels like it."

"That was still really nice of you. To try it."

"It was no hardship. I could tell it would be good. And it was. For a brief moment."

I gaze over at him discreetly. Did he sound sad just then? Does he wish he could eat it? Does he hate being a monster?

"What is it?"

"What is what?" I ask innocently.

"You're holding something back."

"Please with the mind-meld."

"You have something to say. You will say it."

I turn to him as we walk. I want to ask him everything. "Do you miss food?"

"I miss looking forward to it," he says. "The distraction it offered. That satisfied feeling of being full."

"But not eating?"

"Of course I miss that, too."

Something tells me not to press him on this. "What did you think about Berky, in terms of her answers?"

"No hesitation. No deception. Her cake was sabotaged. She is convinced of it. I tend to believe her."

"Me too. When I was doing my online research, I read somewhere that when a cake fails, an experienced baker knows exactly why it failed."

He nods.

"Very loyal to Whitney."

"There's a warrior in that woman. She sees Whitney as an ally, and she'd fight to the death for her."

"Yeah," I agree. "She'd be devastated to learn it was Whitney."

"I'm even more interested in what this Denny has to say now."

"Same. Though he's notoriously ill-tempered, so it won't be easy getting him to talk."

"Perhaps not for you."

"But we're not playing hardball, remember?" I remind him. "We're going to enlist Granabelle's help. And... umm... that's where we're going right now."

"To see your grandmother?"

"And my mother. We're going to the antique store my family owns. It's called Mrs. Morgan's Curios. They'll both be there, and they want to meet you. It's just a few blocks up on the other side of the park. Do you think you're okay to walk? Will your outfit keep you safe from the sun?"

186

"Absolutely." He puts on his hat and gloves, and we set off.

"Mrs. Morgan is your grandmother, then?" he asks.

"The Mrs. Morgan of Mrs. Morgan's Curios was actually my great-grandmother. She started the shop almost a hundred years ago. And I swear to god, I better not catch you looking at either of their necks."

Chapter Twenty-Nine

Alexandru

We pass the town's park—an expanse of unnaturally green grass, wrought-iron benches, and heavy-limbed maple trees, and at the center of it, a pink-and-white gazebo.

Ms. Renfield points out the areas featured in the photos we saw at the wedding expo: where the runaway cart struck wedding guests, and where her friend's ceremony was interrupted by a premature wedding cannon blast.

"My grandmother was pretty unhappy I didn't bring you around the other day," she says.

"They were offended when they heard I brought you to Sloane's shop but not theirs."

"We had no reason to go there."

"Not for the investigation, but it would be customary to bring you, seeing as that you're my employer. My father's friend. The new celebrity in town."

She's attempting to sound casual and failing. There are so many emotions thrumming through her, it's hard to get a read, but there's definitely fear in there. "Why didn't you introduce us, Ms. Renfield?"

She keeps walking, eyes straight ahead. "I think you know why."

"You are worried I will make a meal out of them if we don't catch your killer? You should know that I take people one at a time, not two."

She stops in her tracks. "Not funny."

I turn. I should not toy with her. She has made me an astonishing amount of money. Money is power, and I am not without enemies.

"You can't ever go after them."

I go to her, gazing down into her eyes, chestnut brown with gold threaded through. "Again, you seem to forget who commands whom here."

She straightens up to her full diminutive height. "I'm telling you. If you touch one hair on their heads—one hair—"

"You'll what? Hurl yourself off the cliff? Deprive me of your servitude?" I move closer to her now, voice low. "I know you now. I know what you're made of. I know you'd never do it."

"I'd find a way to make you sorry. You think I can't?"

"I think you could try. I think it would be amusing," I say, voice just above a whisper now.

A flash of anger mixes with her fear.

Somehow, it sits ill with me.

We set out walking again.

Why should I care what a Renfield feels? I remind myself of what her kind has done. What they're capable of.

"Your great-great-grandfather asked me outright to slaughter his kin," I say.

"Oh my god, another 'Renfields are so awful' anecdote. What a surprise. You really know how to hold a grudge."

"It's a bit more than a grudge."

"For whatever my ancestors did that you won't tell me about. That I seem to be paying for."

I adjust my gloves, ensuring full skin coverage. "And will continue paying forever."

The display window of Mrs. Morgan's Curios is arranged with care: a polished silver tea set on a doily. Lace gloves fanned beside a neat row of vintage teacups. A chipped porcelain doll sits propped on a velvet cushion, her glass eyes staring blankly at the grocery store and barber shop across the street.

Ms. Renfield walks in, still angry, and I follow. "And here he is," she says with a wave of her hand. "His Royal Highness. Please, everybody, try to contain your awe."

"Harriet, what is this?" A woman in her fifties comes out from behind the counter. She's a more seasoned mirror of Harriet with strong features, symmetrical and certain, nothing delicate or perky.

Though their hair is completely different. Whereas her mother's hair is coarse and straight, just skimming her jawline, Ms. Renfield has the Renfield curls.

"I'm Lorna." She casts a dark glance at her daughter.

"I'm so pleased to finally meet you," I say, removing my gloves. I look over to find Harriet's gaze glued to my hands, pulse ratcheting up, as though she might see the name of the killer written on my finger.

I fold my gloves and settle them neatly into my pocket.

Mrs. Morgan's Curios is a cheerfully overstuffed Midwestern antique shop that smells of dust and lemon wood polish. Sunlight filters through lace curtains, glinting off the crystal doorknobs in a display case. Shelves are packed with tin toy soldiers and vintage postcards in little stacks. A painted plaster pheasant presides over the cash register.

"You've been keeping my girl pretty busy, Mr. Miramonte," Lorna says. "I was surprised she took on more."

"Your daughter is remarkably industrious. She informed me she intended to improve upon her father's work, and I must say, she has exceeded expectations."

Lorna makes a small noise in her throat, unimpressed. "Her father. Great. And you two were business associates?"

"He was my..." I slide to glance over to Ms. Renfield. "Underling."

Lorna raises her brows. "Doesn't say much for your choice of underlings. Tell me, what kind of man bangs a woman on a train and then jumps into the Carpathians in the middle of the night? From what Harriet's told me, he was a muttering, bug-eating little freak. Yet somehow, he was your employee, and you gave him *bookkeeping* tasks he couldn't understand. Tasks difficult enough to challenge my brilliant daughter, but you had this poor sod doing them. I understand you're a prince or whatever, but what kind of man hires someone that disturbed for something that demanding?"

I arch a brow. "I don't require my assistants to be emotionally sound. I require them to be useful."

Ms. Renfield stiffens beside me. "Such a joker."

Lorna doesn't laugh. "It didn't sound like a joke. It sounded like you enjoy taking advantage of the mentally unwell. And now you've got Harriet tied up in knots."

"I'm not tied up in knots," Ms. Renfield protests.

"And Sloane tells me you're collaborating with my girl on one of her investigations? What kind of game are you playing?"

"Your girl is fine," Ms. Renfield says. "Your girl is right here, capable of applying critical thinking."

"How long is this assignment of yours going to last?" Lorna demands.

"It's permanent," I say.

Lorna's eyes go cold. This woman surprises me. Her fire. She's been through things. "She already has a job. One she loves."

"Mom, I can handle my own business."

"You don't need two jobs. What do you need two jobs for?

Also, who the hell wears gloves in April? What is this? *Masterpiece Theater?*"

At that moment, a voice floats down from the second floor. "Is that my *favorite granddaughter* I hear?"

An older woman descends the stairs with casual theatricality, dressed in a tweed riding jacket, a toucan-print scarf, and what appear to be a boy's jodhpurs. Her gray hair is swept into a regal twist, and she's holding binoculars for some reason.

She stops partway down and surveys the scene with arched brows, and then her gaze lands upon me. "Prince Alexandru Ilie of the Principality of Karsovia, I presume."

"Correct," I say. "And to whom do I have the pleasure?"

"Annabelle Morgan, but you may call me Granabelle."

She descends the rest of the way and comes to me, hand outstretched. I take it and brush my lips over the back with a sly glance toward Ms. Renfield, whose face has gone ashen. "Please, call me Alexandru," I say.

Granabelle beams at me. "So, Alexandru, how are you finding Ashwood? I hope it's to your liking."

"Very much so," I reply. "In fact, I intend to make it my permanent home."

Her hands clap together with delight. "Capital news!"

"Jesus Christ on a cracker," Lorna mutters.

"Has anybody shown the prince around?" Granabelle asks.

Ms. Renfield sighs.

"For heaven's sake." Granabelle sweeps over to me and begins a tour of the shop while quizzing me on the renovation. I answer politely, ever conscious of Ms. Renfield stewing in our wake.

"Hey. What are you doing for a foyer table?" Lorna asks suddenly, from the other room. "You need to buy this one."

"Mom, you can't just tell him what to buy."

"I'm just saying. If someone's doing a period restoration, and from what I can tell, you are, you need to take a look at this dark

192

walnut demi-lune. It's got a lovely marble top. Nice scrollwork on the apron."

"Let's see it," I say.

She leads me to the table at the front of the store, where the table in question stands beneath a gilt-framed mirror. The marble is charcoal gray, the wood dark and warm.

I run my fingers over the edge. "It would suit the entry hall perfectly."

Granabelle lights up. "It *is* a beautiful piece."

I catch Ms. Renfield watching me, brows drawn together.

"And how are you set for linens?" Lorna asks.

Before long, I've selected linen napkins, a pair of brass candlesticks with lions at the base, a set of Eastlake chairs, and something called a "Hepplewhite sideboard."

I arrange to send Gregor around to pay for the pieces and finalize the deliveries.

"These will look beautiful in your home," Granabelle says, wrapping up my candlesticks with paper and string. "The renovation must be breathtaking."

"It's not all that," Ms. Renfield says. "And I don't know when it's going to be done. Oh! I almost forgot." She sets the larger of the two bakery bags on the counter. "We got you pastries from Berky's."

"That's nice," Lorna says warily.

"And I have a question or actually a request." Ms. Renfield turns to Granabelle. "We really want to ask Denny about a few things, and I don't know if he'd talk to us without you there."

"What kind of things?" Lorna asks.

Ms. Renfield gives her mother a hard look. "Mystery things, and don't start on it."

Granabelle looks worried. "Not all this wedding hullabaloo, I hope."

"Yes, the wedding hullabaloo, and for your information, Alexandru completely agrees with me."

"I do," I say.

Granabelle's features light with surprise.

Lorna's do not. "You come to town, monopolize my daughter's time, and suddenly you're on board with her wild theories?"

"Your daughter sees things that other people don't," I say to her.

"The way her father did?" Lorna says. "Because it sounds to me like a fly would buzz by that man's nose and he'd see a cheeseburger."

"Yeah, not like that," Ms. Renfield snaps.

"Your daughter has a brilliant mind for discerning truth in chaos," I say.

"I could bring you over to see Denny," Granabelle says. "He's prickly as an old hedgehog, but he responds to a soft touch."

"Do you think it's possible to go today?" Ms. Renfield asks her.

Granabelle grabs the bakery bag. "Let's give it a try."

Chapter Thirty

Harriet

Granabelle holds Alexandru's arm as we stroll toward my car. The going is slow. She's dragging him from one storefront window to the next, pointing things out, but it's pretty obvious that Alexandru's the one on display like Granabelle's prize pig.

And he's allowing it, for whatever reason.

She was extra delighted that he donned gloves and a hat for the occasion, though she was disappointed he wanted to stay on the shady side of the street. "My skin burns easily," he said simply.

She makes a point of introducing him to people, including Mom's frenemy, Sally Janson, which Mom will be pleased about, even though she really did seem to take a dislike to Alexandru. Does she sense his monster nature? Or is she just taking cues from me? I sometimes forget how street-smart she is.

Granabelle laughs at something Alexandru whispers. I grit my teeth. Seeing them all chummy like this is my worst nightmare.

Maybe that's why he's doing it.

I tell myself to focus on the problem at hand. We need to find the killer. That's how I really ensure their safety.

&a

SCHMIDT MANSION RISES REGALLY at the edge of town just past the Silverton Music Conservatory. It has manicured hedges and a wrought-iron gate, and vines creep up the grand stonework.

"We can't just go in!" I say.

"Nonsense, come!" Granabelle says, pulling Alexandru into the foyer while I follow, because apparently, the granddaughter is chopped liver now that there's a prince around.

The last time I was here was a few years back for Josie's wedding to Derek, the fourth-grade teacher who caught her eye while she was campaigning for city council.

I was so happy for her, and so wildly proud to be her maid of honor. It's a gorgeous place for a wedding, very grand and old-world with chandeliers and elaborate woodwork.

Workers seem to be setting up for an event, hauling lighting rigs and sound equipment around.

Granabelle holds the door open for one of the workmen. "There we are, sweetheart."

A broad-shouldered woman with a clipboard heads over from the side. "I'm sorry, we're setting up for a private event. You can't be here. No public."

Granabelle lifts the paper bag of croissants and puts on her best frail-old-lady smile. "We're just dropping these off to my dear friend Denny. He's working down in the basement today. It won't take but a minute."

The woman frowns.

"He's the one who keeps this place running, and it would mean ever so much to him." She lets her voice crack just a bit.

"Fine." The clipboard woman waves us in. "Don't touch *anything*."

We head for the stairs and go down.

The basement looks like the back room of a used furnishings

196

store—tables stacked on chairs, lamps propped up on aging appliances, and fluorescent lights buzz faintly overhead. At the far end, a man stands at a cluttered workbench, hammering with slow, deliberate force.

"Looks like somebody's hard at work over there," Granabelle sings.

Denny stands, his grumpy face brightening. "Anabelle, what a surprise." He grabs a rag and wipes his hands, eyeing Alexandru. "You look lovely."

Granabelle beams. "I come bearing pastries and a wee request. You know my granddaughter, of course, and this is her employer, Prince Alexandru Ilie of the Principality of Karsovia."

Denny isn't sure what to make of the name, but then he sees the bag. "Berky's!"

Granabelle kisses him on the cheek. "Not the cookies, I'm afraid."

"No, this is wonderful." He looks in the bag. "What's the request? Is that Deco fixture shorting out again?"

"My granddaughter and Alexandru are interested in getting to the bottom of some strange accidents that have happened during wedding ceremonies and receptions recently."

His gaze flicks from Alexandru to me and back to Alexandru. "What do you mean, getting to the bottom of them?"

"We think they're suspicious," Alexandru says. "We think there's something more to them, and we've heard you may share those thoughts."

"Are we talking about what happened at the Creighton Arms? Because I most certainly do share those thoughts when it comes to that." Denny sets the bag on an old piano.

"We'd love to hear about it." I turn to Alexandru. "Creighton Arms is a historic hotel in downtown Creighton. They used to have really fancy weddings there, but they closed after that bridegroom fell to his death off a balcony."

"That poor bride," Granabelle says. "To lose the love of her life..."

"The month before that, the dance floor there caved in, and a few people got very badly injured."

"And I can tell you what I told Anabelle, here," Denny puts in. "My old friend Handy Jack did the maintenance there, and he was one of the best in the business."

"Denny has always admired Handy Jack's capabilities," Granabelle says.

Denny tells us about Handy Jack's meticulous record-keeping. It also turns out that he had seen the underside of that dance floor that collapsed. "I can tell you there was nothing rotten down there."

"You were under there right before it collapsed?"

"Maybe a month prior." Denny takes a croissant from the bag and rips it in half. "Here's the thing: after that dance floor cave-in? Handy Jack went to consult his maintenance records, and they had been stolen. Right off the nail where they always hung on their clipboard."

"Really," I say.

"Yes." Denny points at us with the end of a croissant. "I ask you, who would do that? Somebody who monkeyed with the support beams, that's who. Handy Jack thinks somebody applied sodium hydroxide to the beams. You know what that is? It's lye. It's what they make soap with, and it does a number on wood."

"Could he prove it?"

"Nah," Denny says.

"Is it weird that no one ever investigated?" I ask him. "Who made that decision?"

Denny chews thoughtfully. "Powers that be, I don't know."

I look over at Alexandru and find him staring at me. Have his eyes been on me this entire time?

Granabelle shakes her head. "The authorities wanted none of it."

"And this Officer Cooper had no explanation for the missing maintenance logs?" Alexandru asks.

"He said it didn't prove anything." Denny takes another bite. "The guy who owned the place thought it was foul play, too, but nobody would listen. Poor Jack wasn't sleeping so well after that. And then the next thing you know, the balcony fall happened."

He tells us about that accident from Handy Jack's point of view. How he and Handy Jack firmly believe somebody put some kind of corrosive agent on the metal.

"I'm telling you, there's no way you'd have that level of metal corrosion on Handy Jack's watch. And do you know what else? The new logs that Handy Jack started were stolen again."

"That is suspicious," I say.

"It did a number on the man," Denny says darkly. "He's just broken. It was everything to him, maintaining those buildings. He was proud of his work. Because it was damn fine work. He's down in Florida, now."

"Did Jack have any theories about who could've done it?" I ask.

"He had a few enemies, but no one who woulda had the balls or the know-how." He pulls out another pastry.

"Do *you* have any theories?"

He seems surprised by the question. "Not really. Seems senseless to me." He takes a bite.

"We heard something interesting recently about Whitney the wedding planner. That she sabotaged some chairs here."

"She sure did." Denny stops chewing and stares intensely into the distance. "You think it was Whitney going after Handy Jack?"

"Well, what happened with the chairs?" I ask. "Can you tell us about that?"

"Can I tell you about that? I can do you one better. I can show you."

He leads us into a dusty back room that may have been an ancient cistern and shows us the dusty remnants of some old chairs. He picks one up and turns it over, pointing out where the rungs and legs join. "See these scratches? Somebody deliberately loosened the joints. And that person was Whitney Sternell."

Alexandru watches him intensely. "How do you know it was her?"

"For one thing, I caught her down here the day of the wedding. She said she was looking for some sort of crêpe paper or something, but why the hell look for some fancy paper down in the shop here? Right? I thought it was strange, and then when the chairs collapsed—right at the start of the ceremony—I happened to be up in the balcony tweaking the HVAC. From up there, I could see her face clear as day, and she didn't look surprised at all. Why? 'Cause she did it. It was her beef with Reggie Schmidt."

"Reggie Schmidt is the owner here," Granabelle explains. "Not the beacon of humanity, let's just say."

Denny shrugs. "At least the man doesn't go around ruining chairs. The month before that, she loosened lightbulbs in the chandelier that I had recently changed. I knew there was nothing wrong with those bulbs, but I think she got a telescoping tool and loosened them. Then, when they were discovered to be out, she brought her own guy to change them like a hero, telling everyone who'd listen that the place isn't well-maintained. And another time, she cut the cord to a freezer. You could look at it and see that she tried to make it look like it was frayed, but the closer you got to it, the more you could see it was deliberate. I wish I kept it, but I threw it out."

"Tell them what the beef was," Granabelle encourages him.

"Someone interviewed Reggie for the *Ashwood Gazette*, and he badmouthed her something awful."

"Not by name, but everybody knew," Granabelle exclaims, drifting off toward a dusty puppet theater propped against the basement wall. The paint is peeling off, but you can still see the blues and golds, with sunbursts and crescent moons curling along the arch.

"She lost a lot of business from that article. The chairs and lightbulbs were revenge."

Alexandru clasps his hands in front of him. "Berky is convinced she'd never do such a thing."

"Berky." Denny snorts derisively. "Berky doesn't know her as well as she thinks."

"Interesting," Alexandru says.

For all his complaining, he really does seem to be following these revelations with interest. I'm glad. I want him to be on board with this new way of hunting, for obvious reasons.

Over in the corner, Granabelle has set up her phone on a paint can. She taps it a few times and dives behind the tiny stage for a whimsical pose just as the shutter clicks.

Denny warns Granabelle to be careful and then regards me with a speculative look. "It sounds to me like you're thinking Whitney could've been responsible for the sabotage at Creighton Arms."

"We're exploring all possibilities," I say.

"Whitney." Denny inspects his croissant. "Maybe she enjoyed creating a little chaos. She got a taste of it, and she kept going."

"Came for the vengeance and stayed for the show," Granabelle adds, setting up another shot.

"Be careful back there, Anabelle," Denny warns again.

"You think Whitney could do all that?" Alexandru asks him.

"Whitney is more vindictive than psycho, but I guess with some people it's a fine line," he says.

"Harriet! Alexandru! I need your help!" Granabelle calls.

Alexandru and I wander over. It turns out she needs help getting a photograph of her and Alexandru in front of the puppet theater with Alexandru holding her hand in a courtly way, as though he's about to kiss it, much to Denny's extreme displeasure.

But then Granabelle brings Denny over to do a pose where he kisses her cheek while Granabelle's mouth hangs open in surprise.

Chapter Thirty-One

Harriet

Tres Hermanas smells like garlic and charred steak and warm bread. The dishes and silverware clink as the waitstaff cleans the lunch hour wreckage.

Serena stands, signaling the end of our meeting with organizational wunderkind Malik Thomason. He shakes Serena's hand and then mine, quick and confident.

"I'll look forward to hearing from you both," he says, clutching his tablet. With that, he disappears out onto Commerce Avenue.

We sit back down. Serena sets her phone down. Her home screen is one of her ultra-dramatic architectural photos. She's wild about lines and shapes. "Did you catch that?" she says, twisting her glossy black hair into a bun. "Hearing from us both. He did his research, didn't he?"

"Yes, he did," I say with a sigh.

One of the regional tech blogs recently called me "the shadow COO of InovaSpire," and they're not wrong, though I asked Serena not to give me a C-title. I prefer to work behind the scenes.

"What do you think?" she asks me.

"I think you were right about him," I say. "He's fast. He processes systems fast. He tracks consequences. Didn't flinch when you asked about moving the timeline. And the playbook he suggested?"

"I liked that too," Serena says as she stands again. "He'll be a force multiplier, don't you think?"

"Absolutely."

She gives me a look that's part pride, part sorrow. "He's good, but I swear it'll take more than two people to do your job."

"I'll still be around," I tell her. "Questions, advice, emergency brain-picking—I'm yours."

"I know." Her smile is warm, but it doesn't reach her eyes. She took the news hard. Couldn't believe I'd walk away from a company I helped build just to go organize someone's private empire.

"I always thought you were destined for... something bigger," she'd said when I told her.

From her angle, it *is* a terrible move.

But I can't tell her the truth—that I'm the reason a vampire is in town, and the only way to keep him from preying on my friends and family and neighbors is to work for him.

I can't tell her about the investigation either, or how every lead feels like a chance to balance the scales. To save a life instead of costing one.

"Let's have that offer to him before he gets back to Cleveland."

"On it." I signal for the check. "Go ahead—you've got the media thing."

Serena takes off. I hand the card to our waitperson and ask her to add a slice of cheesecake to go. Then I fire up my tablet and send the offer out.

"Well, well, well." Josie slides into the seat across from me and pulls her son, Angus, onto her lap. He's in a Spider-Man shirt, and his curls are half-wild.

"High five." I reach over the table to meet his hand for a high five, and he tells me about the boat they're going to ride on for his upcoming birthday.

"Are you going to be five?"

Angus smiles. "No, three!"

"*Whaaaat?*" I say, pretending to be aghast.

Angus laughs. He loves being mistaken for an older boy. Our waitress brings my dessert in a box and a little plate of animal crackers for Angus.

"What do we say?" Josie says to Angus.

"Thank you!" Angus starts arranging the animal crackers in pairs.

Josie waves to a few people. She is the ultimate high achiever. In addition to her seat on the city council, she runs a literacy nonprofit. She'll run for mayor someday, not that she'd admit it publicly.

"So. You know everybody's talking about you and Alexandru's investigation, right?"

I keep my expression neutral. "Everybody?"

She ticks off fingers. "City admin chat. Mom group thread. My book club. Just to name a few. People don't know what to think. Some think the prince is enchanted with you and just playing along to stay close. Others think he's this benighted old-world royal who's fallen into your personal murder conspiracy cult."

"Maybe it's both," I joke.

Josie takes a breadstick from the basket that the waitress forgot to take. "You're just a female Svengali, aren't you?"

I shrug. "What can I say?"

"I mean, is he truly on board with it?" She leans in. "Or is he just really, really, *really* on board with *you?*"

I would not marry a Renfield even if the alternative were to be chained to the bottom of the sea to slowly be consumed by eels.

"We have a purely professional relationship."

"It seems weird that your part-time employer would become so invested in this thing. And I still say it's the Snag Tooth Riders."

"Even if the stairway collapse *was* the Snag Tooth Riders, there's still something up with the rest of the accidents." I hold up my hand, stopping her inevitable disagreement. "I know, I know. Bad for wedding tourism."

"Do you have any more proof of anything? Bring me proof, and I'll go down to the police station myself."

"We're working on proof," I say.

She gets a sly look on her face.

"What?" I say.

"Alexandru *is* handsome... in a dashing, surly way. He's very take-me-now-against-a-wall handsome."

"Pass," I say.

"You sure? It's been ages since you broke it off with Maverick. And I can't be the only one who sees some chemistry between you two."

"Not the good kind of chemistry, trust me. Anyway, guys are more trouble than they're worth. Interruptions, distractions, demands—the constant drama—"

"I know, I know." Josie lifts her hands in mock surrender. She's heard this rant before. "Romance is nonsense, relationships are a trap—yada yada."

"They're not a trap," I correct. "They're just a lousy return on investment. More cost than benefit."

Josie smirks. "Only you would put love in spreadsheet terms."

I grab a breadstick just for something to do with my hands. I haven't told her I've quit my job yet. I don't know how to tell her that.

Instead, I tell her about Mom's super side-eye on Alexandru, and she's highly entertained.

"Your mom is the ultimate tough cookie. I can so still see her

206

ordering recruits around and taking no shit." Mom was in the Army for a few years.

"Yeah. She takes even less shit now," I say.

"I know," Josie says softly.

I don't have to complete the sentence, namely that she takes less shit now *ever since James disappeared.*

Josie catches me up on city council gossip, including that jerk, Harlan Delmere, trying once again to ram through the most horrible building project in Ashwood history.

"I thought you guys already voted that down!" I say.

"Now that Deputy Mayor Kazan died, Harlan gets to call another vote."

"Like anyone's going to change their minds," I say. "What a jerk."

"Being a jerk never stopped Harlan Delmere," Josie says, stroking Angus's hair. "The mayor'll veto it in a heartbeat, won't he?" she says to him. "Won't he? Yes, he will! Yes, he will!"

Harlan wants to build a big retail/residential complex on everybody's favorite riverside park, a beautiful and prime parcel right between Ashwood and Creighton. He's trying to do a land swap with some scrubby land down the river.

Nobody's going for it, except the few council members he has in his pocket.

My attention is snagged by a group of college-aged kids over at the large table in the corner. "Hey, there's your cousin Lisa."

Josie twists around. "I think that might be her robotics group. They do some kind of contraption battle thing. Why?"

"Alexandru and I talked to her at the wedding expo, but Kip was right there, and I feel like he sort of put the kibosh on her giving the detailed answers we would've liked to hear."

"Kip likes to be the star of every show."

"Keep this to yourself, but he's one of our suspects."

Josie sits up. "Kip?"

"Kip!" Angus bangs a crayon on the table.

"I can't imagine that," Josie says, but then she looks off like she might be imagining it. "Do you want me to get Lisa over here?"

"I don't want to interrupt her robotics meeting."

"That meeting'll go three hours while they stuff themselves with food before they go back to their workshop and tinker all night listening to goth music." She pulls out her phone and shoots off a text.

Over at the table, Lisa twists around and waves. She holds up a finger.

"OK, she's coming." Josie tucks away her phone and smooths Angus's curls. "Seriously, though, is there anything that will make you conclude that these accidents were just that, accidental? What will it take to make you think that?"

"If that's what the data says to me."

Josie sighs. "You're usually right about things, but if we've got a wedding saboteur on the loose here...? Then I hope you figure it out fast."

"Hey!" Lisa slides into the seat next to Josie and ruffles Angus's hair. "Can I have an animal cracker?"

Angus shakes his head no. Josie cajoles him into sharing just one, to which he reluctantly agrees.

Lisa laughs. "Just kidding!" She smiles at me. "So what's up?"

"I just had a few questions after our discussion at the wedding expo the other day."

Lisa gives me a sassy look. "You and the hot prince?"

"She has him hypnotized!" Josie exclaims, standing and hoisting Angus onto her hip, still holding his crayon. "Let's go see Abuelita in the kitchen!"

Angus lets out a sound of delight as they head back.

I turn to Lisa. "I was curious to hear more about your thoughts on how a perfect storm of vibrations could've made that tower of champagne glasses fall."

"It really is just a theory. But it's like the base beat travelled along structural beams and where the table was unfortunately placed. It's the only thing I could come up with, because honestly, I watched the Stanley people build that thing, and it looked good to me. Those towers are pretty stable when they're built right, and that one was built right. I don't care what Kip says. It was a good tower."

"So you were near the tower the whole time? From when they built it to when it crashed?"

"Pretty much. Right across from them."

"Can you walk me through it?" I ask.

"They brought their own table. You really need something specific for a champagne tower because you need to trust that table. And the actual construction of the tower happens as late as possible, usually during dinner service, because, sure, these things are stable when built right, but someone knocking into it can definitely bring it down. After they built it, two Stanley Catering people stood on each side, guarding it from drunks. Pretty standard. The champagne towers are like a magnet for drunk wedding guests."

"Did you have a pretty good view of it during that time?"

"Oh, yeah. It was right on the other side of the DJ booth, and like I said, people were still eating dinner. Nothing much was happening at the bar."

"How long between when they had it set up and when it collapsed?"

Lisa purses her lips. "Maybe twenty minutes?"

"Did anyone else come around the table?"

"Oh, yeah. A lot of people came over to look at it. You always get a few wedding guests making jokes, like pretending they're tripping or falling. Not funny. And the wedding planner was there adding decor."

"Whitney? Do you remember if it was Whitney Sternell?"

"Yeah, it was Whitney the wedding planner. She always

makes these custom vignettes for the couple, tailored to their interests—a flower, a bell, a tiny bike, or whatever—and she puts them all over the place. All I remember about this one was that there was a Mickey Mouse head involved. Because the couple are Disney fanatics." Lisa bites the side of her lip. "The photographers came over to do detail shots, too, like B-roll shots."

"Was it...?" I wake up my tablet and check my spreadsheet. "I have it down here that Bo Richardson and Roy LaRue were shooting that one. Do you remember which one of them did the close-ups?"

"I feel like they were both doing things around the table."

I nod. "So a lotta traffic."

"For sure. And there were the usual kids asking questions. DJ Sassy Sadie was over there for a while, too, and Kip went over to trash-talk them. Somebody also would've brought over the fake champagne."

"It's fake?"

"Stanley Catering puts cheap sparkling wine in Veuve Clicquot bottles for their fountains. It's not like people drink that stuff. I mean, everyone's fingers are all over those glasses during setup, so it's not exactly hygienic. The tower is just for show."

"I heard that nobody was near the table when it actually fell."

"Correct. Aside from the Stanley people standing on either side to guard it. But they don't stand that close. They don't want to bump it either. At the time of the fall, though, most everybody was watching the groomsmen doing some kind of pretend fistfight on the other side of the room. Bo was photographing the shit out of that, and the tower was collapsing in the background behind them."

"So, you've got a good grasp of mechanical things. Let me ask you, if somebody were to sabotage that champagne tower and make it look like it just spontaneously collapsed, how do you think they would do it?"

Lisa widens her eyes. "You think that's what happened?"

"I think this is one of a strangely large number of wedding accidents around here this year."

"Like Boyd falling off the balcony."

"Yeah."

"Handy Jack was distraught. Everyone thought he'd screwed up."

"You know Handy Jack?"

"Oh yeah. He's kind of Robotics Club adjacent. The man knows a lot about really random tools and techniques. He had an insane clipboard checklist system."

"You know about the checklist?"

"Oh, we all saw waaaaay too much of that checklist. The man thought everybody should use his system. And then some asshole stole it—twice! Most of the people who hang out at Hardware Sam's think it was somebody out to get Handy Jack."

"Wow."

"But the champagne tower would have nothing to do with Handy Jack."

"So if you had to rig the table to make the champagne tower collapse, like maybe by remote control, how would you do it?"

Lisa taps a finger to her lips. "If you could get a solenoid actuator under a leg, you could activate it with a wireless switch to create a sharp sideways movement. Sort of like a pinball machine part."

"How about something that doesn't involve kneeling down by the table? Because the Stanley people would see that, right? What about something that you could stick to the bottom of the table or put on top of the table, like maybe hidden in the flowers."

Lisa nods slowly, warming to the idea. "Yeah, yeah. You could use a gyroscopic device hidden in a floral arrangement. Something that shakes just enough to destabilize the base layer.

Or maybe a small vibration motor affixed to the bottom using superglue or a similar adhesive. Interesting."

"Do you think somebody could have affixed something to the bottom of the table before they brought it out?"

"No way," Lisa says. "The Stanley people make a lot of adjustments on the table before they start building. They would've seen it. You need that thing super level."

"Can you recall anybody spending a weird amount of time around the table and being shady?"

"So you're really thinking somebody crashed it on purpose."

"I'm exploring all the angles."

"Nothing sticks out," Lisa says. "It all seemed very routine. Aside from the champagne tower spectacularly collapsing, glass going everywhere, people screaming because they stepped on glass, and insurance getting involved."

I SPEND the rest of the afternoon at InovaSpire, putting out workflow fires and thinking about what Lisa said. She provided a pretty good list of people who drifted by the champagne tower table during the twenty-minute window where it was on display, including Whitney and Kip.

I'd love to get my hands on the pictures Bo took. He probably wasn't shooting for the whole twenty minutes, but between him and Roy LaRue with his B-rolls, there was probably a lot of coverage of that time span. Maybe he inadvertently caught either Whitney or Kip doing something suspicious. Or Harlan. Or some other person common to all the weddings.

I leave a message with Richardson Photography. Maybe if it's not Kip asking, they'll be more willing to show the photos.

Chapter Thirty-Two

Alexandru

We pull up in front of a red brick building on the southern edge of town. The sun has just set, and the festive lights up and down Commerce Street are flickering to life.

A red and chrome firetruck gleams in the shadows of the open garage. Ms. Renfield glances over and flashes a grin. "Ready to use your bat senses on Chief Knox?"

"Not if you call them bat senses."

She's just shutting her door when her phone rings. "It's Richardson Photography! Lemme get this quick." She turns away to take the call.

I stand and wait.

Ashwood divides neatly along a north-south line, with the central Gazebo Park as its heart. The southern side is polished and charming—wine bars, a gourmet grocer, stylish boutiques, and the cheerful steak and seafood restaurant with its string lights and patio heat lamps.

The north end feels more lived-in. Harriet's family's antique shop is here, along with a bar, a hardware store, the library, a used clothing store, and a few other worn storefronts. The farther south you go, the more the charm fades—until you hit the fire station, the drug store, and an obnoxiously well-lit gas station.

"We just need to take a look at a few old photographs from your archives. We won't tell anybody your uncle showed them to us, and we won't ask to copy them. We just need to take a look."

The voice on the other end questions her. "Why do you need to look at old photographs?"

"It's just really important," she says.

"My uncle would need to have a good reason to open up the archives to prying eyes," the voice says. "Especially the champagne tower pictures. That couple was extremely upset."

Ms. Renfield pleads with him some more, even using the phrase "life or death."

She pockets her phone with a huff. "Bo's nephew, Manny. Apparently, stubbornness runs in the family."

"He called you?"

"I left a message earlier to see if we could take a look at the full set of their photos for the twenty minutes from when the champagne tower was finished being built to when it collapsed, and he's a big no on that. Apparently, the bride and groom were devastated by the collapse and don't want the photos shared."

"That is very extreme."

"People have very extreme feelings about weddings in this culture," she explains.

"I would be happy to convince him to change his mind about showing us the pictures," I say.

"No, thanks. We won't be putting the thumbscrews to Bo Richardson or his nephew."

"Suit yourself."

She blinks. "That's not what you'd really do, though, right?"

"There are so many options," I say. "But thumbscrews do have a certain charm."

I watch Ms. Renfield check her electronic ledger in prepara-

214

tion for our meeting, wondering if she has extreme feelings about weddings.

Did Ms. Renfield want to be a bride? Does she imagine herself having a wedding with things like champagne towers and confetti cannons?

Did she have plans to get married? To have children? The face of Maverick Cooper pops into my mind. She is fond of him, and he of her. Not that it matters. If he so much as attempted to distract her from her duties with me, I would kill him.

"Earth to Alexandru! What's going on?"

"Are you finally done checking your ledger?" I grumble.

"I was done forever ago, but you were somewhere else, and from the looks of it, you were imagining unpleasant things. Let me guess, people being happy and skipping through daisies with their blood flow intact?"

"Are we going to question this fire chief or not?" I ask.

Ms. Renfield stares up at the top of the firehouse. There's a circular medallion sunk into the bricks bearing the year 1989. "I'm hoping to get more details of the curtain fire. We still don't know if Whitney was the wedding planner for that one. And I'm curious about the reason for the lack of investigation. I'm still a little suspicious of Harlan, too, like I know you are."

"I know a blackguard when I meet one." But it's more than that. He's up to something, though men of his ilk always are.

"Right?"

I smile. There really is something satisfying about this mystery game—a small, intricate puzzle to untangle before I feed.

"Harriet!" somebody yells from inside the garage.

"Hey, Sully!" Harriet beelines across the driveway and the large truck and into the garage toward a tall, beanpole of a man. He's wiping a wrench, grinning. He slings the cloth over his shoulder, and they embrace quickly.

I stiffen. A lot of embracing in this village. I do not like it.

Ms. Renfield introduces me as her father's friend. She tells me that she and Sully worked on the high school newspaper together. They exchange pleasantries for what feels like a historical epoch before she reveals the true purpose of our visit.

"We were hoping to get a little information on a fire that happened at the Glassworks Galleria a few months back and maybe talk to Chief Knox about it if he's around."

"He's out on an inspection, but I could try to answer your questions. I was there in the aftermath. It was pretty much of a nothingburger, as I recall."

"We were curious who the wedding planner was."

"The wedding planner? Huh. We could go check the incident report." He leads us deeper into the garage, past yet another gleaming truck and through a side room that's set up with a cooking area and a living area. A husky-looking man with a shaved head watches some sort of sports on TV while eating highly pungent food from a white carton.

"Just checking something," Sully says, though the man did not ask.

We end up in a small back chamber full of gray file cabinets. There's a table in the middle piled with magazines and office supplies, and at the far end is a desk with a brass lamp and some sort of computer.

Sully mutters to himself as he opens drawers and fingers through files. He pulls out a manila file folder and opens it on the table. The folder contains handwritten notes and a few loose sheets of paper. "These are technically public domain. It's not like there was a finding of arson or anything."

"We really appreciate it," Ms. Renfield says.

He seems to find what he's looking for. "Okay, here it is—they didn't have an official wedding planner. They used a day-of coordinator, which was Gabriella Baker."

"Wait—it wasn't Whitney Sternell?" Ms. Renfield says.

"No, it was Gabriella. I got the names myself."

Ms. Renfield's distress is acute. "Is Whitney anywhere there, maybe as a guest?" she asks.

He checks his list. "Nope."

"And you're sure?" Harriet says.

"Yeah, man. Our list is solid. We even cross-checked it against the bride's list and the venue's lists. We didn't know what we were dealing with, so at that point in the investigation, we were treating everything like it was potential arson and taking the names of everybody who'd been through there—guests, waitstaff, wedding staff."

Ms. Renfield studies the printed piece of paper.

"You say you were treating it as potential arson. Did you then rule it out?" I ask.

"Well... the accelerant was too degraded to identify."

I look at Ms. Renfield. Did she notice this wasn't an answer? Did she feel his unhappiness with the situation?

"Anything else about the case seem odd?" Ms. Renfield asks.

"Well, just that Harlan Delmere was telling people that one of the photogs had gotten cleaning fluid all over the curtain. It was a weird accusation that probably didn't happen. And she was pissed."

"Valerie Johnson was the photographer?"

"Yeah. So pissed. She gave me a whole earful about being in this boys' club and getting blamed for everything. Chief Knox told me she was setting up to sue Harlan for libel, but suddenly she dropped it. I was surprised because she was angry as a hornet. Chief thinks her boss, Bo, pressured her to back off, because obviously you don't wanna piss off Harlan Delmere if you're in the wedding photography business."

"Or any business," Ms. Renfield observes.

"What's going on back here?" A large figure fills the door-way. Chief Knox, I assume. He has a big beard, a big belly, and brilliant blue eyes.

"Harriet and Prince Alexandru had some questions about the Galleria curtain fire, and I figured..."

"You figured wrong," Chief Knox says. "These are official records."

Sully looks confused. "It's just an incident report."

"They don't want people in the official records."

Ms. Renfield's interest piques like a silver spire. "Who do you mean? Who doesn't want people in official records?"

"Officials and whatnot," the man barks. He doesn't want to say. Interesting.

"Sorry, Chief," Sully says. "Harriet and I worked at the high school paper together."

The chief scowls at Ms. Renfield and then at me. "What's your interest in the Galleria fire?"

"Do you believe it was arson?" I ask point-blank.

Outrage surges through the chief. "There wasn't enough physical evidence to conclude either way."

"Is that why you decided not to pursue it?" I press.

Ms. Renfield panics.

The chief eyes me square on. "The amount of damage done by the fire itself was negligible. One curtain panel and a singed window frame. It was the sprinklers that did the most damage." This, of course, is irrelevant to my question. He knows it, and he knows I know it.

This man wanted to pursue the arson investigation. Somebody or something stopped him, and his blood is still boiling about it.

Sully makes a sound in the back of his throat. "It was not pretty. A lot of people spent a lot of time and money to look their best, and suddenly it's drowned-rat city."

"Very distressing to people," Chief Knox adds, leafing through the folder. He pulls out a glossy photograph of the fire itself and sets it on the table.

"Wow!" Ms. Renfield exclaims. "That's quite a photograph!" She slides the photo toward me with a significant look.

The image is startlingly clear. The flame is a bright orange column licking toward the ceiling. Guests are mid-scramble—chairs knocked askew, hands raised to faces. But what stops me cold is Kip, caught in perfect focus near the edge of the chaos. While everyone else is stunned or shouting, Kip looks... mesmerized.

"One person seems to be enjoying the experience," Ms. Renfield observes.

Chief Knox grunts.

"Could he have started the fire?" I ask the chief.

"Are you asking if we looked at him as a suspect? No. The investigation simply didn't get that far, and it's not illegal to be fascinated."

Ms. Renfield leans in. "If you had to guess—"

"I don't make guesses like that," he says.

"Kip does look... into it," she observes.

"That man likes trouble. One of his favorite pastimes is tinkering with his Harley-Davidson to make it extra loud and then driving it up and down Commerce Avenue, breaking noise ordinances left and right. You have infants taking naps. You have people trying to concentrate on projects, and this guy thinks it's fun to draw all kinds of attention to himself with his obnoxious motorcycle."

"No kidding," Sully agrees. "Chief Knox was out there with a decibel meter one day, and he clocked that motorcycle at 117 decibels. You know what the ordinance is? Eighty-eight. Eighty-eight decibels is the legal limit."

The chief grumbles. "But does Officer Maverick Cooper care? Not a whit."

"Officer Maverick Cooper is not the most outstanding male in town." I take another look at the photo and point to the corner. "Valerie Johnson, the photographer."

"The assistant must've taken it," Chief Knox says.

Ms. Renfield checks her electronic ledger. "Manny Richardson was the assistant for this one."

I note that Valerie is quite near the blaze. Nearer to it than Kip is.

"Do you have other photographs?" Ms. Renfield asks.

"They'd be on the drive."

She asks if she can see them.

"I'll let you handle this, Sully. What's public is public." Chief Knox leaves.

Sully heads over to the computer and pulls up some files. It turns out to be a great number of photos from every conceivable angle, even before the fire happened.

"I would love to have these," Ms. Renfield says.

"We're not supposed to give copies of files out to people." Sully goes to one of the shelves, grabs a bit of plastic, and sets it down on the desk in front of Ms. Renfield, winking. "Can I get you a coffee?"

"I'd love one, but just the smallest amount," Ms. Renfield says.

Sully leaves, and Ms. Renfield shoves the plastic into the side of the computer.

"What are you doing?"

"I'm copying the photos onto this thumb drive." She pulls the thing out and puts it in her pocket.

Sully returns a moment later and hands Ms. Renfield an empty cup. "The smallest amount of coffee is an atom."

"Amazing. I really do appreciate it." She hands the cup back to him.

Sully shrugs. "No sense in making you file an FOIA. The insurance company has the entire batch of them, too. So does the photographer. Not like it's a state secret here."

Chapter Thirty-Three

Harriet

I STAND at the edge of the fire station lot, pulling my cardigan around me against the cool bite of evening.

"I don't know why you needed the photos," Alexandru says in his BBC accent. "We've ruled out Whitney. It's quite obvious that it's Kip."

"It doesn't feel right. We need more data. Just because Kip ran the bartending operations at every single wedding where there was an accident doesn't mean he caused the accidents."

"You saw the photo. The way he gazed at that fire. His love of trouble and chaos belongs in your motive column."

"Even so, it's not proof. We have six days left, right? If we can just gather more data, the truth will show itself—I'm sure of it."

He steps closer, eyes dark as midnight. "My hunger grows."

"I'm not going to let an innocent person die just because *you're* feeling peckish. You agreed to do it my way, and there are protocols to be followed. Rules on how we should do this."

He looks at me like he's seeing something new in my face. "Rules," he echoes.

"Yes!" I snap.

"You're feeling intense emotions about the rules. What happens when we don't follow the rules, Ms. Renfield?"

"Don't."

"Tell me," he whispers.

A memory flashes. My voice: *I'll be back in a couple of minutes.* James on the monkey bars. His smile—so loving and trusting. The clang of a bell above the ice cream shop door. Bantering with grade-school heartthrob Jerimiah Jacobs. Then the sound of wheels spinning. A vehicle peeling off.

And the grip of fear.

I can feel Alexandru's gaze on me—quiet, intent, measuring.

"Your overlord wishes to know."

"My overlord needs to stay in his lane."

His voice is soft, coaxing. "Tell me."

I spear a finger into his chest—harder than I mean to. "Stay in your lane."

Strong, cool fingers wrap around mine. "Grief. Guilt."

I jerk my finger free, pulse high. "Screw off, Sir Fangsalot. I'm not ready to pronounce a man's death, and there's still time to confirm our assumptions."

He sighs.

"I thought you enjoyed working on our mystery."

"I do enjoy it. But if I take Kip, and the wedding accidents continue, we'll know we had the wrong person by the process of deduction."

"Killing potential suspects and waiting to see if more crimes occur is a horrible investigation method!"

"It's the process of deduction."

"No, it's not! The process of deduction is deducing things," I say.

Alexandru gazes at me strangely, like he sometimes does when I challenge him. "You have a point. It's the process of elimination."

"Elimination by murder. It's completely immoral. Not to mention repugnant."

I stare up at the sky, trying to collect myself. It's not fully dark yet, but the moon is out. "I need to walk a bit." I set off walking, not waiting for his opinion.

"You are distressed," he says, walking beside me.

"How could I not be? We're running out of time, and I feel like we're going backwards. If we don't solve this, somebody innocent will die."

"What does it matter? You humans. Your lives are so short and insignificant. What difference does a few years make?"

"It makes a difference to the person who dies, and to those who love them. They'll miss them every day, and... why am I explaining this to you? We have a deal, and we're going to find this person."

"Perhaps."

"No, we're going to." I cut down to the river walk, heading for my favorite spot, a pretty little bench next to a tree. The land across the river rises sharply, and you can make out the lights of houses through the trees.

I grip the back of the bench, staring at the sky, which is mostly dark with faint salmon-colored streaks. "We can rule out Whitney, but we still haven't seen the guest lists from Sloane. And there are more questions, like Harlan's whole business of shutting down the investigation. Didn't you think Chief Knox was acting a little sketchy about it?"

"If by sketchy you mean full of outrage, then yes, I would have to agree."

"You got outrage from him?" I ask. "That's a strong emotion."

"And that emotion felt bottled up. I believe that he wanted to continue the investigation and was prevented."

"By Harlan," I say. "Interesting. Could our culprit be Harlan? He attends a lot of weddings, but I don't think he's at every wedding. Though he *was* at the confetti cannon wedding, and he was definitely at the stairway collapse wedding. But what about the others? I can't believe Sloane just won't turn over the guest lists. What would Harlan's motive be? I can't imagine."

Alexandru leans against the bench in a pose that might be described as "Italian menswear model staring animalistically into the distance." Who knows what he's thinking. More dark thoughts about humans, probably.

"I wish we could see what the police have turned up," I say. "I feel like they're focusing too intently on the motorcycle gang. They might have evidence for one of our suspects and not recognize its significance because it doesn't have to do with the Snag Tooth Riders."

"I could get it out of Officer Cooper within seconds."

"No, thanks. Has Gregor gotten the package from the overseas seller yet?"

"Some packages did arrive recently."

I text Gregor.

> Did a package arrive from Sweden recently?

Reply dots appear immediately, because, of course, Gregor gets back right away when the overlord is involved.

"And don't forget about Valerie. You thought she was being super weird about the archives, and she was definitely in a prominent position by the fire."

Alexandru raises a brow. "You said you ruled her out. Because of your spreadsheet."

"All I'm saying is it's too early to nail Kip."

"Perhaps it's two people working together," Alexandru suggests. "We could rule Whitney back in that way."

"Serial killers don't work together. That's not a thing."

"Never?" he asks, and I don't have to be looking at him to know he's got one eyebrow arched.

His ability to read me is getting annoying.

"Behavioral profiling says the average serial killer is wired for secrecy, control, and personal gratification. Team dynamics doesn't work for somebody like that."

"But it's not impossible. There have been pairs. You've read about them."

I groan inwardly, frustrated. Which I'm sure he can also read loud and clear. "It's rare for them to work in pairs. When it happens, it's usually an alpha who is the killer and a lackey. So yes, it *does* happen."

"Overlord and underling. Like us."

"Uh, no—not like us." But then I think about it and realize it is a little like us. He's the killer and I'm the lackey.

How is this my life?

There's a rumbling in the distance. "Oh, goodie, here they come," I say.

"Who?"

"The Snag Tooth Riders themselves, in all their annoying loudness." I turn and lean with my butt against the back of the bench as they ride up from the south. I put my fingers in my ears as they near.

Alexandru folds his arms, shifting his pose to "Italian menswear model annoyed by noise."

There are a good dozen of them in their full leather regalia, riding two by two on their shiny bikes.

"It's called a muffler," I yell as they pass. "Look into it!"

Alexandru's lips quirk.

My phone vibrates and I check it. There's a single word from Gregor: *arrived.*

"Our bribe for Sloane is in. We can bring it to her tomorrow."

"Excellent."

We set back off to my car.

"Do you think Gregor hates it when I greet him in a friendly manner?"

"No doubt about it."

"Do you think he actively wants me to ignore him?"

"Gregor doesn't actively want anything."

"He must want something."

"He wants the status quo he now has."

My mind drifts back to our interview with Sully and Chief Knox. "I have a new thought. Did you catch how Sully mentioned that insurance has all the photographs from the curtain fire incident?"

"I did."

"And remember how Lisa Galindo mentioned that insurance got involved in the champagne tower collapse?"

Alexandru's eyes sparkle.

I smile. "Bo Richardson refuses to show us his precious champagne tower collapse photos, but I bet you the insurance company has them. Why didn't I think of that sooner? We have to get pictures from them."

"Judging from your late father's grumbling, insurance companies are not entirely helpful," Alexandru says.

"No, they're not, but I'm going to see what I can do. I've got admin girls everywhere."

"What is an admin girl?" Alexandru asks as we turn toward Commerce Street.

"Somebody who runs things without people realizing they're running things. I'm part of a whole admin girl mafia in Silverton Valley, and we are low-key very cooperative with each other."

"Admin girl. And this is what you do for Serena?"

"Oh my goodness, stop the presses! Is the great overlord stooping to ask yet another personal question about the life of a lowly and despicable Renfield?"

"I am requesting information."

"Sounds like a personal question to me."

"It is pertinent to your employment with me."

"Is it, though?"

Alexandru casts me an imperious gaze. "You should pray that there doesn't come a time when my annoyance with your insolent attitude outweighs the value that you bring."

"What? Is that something you're constantly evaluating and weighing? Insolence versus value?"

"It is."

I suck in a breath. Is he joking or what?

§

AFTER A SHORT AND SILENT DRIVE, we're at the gates of Kingston Manor. I hit the remote to open the wrought-iron gate that surrounds the gloomy grounds and continue up the circular drive that's flanked on either side by trees.

I get out and head to the double front door with its carved mahogany design, luckily not serpent-forward enough to frighten the delivery drivers of Silverton Valley.

Gregor opens the door, and I give him a curt, businesslike nod as we enter the mansion of doom.

I spot the package on the foyer table and rub my hands together. "Behold, the key to Sloane Cunningham's cooperation!" I open the box as Alexandru looks on. Carefully, I ease the treasure out and hold it up for him and Gregor to admire.

"*Mystery Date?*" Alexandru says. "What is that?"

I flip it over to read the back, in no hurry to answer his questions.

Gregor rushes in with an answer, fearing his overlord's discomfort. "It is a board game from the seventies."

"It's a rare, totally ridiculous version from the 70s, and Sloane's going to lose her mind. She collects retro board games. She has a whole room dedicated to them."

Tomorrow, after work, we get the guest lists.

Chapter Thirty-Four

Harriet

My office at InovaSpire is calm and orderly, just how I like it —all clean surfaces and neat screens and a great view of the Silverton River. I've worked here for eight years. I'll miss this office.

A bag I nabbed from the antique store leans against the wall. It's a vintage train case, its soft leather burnished from decades of handling. The thing is big enough to hide a throw pillow. But today it contains a certain board game swathed in bubble wrap.

I sign off on a speaking engagement for Serena and tweak a budget bump for the backend crew.

I check my phone. Ten minutes until a Zoom with the West Coast crew. I go to another tab and pick back up on my research from this morning, and the second time's the charm. I zoom in on a tiny line item in a scanned claims form:

Policy underwritten by Creighton Mutual Insurance Group.

Finally! The name of the insurance company that dealt with the champagne tower collapse. And it's local!

And I just happen to know somebody inside.

I pull up LinkedIn. Who needs to get the photos from Bo Richardson when you have the admin girl mafia?

There she is: *Kat McClellen–Claims Admin Specialist at Creighton Mutual.* We chaired some networking events together and bonded over some unbelievably annoying venue policies. Best of all, I let her use some of our deep research firepower for a family situation she had.

This is happening.

I grab my phone and fire off a text:

> Hey stranger, it's Harriet. Question for you. Wanna catch up over lunch this week? My treat.

I watch the dots appear, pause, vanish, then return.

> I was just thinking about you! Also have tea 2 spill. Thursday? Noon? Greek place on 5th?

> Perfect. See you then.

I set the phone on the desk and spin slowly in my chair. It's a big ask for the photos from an old insurance claim, even if it was just a wedding disaster. But I'll tell her what it's for and assure her it won't get back to anyone official. We just need to examine the background images. See if there's anything to see.

A soft knock on my open door pulls me out of my thoughts. Serena steps inside, immaculate as ever in cuffed trousers and a stylish blouse. "Got a minute?"

"Always," I say, straightening instinctively. Something's on her mind. "What's up?"

She closes the door behind her. Never a good sign. "I ran into Harlan Delmere last night at that new wine bar over in Creighton."

"Okay."

"He stopped by my table and said—jokingly, of course—that

I must not be giving my employees enough to do because apparently one of them is out there investigating crimes that don't exist."

In my head, I'm thinking *Gasp*! But I keep my expression neutral. "Really."

"He said," she continues, voice tightening, "that he doesn't mind a woman having hobbies—his exact words—but it starts to get concerning when those hobbies threaten to spread rumors that affect tourism in the valley. Or interfere with an active investigation like the attempted assassination of Ashwood's mayor."

"That's what he said?"

Serena nods.

"Do you think it was a threat, like he would try to get some business yanked?"

"I think that's exactly what it was. The way he looked me right in the eye, ensuring that I got the full subtext? Just really intently looking at me, you know?"

"Shit. I'm so sorry. Alexandru and I are looking into some things, but I swear, I'm not interfering in any investigation. If anything, I'm supplementing the police investigation."

She snorts. "Said no police officer about an amateur sleuth ever. What's really going on, Harriet?"

I give in and tell her about the investigation. Turns out Serena was at the wedding where the dance floor caved in. "You're saying you suspect a pattern in the accidents?"

"I know there's a pattern."

Serena's eyes sparkle. "I'm gonna go out on a limb and guess that you have one hell of a spreadsheet going for it."

"Oh, you have no idea," I whisper. "And the stairway collapse is part of it."

"And you don't think it's the Snag Tooth Riders? Everyone's been saying it's payback for shutting down Fight Nights. Supposedly, there's evidence and everything."

"Supposedly," I say.

"If you're right, this is serious stuff. Like serial killer territory."

"There have only been two deaths so far, and it's not a serial killer until three, but a budding serial killer? That's where this is leading. But I never meant for any of this to affect the business," I say. "I guess I need to do some damage control on it."

Serena waves that off with a flick of her fingers. "You'll do nothing of the sort. Harlan thinks he can look me in the eye, deliver a veiled threat, and I'll come running to shut you down? He can screw himself."

My eyebrows lift.

"Also? I find it suspicious he'd care. Don't you think it's suspicious?"

"Highly," I say. "And it's not the first time he's intervened. There was a curtain fire at the Glassworks Galleria that was probably arson, and he shut it down tight. What is he hiding?"

Serena twirls a pen. "But why would *Harlan Delmere* set a fire in one of his own properties? Why sabotage the wedding industry he so richly profits from?"

"Whoever's behind this probably has a reasoning process we can't comprehend."

"'A reasoning process we can't comprehend'? You mean the person is batshit bonkers?"

I snort.

Serena shoves the pen in her bun. "Well, be careful. And I don't mean be careful about InovaSpire. Harlan Delmere can call every boardroom buddy in the region to cancel our contracts, and it wouldn't dent our bottom line."

I smile. Our firm is a force. "Thanks."

"But you should be careful for yourself and your family and your hot new friend. If you're right, this person is dangerous."

"Thanks. Will do."

"Of course. And let me know if you need anything. I got your back." With that, she turns and leaves.

I gaze out at the river. Could Harlan actually be behind it all? Hopefully, we'll get the guest lists today, and with any luck, Harlan will be on each and every one of them.

Though her question is a good one. What does he get out of sabotaging weddings?

Chapter Thirty-Five

Alexandru

Ms. Renfield and I walk to Sloane's, her carrying a leather satchel containing the game.

Her steps are brisk, and as usual, she holds herself like a military general, inhabiting every inch of her small stature. She's nervous but pretending she isn't.

She told me about Harlan threatening her boss. But her nerves aren't about Harlan—it seems that they're about Sloane.

"Alexandru, can you help me understand how this'll work?"

I arch a brow. "This?"

"The bribing process. What do you recommend? Do we just go in and I say, 'Oh, if only we had the guest list database!' and then show her the game?"

I smile—slow and amused, just enough to irritate her.

"What? I'm sorry I'm not a centuries-old menace and don't know the ways of your menacing menacehood."

"How I envision it," I say, "is that you place the game on the counter. And then you simply wait."

"I don't say anything? That seems weird. Just wordlessly tempt her?"

"Say as little as possible, and don't propose the deal yourself.

You want to let her take the lead with that. Sloane likes to oppose you and refuse you things and make demands. Let her make a demand."

"Wow." Ms. Renfield's tone is the shocked one she gets when I exhibit knowledge of human nature. "Sloane *is* my ultimate contrarian."

"So it seems."

"So I give her nothing to be contrary about."

"Exactly."

The bell over the door rings as we walk in.

"Alexandru! How are the cards working out?" Sloane asks. "I trust your assistant handed them off without incident?"

"That he did, and they're perfect. Not many people use that style of letterpress anymore."

"Understatement of the century," Sloane declares.

Ms. Renfield sets her bag down on the floor in front of the counter and pulls out the bubble-wrapped box.

"What's all this?" Sloane asks her.

Wordlessly, Ms. Renfield unwraps the box. Sloane's interest grows keener with the removal of each layer of bubble wrap, and she gasps when Ms. Renfield finally reveals what's underneath.

"No. Harriet. Is that real?"

Harriet shrugs. "Should we open it up and find out?"

"Don't you dare break that shrink wrap!" She stares at it. "It's the Sears holiday edition."

Ms. Renfield says nothing.

"What are you doing with this?"

"You were interested in this game way back when..."

"Oh, I suppose... maybe at one time," Sloane says, which could not be further from the truth. She's vibrating with excitement. "May I?"

"Go ahead."

Sloane picks it up by her fingertips like it's a fragile relic.

She turns it over and examines the picture on the back. "The woodsman," she says reverently. "And you're showing me this, why?"

"I thought it would be fun for you to see it before Mom put it on eBay."

Sloane's eyes widen. "You can't. No."

Silence.

"But you're not going to, are you? You know what I think? I think you want those lists of wedding guests. You think I'm gonna make that exchange."

Ms. Renfield shrugs.

"You're not fooling me," Sloane says. "I have something you want, and now you have something you think I want."

It's hard for Ms. Renfield to maintain silence in the face of this; she's desperate to fill it. To just say anything. She thrums with emotions, but her self-control is admirable. For a Renfield.

I wonder again—with the mildest curiosity—what happened between them.

Sloane slides her fingertip lovingly over the edge. "Weddings where there were accidents. You really think someone's doing it on purpose?"

"I know someone's doing it on purpose," Ms. Renfield says evenly. "I know it for a fact."

I feel the corner of my mouth twitch. My little Renfield knows her hunt.

"I suppose I could give you the databases that you want," Sloane says. "It's not like it's private information, being that these weddings were in public venues. But I want something more than this. You'll give me this game, and while I assemble the databases for you, you'll go get me a chocolate salted caramel Berky Bomb."

Ms. Renfield sighs. "Fine."

Sloane smiles. "Got a thumb drive on you?"

Ms. Renfield has one, naturally. She always comes

236

prepared. She hands it over, along with a list of the weddings in question.

Sloane gets to work on her laptop. "Sadly, you left out one of the weddings that you should've requested a guest list for."

"Excuse me?"

"My friend was married in Creighton last fall, and there was quite an egregious accident. Quite notorious."

"What happened?"

A slow smile spreads over Sloane's face. "They rented out the courtyard of that Italian restaurant by the marina. It was a midnight courtyard ceremony, very romantic and intimate. Sparklers lining the stone walls, twinkling fairy lights, candle-light... lovely!"

Harriet blinks. "And?"

"The sparklers detonated," Sloane says, relishing the memory. "Somebody added actual firecrackers, so instead of a soft, festive glow, it was the battle of Bunker Hill. *Boom boom boom*. Half the guests hit the ground. Somebody's great-aunt pushed over the mother of the bride."

Ms. Renfield stares. "You're making this up."

"I was there," Sloane says. "They never did get to the bottom of how it happened. The fireworks company said someone from the wedding tampered with the sparklers after they were set up. The groom thought it was a disgruntled fire-works employee. However, my friend, who was the bride, loved the pictures. She said it made her wedding "memorable." She actually had this wedding photo that was just utter chaos up as her Facebook header forever. All these people panicking, and she and her man up at the front, jaws hanging open while the officiant crouched behind a floral display."

"Is it still up on her Facebook profile? I would love to see it!"

"Sadly, their wedding planner messaged her privately this past weekend and asked her to take it down. Said it was giving her business a bad look. She was all weird about it."

"Just this past weekend?" Ms. Renfield can barely hide her excitement.

"Do you recall who the planner was?" I ask coolly.

"I think it was Whitney Sternell."

Ms. Renfield's so thrilled, it's a wonder she doesn't explode like a little firecracker herself.

I have to admit, it *is* interesting. An unexpected twist in this pre-meal puzzle.

"Does that fit into your scheme?" Sloane asks coolly. "Your little pattern?"

"It does," Ms. Renfield says. "Is it possible... Could you grab your phone and pull up her Facebook header?"

"I told you, the picture is down," Sloane says.

"I would love it if you could send me the URL. I might be able to access it on the Wayback Machine."

With a sigh, Sloane pulls out her phone. They fiddle with their electronics together while I examine envelopes.

The next thing I know, Ms. Renfield lets out a gasp of dismay.

"Removed?" Sloane asks.

"Scrubbed."

"Maybe try cached Google images?" Sloane suggests.

"No dice," Ms. Renfield says after a beat.

"Well, those things aren't foolproof," Sloane says. "I suppose you want *that* guest list, too."

I step in. "We would appreciate it."

"And you're on board with all this," Sloane says to me.

"I am."

With a weary look, Sloane taps a few more keys.

"Sloane," Ms. Renfield says. "Do you think the bride might be willing to send us a copy of the photo?"

"Of course she would. She is a very close friend."

The strong emotion that spears through Ms. Renfield

surprises me. I'd expected anger at Sloane's high-handed treatment, but it's something more like sadness. Loss. Longing.

"We really think something is going on," Ms. Renfield says.

Sloane examines her fingernails. "I gathered as much."

"The pattern is clearly manufactured. The escalation is undeniable. If you look at the spreadsheet covering the last year—"

"Do I want to see the Excel embodiment of a cry for help? Is that what you're asking me?" Sloane says. "No, thanks."

"It's real. People could be in danger. There will be a next victim."

"Well, you be sure to get all that data down. There's nothing more important when it comes to fighting for justice than a complete data set."

I'm thinking that Ms. Renfield does indeed require an exhaustive amount of data, but something more is going on. Ms. Renfield straightens her spine. "I'm glad you think so."

That's not what she wants to say. She wants to argue, to plead her case—badly.

Sloane has touched a nerve of some sort, and for some strange reason, I feel affronted.

What do I care?

She's nothing but a Renfield. A tool.

"Whatever," Sloane sniffs. "However, I am a little thirsty for a double-froth vanilla crème brûlée latte from Berky's. I suppose if one were to show up on my counter in the next twenty minutes, along with the Berky Bomb, I might be in a good enough mood to text her and get that photo for you. Since you're so desperate to see it. She does love to show it to people."

"Could you find out who the bartender was as well?" I ask.

Sloane keeps her gaze on Ms. Renfield. "If you add another Berky Bomb. Make it a lemon ginger. Alexandru can remain behind. I have some paper samples to show him."

"Did she really just want to show you paper samples?" Ms. Renfield asks as we head toward her car after leaving Sloane's.

"She would like me to bed her."

She makes a sound in the back of her throat. An objection? Disbelief?

"It is not uncommon," I inform her. "Females sense the exquisite pleasure I can bring."

Heat suffuses her cheeks. "When they're not running for their lives!"

"One can turn into the other."

"Oh my god, whatever." She stops and turns to me. "That was some very interesting information about Whitney asking for the picture to be taken down, right? And just a few days ago? How is that a coincidence? What does she not want us to see?"

"What concern is it of ours? Did we not rule her out?"

"We did, but I find it suspicious."

"Is there a reason you want to look anywhere but in the direction of Kip the bartender? We're like old ladies, embroidering the edges of this hunt."

"But there's so much more to learn. This Whitney thing—"

"We ruled her out, did we not?"

"I will grant you that if Sully thinks that list is complete, I'm inclined to believe him. I knew Sully pretty well in high school. He's very detail-oriented. Still, we have the guest lists to go over."

"Tell me, is barkeep Kip's tavern around here? I am ready to see him."

"Wait, what? What are you going to say? We can't tip him off that he's a suspect until we know more. You're not thinking of cornering him, are you? We still have five days!"

"You say you want more information. Cornered prey sometimes offers things up without being asked."

"I feel like that's a way to say that you want to toy with your food."

"It is one of the best parts of the hunt. What's more, it is my understanding that you can look at these lists of Sloane's anywhere once you insert the thumb thing into your electronic ledger."

"We should at least wait until we see what's in the picture before confronting anyone. If Sloane can get it from her BFF soon," she adds bitterly.

"What happened between you two?"

"Asked and answered: none of your business."

"It is my business if it affects your duties."

"I don't see my past with Sloane as being germane to my duties."

"It's germane if your overlord says it's germane. You were friends once."

"And now we're not," she says. "Look, you know what I'm thinking? I could use a beer. Or two. Maybe three. Let's see if Kip is at his bar."

A clumsy ploy to redirect my attention, but I allow it.

She wants to keep her secrets. I can understand that.

Information can always be used against a person; I am pleased that this Renfield understands this. Indeed, I regret much of what I told Algernon, Duke of Densmere, for that very reason—though he paid dearly for it, and will again, should he ever crawl out of whatever sordid, velvet-draped den he's hiding in.

It comes to me that he hasn't made his presence known for some decades now.

Unsettling.

Algernon rarely stays quiet this long. He usually finds a way to slither into my affairs by now. Baroque sabotage is his art form. He doesn't lash out; he orchestrates.

Not twenty minutes later, we're on barstools at a tavern

called the Muddy Pint. The place was built too close to the river, and the walls brag about it—photographs of past floods lined up in frames, each one showing the water covering the floors. The years are scrawled beneath, like tally marks in a long, unfortunate game.

"It is so strange how humans crow about their follies."

"It shows they got through something together," Ms. Renfield says.

"Hey there!" A young barmaid sets a napkin in front of each of us. She greets Ms. Renfield like an old acquaintance, but her wide-eyed gaze keeps straying back to me. Instinct warns her to keep her distance even as something in her wants to step closer.

She pours us two beers and sets them in front of us.

"Is barkeep Kip Kidderson here tonight?" I ask.

She straightens. Surprised, perhaps, that she's being addressed by me. "No, he went off on his Harley. It could be a while."

I nod. She scurries off.

Ms. Renfield takes a big drink of her beer and smacks her lips. "Aah!"

She then proceeds to write on her electronic ledger with her white pencil, working diligently.

She seems troubled, even a bit wild—I suspect it's her interaction with Sloane.

She reads, white pencil hovering, then presses the end of it to her lower lip, breathing around it, thinking, that clever brow drawn tight. When she moves the pencil away, there's a glossy crescent of red from her lips.

Then she puts it back between her lips.

I blink, watching.

All of a sudden, she pulls it out and taps on the screen. Her expression brightens a bit.

She likes what she sees.

She truly is formidable in her own way. I try not to smile, remembering how she yelled at the biker gang.

It's called a muffler! Look into it!

"Okay, then!" She taps her ledger with a flourish and then turns it to me.

Four names are displayed. "These are the people who were at all of the weddings. We're going to have to add these names to our suspect list. Though some of the sabotage incidents required access prior to the ceremony, so they're still a little iffy as suspects."

"Then why did we go through all the trouble to get these lists?"

"For this reason." She taps some more and then presents me with another list. "Vendors who were guests. For example, Bo Richardson was a guest at the confetti cannon wedding. I'm going to have to add him to my spreadsheet. That wedding was photographed by Roy LaRue and a freelance assistant, but we can add Bo in there as a guest."

"But there are other accident weddings where he wasn't present."

"Well, it's a data point. Our picture is becoming clearer, even if it hasn't shown us the killer yet. All the little data points will reveal our killer."

She switches beers with me and drinks from mine, then does more screen tapping.

At one point, she stops and looks over at me. "You love to sit still and stare daggers into nothingness, don't you?"

"I'm not staring daggers, and it's not nothingness. It's a wall of signs and bottles."

"But isn't it boring just to look over and over at the same thing?"

"It is my way," I say.

She mumbles something about a cure for squirrel brain and

keeps poking around in the file. "Check this out! Harlan was invited to all but one of the weddings."

"People do not like Harlan," I observe. "They invite him to show fealty."

Ms. Renfield's eyes sparkle, and in the light of the beer signs, you can see the gold threaded through the brown, like trapped flame. "I say we don't invite him to our fake wedding, darling."

The drink is indeed affecting her.

"It really *is* weird that Harlan warned Serena like that," she says. "Did he think that would make her tell me to stop? He really doesn't like us investigating. Very suspicious. I would love it if he turned out to be the killer."

"Because you don't like his wealth?" I ask. "Or because you don't like that he stifled the curtain fire investigation?"

"I don't like the way he throws his weight around. The way he tries to bulldoze people."

"People like Chief Knox?"

"That's just one example. He's also trying to build this residential office complex on the river, where there's currently a park that everybody loves. People keep voting it down, and he keeps bringing it back up. Such a jerk."

"He showed his hand with that warning," I say. "He is up to something."

The barmaid comes by, and Ms. Renfield asks for a glass of water. The barmaid puts it down on a little napkin.

"So, how do you like working here?" she asks the girl.

"It's fine."

"Kip seems like he'd be a fun person to work for."

"He's fun enough," she says, wiping down the counter. "I mean, as much fun as a boss can be. A boss is a boss."

Ms. Renfield points her thumb at me. "Don't I know?"

The barmaid looks alarmed. "I didn't mean all bosses."

"I am not her boss. I am her overlord."

The barmaid smiles uncertainly.

"There. You see what I'm dealing with?"

"I understand Mr. Kidderson is quite the motorcycle aficionado," I say.

"You have no idea." The barmaid shakes her head darkly.

"You're not a fan?" Ms. Renfield says.

"I got no problem with motorcycles. It's some of the dudes who ride them I'm not a fan of."

I lean in. "What do you mean?"

She glances around and lowers her voice. "You know. The Snag Tooth Riders? Kip gets really excited when they come in here. He's even been encouraging it, but they completely suck. They make a mess. They do not tip. They scare the tourists who actually do tip, and they take up all the good tables—*and* all the best parking spaces."

"I guess I have been seeing motorcycles here a lot this spring," Ms. Renfield says. "Why do you think he encourages it? Considering it's so bad for business."

"He's into them. He's always talking about how he'd like to wear the colors and knock some heads around and all that. You see that nachos item on the menu up there? The Widowmaker nachos?"

Ms. Renfield squints at the menu posted on the wall. "Double-fried tortilla chips layered with smokehouse brisket, pork belly burnt ends, and crumbled hot sausage with an American cheese drizzle and bacon fat crema. Whoa."

"Gross, right? He created that for them. It's their favorite thing ever, and it's disgusting. They get it all over their beards. We're talking bacon fat crema here. I don't even know what bacon fat crema is or where Kip gets it. The normal restaurant supply place would never have that."

She grabs a napkin and heads down to the other end of the bar.

Ms. Renfield turns to me, eyes bright. "Are you thinking what I'm thinking?"

"I think you're thinking about the stairway collapse. Most of the villagers blame it on this Snag Tooth Riders motorcycle gang."

"Yes." She smiles conspiratorially. "But what if it's the Snag Tooth Riders' biggest superfan who wants to be in their club? Maybe he thought if he killed the mayor or deputy mayor on their behalf, they'd let him in?"

"But what about the accidents before that?"

"Maybe he was responsible for the sabotage all along and decided this latest one was for what he saw as a good cause?"

I consider this. "There was a man during the Wallachian campaigns—Iancu of Moldavia. He wanted to defect to the Ottomans, but they didn't trust him. So he began delivering heads—their enemies' heads. Left them on pikes at the enemy gates. As proof of worth."

"Proof of worth," she murmurs. "Did it work?"

"No. They killed him."

She laughs. "That's not even funny! But it is."

I tilt my head. "What, precisely, does a motorcycle gang do?"

"They brawl. They drink too much. They hook up with each other's girlfriends and ride around acting like they're in high school. They sell drugs and guns and apparently eat gross nachos."

I push my glass away. "Kip would not want to join a gang such as that."

She blinks. "What do you mean? He's clearly doing everything he can to get in with them."

"Kip's the sort of man who wants the *look* of belonging. He wants to orbit danger; he does not want to live it."

Ms. Renfield's eyes shine, and she taps a forefinger upon her faintly smiling lips, something she does when pieces of our puzzle come together. She really is so different from past Renfields, who would just seem relieved when something went their way.

"Thoughts?" I ask.

"I'm thinking you're right. Kip is one hundred percent not the brawling type. And he's not a giant beard guy, either. He's a fashionable-stubble guy who wants a whiff of danger, but not the actual danger. Not an actual beard."

I nod.

"But that doesn't rule him out. Maybe he did it as a favor to the gang."

I meet her gaze. "If Kip is our saboteur, then he's no fool. He's gotten away with it this long, which suggests a healthy sense of self-preservation and calculation. If he caused the stairs to collapse as a favor to the gang, he would have to let them know he did it. A careful man like that does not confide his crimes to a pack of drunken brawlers who owe him no loyalty."

She toys with her necklace pendant, a small gold key. "Good point. He's a showboater Snag Tooth guys eating nachos in his bar is probably gang-adjacent enough for him."

"He could still be our culprit, of course," I say, thinking again of his rapt expression. "He loves a show."

Ms. Renfield calls the barmaid over and asks if Kip ever went to the Friday night fights out at the Snag Tooth Riders' farm.

"Oh yeah. He loved them," she says.

"Was he upset when Fight Nights got shut down?" Ms. Renfield asks.

"Very." The barmaid wanders off to serve another customer.

Ms. Renfield takes a sip of beer and then licks a stray bit of foam from her lips. "So maybe he targeted the mayor as an anonymous favor to the Snag Tooth Riders but didn't intend to ever let them know."

"Perhaps," I say.

She lowers her voice. "If that's what happened, it backfired, because he kind of got them in trouble. Everybody really does think it's them."

Chapter Thirty-Six

Harriet

I see Kip the next morning at the grocery store. He's with a pretty young girl with bleached-blonde hair and a black tank top, all very motorcycle chic. Is she in the Snag Tooth Riders' orbit? Or are these just two people who love the motorcycle look but not the life?

I watch them compare bagged potatoes to single potatoes. He looks up, seeming to sense me watching him, and smiles. I wave. He goes back to the discussion.

It's hard to imagine him as a killer. It's honestly hard to imagine anybody at all as a killer, even Harlan. But maybe I'm just naïve. Clearly, somebody's killing people. I know those accidents are not real accidents.

I'm heading out to the parking lot when I get a call from Bo Richardson. "Manny says you've got a request. That it's a matter of life or death," he says. "Color me intrigued."

"Hey, yes, thanks so much for calling me back. Do you think Alexandru and I could stop by? We won't take up much of your time."

We arrange to stop by around six, after I get off work.

I HEAD HOME AFTER WORK, switch out my outfit, and try to make my exit as stealthy as possible, but Granabelle flags me down from atop a ladder. "I hear you were out on the town with your handsome boss last night!"

"It was just work stuff," I say.

"Why don't you invite him for dinner?" she says.

"We're not having some random dude in here for dinner," Mom says.

"He's not some dude; he's her boss and paramour."

"So not my paramour," I say.

"Glad to hear it," Mom says. "Any man who was in cahoots with your father is sketch city. I don't care if he's a prince."

"If you were to marry him," Granabelle wonders aloud, "would you become a princess?"

"Princess of the idiots," Mom says.

I was twelve when James was stolen away from us, too young to really understand adults, so I don't know if Mom was as jaded and cynical back then or if her attitude came from having lost a child. But right now, I love that she's one of the few people in town not falling all over themselves for Alexandru.

The conversation devolves from there, with Granabelle yet again floating the idea of a photo shoot at Kingston Manor. "I would be happy to unveil his renovation project to the world through my Instagram account!"

BO RICHARDSON's photography studio is located on the bottom floor of a refurbished warehouse on the posher north side of Ashwood.

"What do you imagine we'll see in these photographs?" Alexandru seems surlier than usual.

I put the car into park and turn to him. "Remember how you told me that if you go for a month without feeding, you 'hit the edge of your restraint'?"

"Yes, of course."

"That's four days from now. Are you starting to feel the effects?"

"Best we settle on a culprit," he says.

"That's not a no," I say.

"And that's not an answer to my question," he says.

Hangry, I think.

"The photographs. Fine. What I'm hoping to see is somebody acting suspicious around the champagne tower table during the twenty minutes between when they finished building it and when it fell. Maybe Whitney the wedding planner. Maybe Kip the bartender. Maybe Harlan the rich jackass or one of the guests on our short list. There has to be some photographic proof in there."

We get out.

"I thought your admin friend was going to be giving you the photos from the insurance company."

"We went out to lunch, and she said she'd try and get it. I haven't heard from her yet. It's a little tricky to do that sort of thing. She has to wait for some other excuse to go into the archives. So, I say let's strike while the iron is hot. Bo offered to possibly help, so let's go for it."

The inside of Richardson Photography is all concrete floors and high ceilings. Scattered vintage props—a velvet chair, a fainting couch—dot the space, along with sheer curtains and lots of moody lighting. The walls are plastered with giant photos of happy brides and grooms in seemingly uncensored moments.

Bo comes out from behind a desk at the end of the space that holds several computer monitors. He's in all black except for his bright red suspenders, which he doesn't really seem to need to hold up his pants, but there you are.

"I'll admit, I have a hard time believing any photos of ours are a matter of life and death," he says with a wary glance at Alexandru. "But that's what Manny told me you said."

"Just between us," I say, "Alexandru and I believe that somebody is staging accidents at area weddings."

Bo raises his eyebrows in surprise. "Are you talking about the deputy mayor's death?"

"We believe that was the one accident where the culprit lost their opportunity to retrieve their equipment," Alexandru says. "That is why the villagers see it as an assassination attempt."

Bo blinks, and I make a mental note to talk to Alexandru about calling people villagers and peasants. "Umm... but the *Gazette* said it's the motorcycle gang."

"We disagree," I say.

Bo's brows knit thoughtfully. "I know that you're something of a hobbyist when it comes to true crime, but this is real life. Do you have any proof of your theory?"

I grip my tablet. "There have been at least ten recent incidents staged to look like accidents. People would've thought the stairway collapse was due to poor maintenance if they hadn't found that hydraulic device."

Bo ponders this, looking alarmed. "The curtain fire at Glassworks Galleria. And when the dance floor caved in. My god."

"And of course, the champagne tower collapse. That's why we're so eager to see the photos. We feel like there could be a clue there."

"How so?"

"The timeframe where the culprit could've monkeyed with the table is just twenty minutes, and we think you were taking pictures of the groomsmen in that area most of that time."

Bo looks upset. "Do you feel that my crew or I am in danger?"

"We plan to get to the bottom of this quickly," Alexandru says. "We will be eliminating suspects within the week."

I shoot him a glance because that sounded a bit weird, honestly.

Bo looks ashen, not that I can blame him. He's been at a lot of those weddings, rubbing elbows with a killer.

I say, "We're interested in all of the photos from when they brought out the table to when the collapse happened. Even photographs that have only part of the table visible could be a great help to us."

"Well, I can certainly make an exception here—this is all very troubling." Bo strolls back behind the desk to stand in front of one of the monitors. "Can I ask who your suspects are?"

"We're still gathering data," I say.

He shoots a nervous glance at Alexandru, who is following his movements like a dog following a kid with a plate of steak. "So you don't have any suspects?"

"We're working it out," I explain.

"I get it, you don't want to say. I suppose I could pull up what we have for the champagne tower photos. Do you want to see my photos from the wedding where Deputy Mayor Kazan died?"

"Were you taking photographs after the collapse?" I ask.

He frowns at the monitor and taps a few keys.

"Photos of the aftermath could be very helpful!" I add. "We might even be able to see the culprit trying to find the device!"

"Obviously, I wasn't shooting after the collapse," Bo says, ever so shamey. "I was helping the victims... It was chaos. Terrible. And poor Deputy Mayor Kazan..."

I ask, "Do you recall anybody who seemed to be pawing through the debris in a way that didn't make sense? As if they were trying to retrieve something rather than help?"

"Maverick Cooper asked the same thing, and I'll tell you what I told him: I was working on pulling a beam off of Glenda Shepherd's legs, and that's where my attention was. Wait." He looks up. "That groom falling off the balcony out at the Creighton Inn—so you're suggesting that was a murder?"

"Yes," Alexandru says, gaze sharp on Bo.

"I didn't shoot that wedding. It was Roy with Manny assisting, but they were both pretty upset. Roy felt a little bit responsible because he had been urging them to do comical poses up on that balcony. Of course, that's sort of a tradition with couples. These two people were just starting their lives together... Roy couldn't work for a week."

"We understand that your employee, Valerie, was also blamed for that curtain fire at the Glassworks Galleria," Alexandru says.

"That was bull crap," Bo says. "The whole thing about lens cleaning fluid. They didn't do anything wrong."

"We heard there was talk of a lawsuit."

Bo continues scrolling through images. "Valerie was pretty upset. One specific person was circulating that rumor, and she wanted to bring them to court."

"Harlan?" Alexandru says. "Did you instruct her not to sue?"

Bo pauses what he's doing and looks up. "Harlan owns half of Ashwood, including one of the top wedding venues. You bet I instructed her to back down."

"Did Harlan ask you to do that, or did you do it of your own accord?" I ask.

Bo hesitates—just long enough. "I don't see how this is relevant. I thought you came here to see champagne tower pictures."

"We did, and we still want to see them," I say quickly. "We're just curious about these incidents. You tend to be at a lot of weddings, and you observe people with a photographer's eye. Did you ever notice anything strange? Somebody looking around somewhere where they shouldn't be? Or acting nervous or suspicious? Anything off at all?"

Bo exhales. "I photograph hundreds of weddings a year. Emotions run high. People drink. Cry. Pass out. Fight. Marry people they shouldn't. Pretend to feel things they don't. Pose for photos as if they're having carefree moments that are anything but."

I look over at Alexandru, curious what he's getting from all this, because from where I'm sitting, someone needs to take a break from the wedding photography business.

"What about the vendors?" I ask. "Caterers. Planners. Tent crews. Bartenders."

Bo's eyes flick to my tablet. "That's your focus?"

"Not solely," I say.

"Here we go. Here's the set." He invites us to stand next to him as images of groomsmen in the foreground and the champagne tower in the background fill the screen.

There are a lot of them.

The first one is actually just the groom standing there alone. In the corner, you can see the Stanley people finishing the tower. More of the groomsmen get into the shot, and the tower is there in the background. Later images show the groomsmen raising glasses in a toast, drinking, making faces, and then play-fighting. The tower is still visible in the background corner.

"These men would be utterly unfit for battle," growls Alexandru.

"To say the least," Bo says in his judgey way. Definitely one of the fake carefree moments he disdains.

I spot a shot of Kip talking to the Stanley Catering people. And he's right near the table. I lean in. "Would you be able to enlarge that part with Kip?"

Bo hits a few buttons, and we study the shot.

"Can you zero in on Kip's hand in all of these?"

Bo complies. Kip touches the table now and then, and at one point, he crouches down and looks at something, but you can't see his hands.

"I wish we had another angle," I say.

"Those caterers are both watching him," Alexandru says. "They would see if he did something to the table, would they not?"

"So you think it's Kip?" Bo asks.

"Anybody interacting with this table is a suspect," I say.

"I see," Bo says in a tone of voice that suggests he really, really thinks Kip might be a suspect.

The images sharpen, shift. Kip's mouth freezes in mid-sentence here and there. "Seems like he's trash-talking," I observe.

"I wouldn't doubt it," Bo says.

Sadly, there's nothing that shows Kip up to something, though the one where he's crouching is a bit suspicious. But according to Lisa, he'd have to be affixing something to the table and the men are staring at him.

We spot one where Whitney comes into the frame, and I ask Bo to zoom in on her as she places the vignettes, as Lisa called them. We ruled her out because she wasn't at the wedding with the curtain fire, but I want to see the vignettes. They're a perfect place to hide something.

Bo's voice is sharp with interest. "Whitney, huh."

"As Ms. Renfield said, anybody interacting with this table is a suspect," Alexandru says.

Is Alexandru annoyed with Bo, or is it his hunger?

Bo gives me a confused look. "Ms. Renfield?"

"My father was a Renfield," I say, though that doesn't really explain it because... NOT MY NAME!!

There's a shot where goth Lisa brings one of the caterers a drink and toys with one of Whitney's garlands, chatting.

It couldn't be her, though, being that she was only present at two of the weddings, though she'd be an amazing suspect, considering her engineering and tech gadget know-how.

None of the guests on our short list show up, though there are gaps when Bo wasn't shooting.

"Can you recall Harlan being there?" I ask.

"Harlan." Bo stares at a window, thinking. "Not specifically, but he is everywhere."

"Where is the actual collapse shot?" I ask, eager to see the picture that Kip was so excited about.

"Here." Bo enlarges a shot of the glasses in a low pile with blurs above it.

"This is the picture Kip was so enthralled with?" I ask.

"I suppose," Bo says.

"Wow. Okay. No offense, but he acted like the collapse shot was the most amazing photo he'd ever seen. Like it belonged in a gallery."

Bo smirks. "I think there was a bit of schadenfreude happening there. Kip is usually the one to build these towers, but the groom wanted the Stanley Catering crew to do it. Kip was pissed that he was passed over, so he loved that it fell."

"So you didn't get any shots of the cleanup?"

Bo screws up his lips. "Wasn't really the kind of moment I was hired to photograph."

"Can you describe what you saw?"

He furrows his brow at the wall where there's a giant print of a bride and groom swinging on a swing set. "People were crowding the perimeter, though some idiots walked in it. Staff went in with brooms and towels, trying to contain the damage. Bride was crying."

"Anyone stepping in to help in a way that seemed off?"

Bo shakes his head slowly. "Not that I saw."

Then I ask him about the fireworks wedding.

"My god, how many weddings did this person ruin?"

"A lot," I say.

Bo hits a few buttons. "Looks like Roy hasn't gotten them

into the cloud yet. So these are your suspects? Kip and Whitney? That's who you wanted me to zoom in on."

"Whitney wasn't at all the weddings in question, such as the curtain fire wedding," I tell him. "One of her employees was the planner there, so we've ruled her out."

Bo winces theatrically. "I hate to say this, but if Grace was there, Whitney was there. She would've at least stopped by."

"They only hired Grace. For the day of," I say.

"Doesn't matter. Whitney doesn't trust her staff."

I perk up at that. "Really? She wasn't on the list..."

"Trust me. It's a known thing among brides that when you hire one of Whitney's assistants the day of, you get at least a little bit of Whitney. It's a cheap way to get Whitney involved in your wedding without paying for Whitney. She's a notorious micromanager. Always manages to sneak in and critique things."

"Really?"

"Notorious. They hate it."

Chapter Thirty-Seven

Harriet

"Well, that was enlightening," Alexandru says, settling himself into my car. "Whitney was at the curtain fire wedding. *And* she requested that Sloane's friend take down the picture from the sparkler wedding. Very suspicious."

I'm thrilled that he seems to be taking such an interest in the mystery.

"It's Bo's word against those firefighters who made that list of who was there at the curtain fire wedding. They are very detail-oriented officials," I point out. "It's unlikely they missed getting somebody on there."

"Did you not hear what Bo said? It is Whitney's way to sneak into the weddings of her underlings."

"True. Did he mean it literally, though?"

Alexandru shrugs.

"In any case, it's enough to put her back in the running." I make a note on my tablet. "Did you pick up anything else from Bo?"

"Fear. Alarm."

"Because a killer has been in his midst?"

Alexandru looks like someone parsing out flavors, his striking face unmoving except for his coffee-colored eyes, alive with dark intent. "His fear was the kind that prey would have."

I put on my seat belt. "Prey for us or prey for the killer?"

"Prey for us. It's something about the archives."

"What is up with those archives? It's the same thing as Valerie's weirdness about the photo archives."

"A bit. Perhaps he and Valerie are working together."

"That can't be. Neither he nor Valerie was at the sparkler wedding."

"Maybe we need to talk with Roy and Manny. Perhaps they are involved. Somebody from Richardson Photography was at every wedding."

"Oh my god, if we're going to start suspecting a serial killer photography gang, I'm going to need a new spreadsheet. No—scratch that. I'm gonna need a new spreadsheet, three beers, and ten Berky Bombs. And a lobotomy. Because it can't be a whole group."

"You're the one who always says to keep an open mind. To follow the data."

"All we know is that they're feeling weird about something in the archives. It could be something that's not murder. And Bo showed us all of his champagne collapse pictures. Totally forthcoming."

We head north on Commerce, past the music conservatory and the sprawling grade school playground. You can tell that the tourist trade is ramping up by the length of the line at the ice cream shop across the street.

"It comes from here," Alexandru suddenly says. "The guilt that you feel."

"What? What are you talking about?" But I know what he's talking about.

"The ice cream shop. You hate it. What happened there? What is that place to you?"

James actually disappeared from the school across the street, but the ice cream shop was the scene of my crime—I went there instead of grabbing James and walking him home.

"Maybe I still feel bad about the great butter brickle binge of twenty nineteen," I say with a lightness I do not feel.

"You will tell me."

"I'm sorry, are we trying to solve the case of Harriet Morgan's random life events? 'Cause I thought we were working on the case of 'let's find that killer before Alexandru goes monster mash on the town'?"

I can feel his dark gaze on the side of my face. His power fills the small space. He's relentless. Ancient. And he sees everything.

"What happened?"

"Can you please leave me alone on this one?" I turn to him. "Please?"

Something strange flickers across his face.

"It's something from a long time ago," I add softly.

"Pull over," he says.

"I'm not talking about it."

"No. Back at the Tres Hermanas restaurant. Whitney was there."

"You realized that just now?"

"Yes."

"You picked her out of that crowd?"

"We will question her."

"I don't want her to know she's a suspect," I say.

"Pull over," he commands again. "I have a plan."

I do a U-turn and pull into a space in front of the tea shop. "Let's hear it."

"We pretend to dine out there. We strike up a conversation with her and gather impressions."

"I don't know if we can do it that naturally, though. If we tip her off that she's a suspect before we have our ducks in a row, it'll be harder to bust her."

"At this rate, we will be getting our ducks in a row forever."

"You only get one chance to do a thing right," I say. "We should at least see what's in the photo that she wanted hidden from the world!"

Alexandru brushes an invisible speck of nothing off his perfectly tailored jacket sleeve. "The last I checked, Ms. Renfield, you are not my overlord, and I tire of your tentative ways." With that, he opens his door and gets out.

"Oh my god, what?" I grab my bag, lock the door, and catch up to him. "We need to plan our approach."

"Ten centuries and I've never needed a plan to talk to villagers. I don't feel I need one now."

He heads for the restaurant. There's no stopping him.

Also, *ten centuries?*

The Tres Hermanas front patio is full of diners underneath elegant white lights strung overhead like stars.

Josie's mother, Rita, meets us at the door. I introduce her to Alexandru, who takes her hand with his usual dangerous charm. She seems to be both enchanted and terrified, which I suppose is as rational a response as any.

She congratulates him on how tasteful the Kingston renovation looks from afar and tells him how she used to play there as a child, something he's definitely been hearing a lot of.

"Could we sit on the porch?" I ask.

"We would like to sit near where Whitney Sternell is sitting," Alexandru says.

"We met her at the bridal expo, and we wanted to..." I end my sentence in some mumbles with the words "you know" thrown in a few times, all in all doing a poor job of smoothing over the impression that we want to harass Whitney, which is what we want to do, I suppose.

"Yes, I heard about you being at the bridal expo. You'll be happy to know Josie is in full zipped-lips mode."

Rita leads us across the dining room and out to the porch, seating us at a lovely table next to the colorful planter boxes that separate the sidewalk from the diners.

"There's really nothing to report," I say to her.

"I understand. You and the prince simply want to say hello to the wedding planner that you met." She winks.

"He's not really a prince."

"I am technically a prince," Alexandru says once she's gone.

"Prince of Dorkness."

"She seemed nice," he says.

"You will never, ever, ever go after her. Do you understand me?"

"The list of people I'm not to go after is getting annoyingly long."

"I'm not fooling around. I will hunt you to the ends of the earth. I will so kill you."

He looks amused.

A baby at a nearby table bursts into tears.

"I want you to promise."

"Fine. Who is she?"

"That's Josie's mother. She was like a second mother to me growing up. I practically lived with them at one point." I pick up a menu. "We have to eat inside one day. It's really retro with awesome art from the 1930s, and sometimes they play Frank Sinatra. I know that's probably a little too mod for you."

He gives me a dark look.

"Whitney looks like she's about to get her check. Are you ready?"

Our waitperson comes over, and I order two beers and two crab cakes.

Whitney looks over, and I wave to her excitedly. She smiles and waves and holds up a finger.

"Shall we go over?" Alexandru asks.

"She'll stop by here on her way out," I say.

"How do you know she'll stop?"

"Because I waved energetically, and she held up a finger. She'll be right over."

Whitney does indeed stop by right after our beers arrive. She's got a big to-go box and an even bigger grin. "Harriet and Prince Miramonte, out on the town again."

Alexandru stands. "Ms. Sternell."

"Oh, please, don't get up on my account. How are you settling into Kingston Manor?"

"Very well, thank you," Alexandru says.

"Yes, it's all very gloomy and gothic," I joke.

"Perhaps some decor changes will be in order soon once you've completed *the mystery*," Whitney says.

"Excuse me?" I say, confused.

She gives me a sly look. "You know, the 'wedding mystery' you were investigating at the wedding expo? Though I must warn you, most *mystery* venues, at least the good ones, book up eighteen months in advance." She winks.

"We need no venue for our mystery," Alexandru says.

"She means like wedding venues," I explain to him. "Like for us."

"But we are not betrothed," Alexandru says.

"Don't worry, I won't tell." Whitney leans in. "I know the royals don't like their people marrying commoners. No offense, Harriet."

"No, I get it. Some royals would rather be chained to an ocean floor and eaten by eels than marry one such as me!"

I look over at Alexandru. His brown eyes are full of something fierce and tightly caged.

"Oh, well, I'm sure nobody feels like that," Whitney stammers.

I gather my courage. I'm going to ask her a blunt question,

just like Alexandru sometimes does. "What's your opinion on the Schmidt Mansion as a wedding venue?"

Whitney blinks. "It's lovely. Full of old-world charm. It's the perfect place if you're envisioning a more intimate ceremony. Though they do tend to book out." She pulls out her phone. "Currently, they're booking out a year and two months, though I have a line on a November date for this year. Holiday weddings can be magical."

"And there are shorter days," Alexandru says.

"Right, yes, of course," Whitney says, like that's a big concern for many grooms.

"I've heard there's a lack of upkeep there," I say, hoping that Alexandru takes note of the way I'm leaping without looking, ducks all out of their rows. His commentary on my tentativeness has really gotten annoying.

Whitney straightens. "There may have been issues in the past, but I highly recommend the venue. I always do."

"I understand somebody got hurt when some chairs collapsed," I press.

"Yes, that was extremely unfortunate. Just awful. But I promise you, they're a first-rate operation. Truly. Granabelle's friend Denny Cole does maintenance there, and he's one of the best. The chairs..." She shakes her head, hard, as if the collapsing chairs and someone getting hurt were a total fluke. "It's the most elegant place in the area for a wedding under three hundred. If you ever want to talk—just hypothetically, in the spirit of *mystery solving*—I'd urge you to make an appointment. People who wait until the last minute usually end up with... less than ideal options."

"There is also the Glassworks Galleria," I say, feeling Alexandru's attention on me. "But they had that awful fire there where everybody got wet from the sprinklers. Do you remember that?"

Whitney stills, looking from Alexandru back to me, back to Alexandru.

Am I being too forward? Have I gone too far?

"A bit of advice," Whitney says. "You can't avoid every potential pitfall. A wedding is a celebration, warts and all. Though... here's an idea!" She points at Alexandru. "I could envision a casually elegant engagement party at Kingston Manor. It would be quite the ticket. Did you restore it to its original condition as you did with your London residence?"

"The third floor was restored to its original condition," Alexandru says.

"Somebody has done her homework," I joke, actually surprised that she knows about Alexandru's large London residence.

"Prince Miramonte is the talk of the town. Everybody's been googling you. I must say, it's a beautiful story, the way your tragedy with your father brought you together with the prince."

"Do you recommend the services of Kip the bartender?" Alexandru asks. "Do you find him to be a trustworthy person?"

"He is the default beverages person," Whitney says.

"That doesn't seem like an endorsement, exactly," I say.

"Well, he is the homegrown choice, let's just say." The way she says homegrown is not exactly approving. "If you are envisioning a more jet-set or sophisticated crowd coming in from all corners of the globe, you might look to Cleveland for a slightly upscale beverage service."

"Do you find him trustworthy in general?" I ask.

She narrows her eyes. "Why would you ask?"

Our waitperson comes and sets down our crab cakes.

"I should let you go so I can catch up with my friend," Whitney says. "But if you want to call to make an appointment, I have a good deal of flexibility in the upcoming week." With that, she takes off.

I sip my beer, conscious of all eyes on us. "Us out at a restaurant talking to a wedding planner. My god, the rumor mill. Can you feel it?"

Alexandru raises an eyebrow. "The intensity of the interest around us is quite striking."

I take a crab cake, put it on my little plate, and lean in. "Take a crab cake and put it on your plate like you're gonna eat it. Maybe cut it in half or something."

"Will the villagers rise up with pitchforks if I don't appear to be eating?" he asks.

"I don't want to insult Josie's mother," I say. "She'll feel bad if it looks like you don't like the food."

Alexandru places a crab cake on his plate with a look of great put-upon-ness. "Our friend Whitney most definitely feels guilt about the Schmidt Mansion accidents. Extreme guilt. So much deception. Fear."

"Really?"

"I'm no psychic, as you like to remind me, but I feel confident she sabotaged those chairs."

"But the way she fell all over herself to recommend the Schmidt Mansion, it almost felt like she was trying to make it up to them or something. Is that the behavior of a serial murderer?"

"Some killers feel guilty after they kill. Some find only pleasure in it. Others do it because they're compelled for whatever reason, and it bedevils them afterwards."

"Huh. And what did she think about the curtain fire incident? Did she have any feelings about that?"

"Frustration, mostly," he says. "However, her frustration might be toward you for mentioning all of those accidents. She thinks you are too timid."

"I think you're letting your opinions color your reading of her."

"No, in truth," he says. "I believe it's what she thought."

"Did she also think I take forever to get my ducks in a row?"

This earns a rare smile from Alexandru. "I am telling you what I felt from her."

I take a bite of my crab cake. Alexandru cuts his apart some more.

"Sadly, we still don't know if she was actually there for the curtain fire wedding. I really wanted to find a way to ask her without being too obvious."

Alexandru fixes me with a hard look. "Whitney is almost certainly the one who sabotaged the chairs. The guilt and nervousness rolling off of her was extreme. As you said, once we catch the culprit behind the small accidents, we shall know the culprit behind the larger accidents."

I cringe inwardly. "I did say that, didn't I? But we need confirmation, and it still could be Kip. We have four days left."

Alexandru gives me a warning look.

"What? I want to feel a hundred percent. We should at least get a look at the photo she wants hidden so badly. In fact..." I grab my phone and text Sloane. "I really hope Sloane's not gonna be playing games and dragging her feet in getting it to us."

When I next look up, Alexandru seems stormy and distracted.

"Is it the hunger? Are you going to last?"

"Of course I am."

"What happens between now and the point where you lose all restraint?"

"All restraint might be a little extreme," he says, switching our beers. "Don't worry about it."

"Okay," I say, but I am worried about it. Is he fighting to keep his restraint even now?

I decide to distract him with updates on his billion-dollar holdings. I'm just describing how I've located the best possible property manager for his downtown Athens holdings when I hear a familiar voice.

Josie's mother, Rita, is working her way across the patio, greeting diners and making sure everybody's happy and content.

"Quick!" I whisper. "Switch plates with me."

We do a quick switcheroo so that he gets my mostly empty plate of crab cake debris and I get his cut-up crab cake. I plop on some sauce and take a swig of his beer.

"I'm eating and drinking for two now," I joke.

A woman at the next table gives me a dirty look and eyes my beer.

"Joke," I say.

Rita walks up, beaming. "I hope you two are enjoying yourselves."

"We are!" I say.

"Very much," Alexandru says.

It's clear she thinks we're a couple, which she's quite thrilled about. I'm sure she thinks it's an amazing boon to become arm candy to a charming, three-piece-suit-wearing prince.

Sadly, this kind of prince eats his arm candy.

Chapter Thirty-Eight

Alexandru

Ms. Renfield takes another swig of beer and sets it down with enough force that some of it splashes over the rim. "I'm not kidding around about her. Off-limits."

"There are other people on my shortlist," I say. "Plenty to last me."

Ms. Renfield follows my gaze to Officer Cooper, striding out the front door of Tres Hermanas with a large takeout bag stamped with the restaurant's logo.

He spots us instantly. Despite the look I shoot him, pointed and warning, he pivots and heads our way.

"Groan," Ms. Renfield mutters.

There's a little fence with flower boxes all around the patio, and Maverick stops on the other side, his jaw tight. "I trust the two of you are enjoying a nice evening," he says, voice clipped. "One entirely free of interfering in active police investigations?"

"We are enjoying a very nice evening," Ms. Renfield replies tauntingly. "Thank you for asking."

"I'm not kidding," he says. "It's my job to keep people safe, and I can't do that if private citizens go around trying to solve crimes they have no business with."

"Her safety is not your concern," I inform him. "Anyone who moves against her will have instant regrets. Regrets that they never knew they could have."

"What exactly does that mean?" Maverick asks, voice low.

"Nothing," Ms. Renfield says. "Are you making any headway on identifying who purchased that device?"

Maverick frowns. "I'd be happy to answer that, Harriet, as soon as you let me know your badge number."

"Because we have it narrowed down to three suspects," she says.

I sit up, surprised at this. What is Ms. Renfield doing?

"I'm telling you, Harriet," Maverick warns, but he's brimming with curiosity.

She gives me a significant glance. There's an energy about her that is not unpleasant. She turns back to Maverick.

"Suspect number one is Whitney Sternell."

"Whitney?" Maverick balks.

She tilts her head slyly. "No? Our second suspect is Kip Kidderson."

She waits. Maverick stands there frowning, surprised and suspicious. He does not think Kip makes a viable suspect.

Of course, I see what she's doing.

"Our third and final suspect is Harlan Delmere."

Maverick barks out a laugh that does nothing to conceal the shock that flows from him, as well as anger and a bit of loathing laced with fear, but it's a protective fear. Is it fear for Ms. Renfield?

"I'll have to give you points for creativity," Maverick says coolly. "Being that every single piece of evidence points toward the Snag Tooth Riders. Do you have some sort of evidence for your so-called suspects? Because if you have evidence and you're withholding it from me, we're gonna have problems."

"I'd have to get your badge number first," Ms. Renfield says.

"I mean it about withholding evidence," he says.

She grins. "Okay."

Maverick frowns. He wants to know more about why we suspect Harlan, but he's clever enough to see he won't get it—not without giving something up himself. "Look, if I catch you two trotting around and harassing citizens, that's something I might have to haul you in for." He knocks twice on the edge of the flower box. "Don't make me do it." With that, he strolls off.

I pick up my glass and gaze at the bubbly amber liquid.

"Anything?" she asks me.

"Fishing without a plan. How very unlike you, Ms. Renfield."

"I know! It is so unlike me. But what the hell, we did it with Whitney. Why not Maverick? Because I can't stop thinking about Harlan. What did you think?"

"Clumsily done," I say, but I did rather enjoy being surprised by her.

"Oh, wow, thanks," she says sarcastically. "Did you get anything?"

"Your Maverick Cooper does not believe it could be Whitney or Kip."

"He's not *my* Maverick Cooper."

Was he hers? There's something there.

"What about Harlan? Did Maverick have feelings about Harlan?"

"Oh, yes. Surprise. Righteous anger. And if I'm not mistaken, there's a bit of fear for your safety." I set my glass neatly in the center of my napkin. "It's as if the man is completely unaware of your throat-stabbing skills."

Ms. Renfield narrows her eyes at me. "So, do you think he actually suspects Harlan? Or just fears and loathes him?"

"He was surprised that you would think to name him," I say. "He's not surprised at Harlan being involved. I feel like Harlan's name was already there for him as a suspect."

Her smile is wide and infectious. "Are you saying my little trick worked?"

I sigh. "I suppose it did. You now know that the police have their eye on Harlan. At least a little bit."

She leans back in her chair, the lantern light skimming over her cheek. The quiet contentment in her expression is oddly pleasing.

Chapter Thirty-Nine

Alexandru

"Ms. Renfield seems to think you've taken a dislike to her,"
I say.

Gregor lifts his head slowly, as if the motion costs him. His
expression doesn't change—still that flat, gray blankness—but
his eyes are cautious. "I have no opinion on the human world."

It comes to me here that I've been ignoring Gregor.

Neglecting my duties to Gregor.

I take a step closer, voice low. "And yet you've managed to
give her the impression that you do. That you have an opinion
on *her*. Tell me, Gregor—who are you to have opinions?"

His gaze drops to the inlaid marble floor. "I am no one, my
lord."

"Precisely." In truth, I don't know if he has any opinion on
Ms. Renfield or anything at all. He's one of the few beings I
cannot read. Not because he's shielded, but because there's
simply nothing left to read. He's a muttering, gray shadow of
what was once a man.

"She's just another Renfield, no different than the ones
before," I say.

"I understand, my lord."

"Did you clean the dungeon?"

"Of course, overlord."

The dungeon spans the entire footprint of the mansion, deep in the ground. We had a tunnel dug to the side of the cliff, all the better to throw body parts into the river. The perfect automatic waste disposal system.

"You will clean it again," I say. "This time you'll use a toothbrush from the guest bath on the east wing."

He blinks.

"On your hands and knees. No gloves. No light. You will not eat until it is done. And if I find so much as a speck of filth clinging to the mortar, I will hang you by your ankles and let the rats decide how much of you they want to keep."

"I hear," he says, voice soft and toneless. "And I obey."

He turns, dragging his ruined soul behind him, just the slightest tremor in his step.

Good. Let him fear. Let him remember what he is.

❧

I DON'T SEE any more of Gregor until the next evening when he emerges from the dungeon, knees bloody, face drawn. "Don't tell me you're done already." The last cleaning took at least three days, and he had a mop to use.

"No, overlord." He holds out my phone in a shaking hand. "Ms. Renfield for you. You were not answering, so I took the liberty—"

"Very well." I snatch the phone from him. "Proceed." I point at the dungeon door, cleverly disguised as part of the wall.

"Alexandru," Ms. Renfield says breathlessly. "I just got home from work, and Roy LaRue is here in our store. You know, the photographer who works with Bo Richardson? I really want to question him about the archives and maybe get the sparkler picture since Sloane probably isn't gonna help us. Can you get Gregor to drive you here?"

"Gregor is busy. You will come and get me."

"I can't trust Mom or Granabelle to stall him. Can't you make Gregor tear himself away from whatever he's doing?"

I clench my jaw. "I'll drive myself."

"What? You know how to drive?"

"Of course, I know how to drive. I am not a child."

"Then why were you making me drive you everywhere?"

"Because it is your place to serve me." I hang up without further explanation.

I probably shouldn't be driving, considering my present state, but I descend into the garage and select my black Alfa Romeo Spider—a gift from a Baltic heiress in the 1960s. She was a wild redhead with a passion for diamonds and danger. Even then, sex with women had become as routine as the hunts. Just a simple means to an end.

When I arrive, Roy is wearing a pinstriped gangster cap and hoisting an oversized jug labeled XXX, while Granabelle lounges beside him in a flapper dress, a string of pearls nearly to her knees, pretending to sip from a silver martini glass.

Ms. Renfield is taking pictures. So this is how they've kept Roy here.

He regards me nervously as I stroll in.

"That's enough," Ms. Renfield says. "Thank you, Roy." She slides her gaze to me, red lips pursed, still annoyed at the news I can drive, I suppose.

Granabelle clasps Roy's arm with both hands, eyes twinkling. "You make an old lady's heart pitter-patter like a flock of butterflies."

"My pleasure," Roy replies, visibly calculating the fastest route of escape.

"Prince Miramonte!" Granabelle turns to me, beaming. "I have a derby hat that will be *perfect* for you for this shoot!"

"Not happening," Ms. Renfield cuts in.

"Oh, you can't blame an old woman for wanting a bit of fun," Granabelle says, fluttering her hands a bit.

Ms. Renfield's mother, Lorna, grabs a phone and some papers. "Harriet, could you ring Roy up? Your grandmother and I have business upstairs." She takes the silver martini glass from Granabelle's fingers, whispering, "A deal is a deal, now come on."

Whatever deal they made is certainly powerful, being that Granabelle is not one to leave me alone. What's more, Ms. Renfield's mother is not one to refrain from cutting remarks. The women in this family possess a good deal of bravery. Though sometimes bravery is foolishness.

"You were an amazing sport," Harriet says to Roy.

"Bringing joy to elderly women everywhere," Roy jokes, again glancing nervously in my direction.

I nod my acknowledgement as Ms. Renfield goes around the counter. "Let me give you a little discount on the armoire."

"Not necessary," Roy says.

"Granabelle would insist, and so do I!" She rings him up and hands him a wrapped candy from a bowl. "Saltwater taffy. Not an antique, I promise. But I do have a favor to ask."

"Lemme guess," Roy says with another glance in my direction. "You're hoping for pictures from the Bamberg–Greyhorse wedding, aka the exploding sparklers."

He already knows. I tilt my head. "Did Bo tell you?"

"Yeah. Bo said I didn't upload, but that's not true—I did. But our server's been glitchy, and sometimes the files don't show up on his end. That's why I stopped in, to let you know we're figuring it out. I know you wanted to see them. We'll get it worked out eventually."

Ms. Renfield offers him a smile. "No, that's fine, I appreciate the effort."

The smile lies. She's disappointed and suspicious.

It *is* suspicious. Good god, are we going to get another suspect?

Breezily, she says, "I'm surprised you all don't keep your images on backup devices."

"We generally send our photos to a central server," Roy says, "but Bo's converting systems, and it's a whole thing. I know. It's bad timing. He thought it might even be a hacker."

"A hacker right when you're doing a systems overhaul really *is* bad timing," she says.

"A hacker?" I say.

Harriet turns to me. "It's when somebody compromises your system. They hack past the firewalls, like breaching the gate that protects a village."

"Ah," I say. "And then these hackers are inside. They string the nobles from the trees and crown the young survivors with bloody entrails. Like the Mongols."

Roy laughs nervously. "Let's hope not!"

"They may well plunder your archives," I point out to him.

Roy blinks, fear and nervousness emanating from him. "Bo told me that you have a theory that somebody's been deliberately arranging accidents at these weddings. Do you think that's who could've hacked us?"

"Possibly," I say.

Dark emotions roll through Roy. "I was there when Boyd Halverson fell to his death. It was awful. And fireworks suddenly exploding during a ceremony..." He shakes his head. "We're lucky nobody had a heart attack. If there's anything I can do to help you identify this culprit, count me in. And as soon as we get access back, I'll get you the image sets."

Ms. Renfield looks Roy in the eye. "We heard about some kind of action shot you took where the fireworks had just gone off and people were freaking out..."

"Yeah, that shot was wild. Nothing you'd expect to take at a wedding."

"We heard that the bride displayed it as her Facebook header for a while."

"She loved it," Roy says.

Ms. Renfield slides a glance my way. "We also heard that Whitney the wedding planner recently asked her to take it down. Apparently, it was bad for her business?"

"Whitney? No way." Roy is genuinely astonished. "It was great for her business. She'd joke about how many referrals she got from it. You're telling me she personally requested—"

"She called the bride herself," I say.

"Well, that's bizarre," Roy says.

Ms. Renfield adjusts her glasses. "Can you recall anything in the photo that might have made her look suspicious somehow?"

"Hold on a moment. You're not thinking Whitney would be causing these accidents, are you? No. She would never."

"No?" Ms. Renfield says.

"Not Whitney! Look, we were also both there when Boyd fell off that balcony, and I can tell you she was as horrified as anyone. That lady doesn't have a malicious bone in her body. She loves people. She loves weddings. She's into it."

I say, "We understand she sabotaged some chairs last year."

Roy shakes his head vigorously. "I know that's the talk out there, and I can't speak to it, but what I can tell you is that she'd be the last person to do any of this."

"Was Kip Kidderson at the firecracker wedding?" I ask. "Was he the barkeep for that wedding?"

"I don't know. Weddings kind of all blend together."

Ms. Renfield taps her white pen to her red lips. "Do you remember anybody behaving oddly at that wedding?"

"Oddly? It was mayhem. People crying. Manny up front, crouching and shooting like a battlefield photographer. It was a lot of odd."

"Manny got a different angle? Are Manny's shots in the hacked archives as well?" I ask.

"Yeah, they were in a group with mine. People were miffed that we kept shooting, but we were hired to document the day and document it we did."

Ms. Renfield examines her electronic ledger. "You were also a photographer for the wedding where the champagne glass tower collapsed. Do you recall anyone behaving oddly around that table beforehand? Bo says you were shooting B-roll."

"It was such a long time ago. I can't say anything sticks out. I guess Whitney was at that one, too."

Ms. Renfield presses him on other weddings he was present at: when the confetti cannon blasted off inappropriately and when Berky's cake collapsed. He is of very little help.

She slips her ledger into her satchel. "Do you think Manny would be willing to talk to us?"

"Manny? That's doubtful. Manny doesn't have much in the way of social skills," Roy says. "By which I mean, he lives in his family's basement and rarely talks."

"He returned our call the other day and seemed normal enough," she says.

Roy lifts his brows in surprise. "Manny returned a call?"

Ms. Renfield straightens, sensing something interesting. "Is that weird?"

"Yeah. Usually, you can barely get a mumble out of Manny. Don't get me wrong, he's a decent photographer and all. He's actually quite gifted, just like his uncle, but he's antisocial. Hair covering his face, always wearing that feed cap and shaded glasses. Bo would never put Manny in a customer-facing situation. He doesn't even seem to like him, honestly."

"How so?" Ms. Renfield asks.

"I don't know. Bo's just weird about the guy. Like I said, Manny does good work, but Bo will never use him as his own

assistant. It's always us. He avoids him like the plague and pays
him off the books. Some strange family dynamics, I guess. I'm
sure Bo wouldn't mind if I gave you his info."

Chapter Forty

Harriet

I give Roy his receipt. He scribbles Manny's number on a card and asks if we have a dolly. "That's my truck right out there."

"Let me grab it and help you!" I say brightly.

Alexandru looks annoyed. "I'll carry it. You will open the door."

I give him a warning glance, but it's too late. He just hoists the thing up and carries it out of the store like it's nothing.

Erp.

"Wow," Roy says, following him out. "Guessing you got quite the gym up there in Kingston Manor."

Alexandru places the thing in the back of Roy's small truck without answering, while I stand there shocked.

"Dude," I say once Roy drives off. "Have you not learned to hide your super strength over the years?"

"A human male should be able to lift such a thing."

"You might need to dial down your assessment of what a human male can do. Maybe way down from battle-hardened crusader to something more in the realm of couch potato. And also, since when do you help the peasants with menial tasks?"

He scowls, and I can see this didn't occur to him. Was he operating outside of his normal monster mash parameters?

I smile. "I think you didn't want Roy to see you standing by like a slouch and watching your beautiful fiancée struggle."

"You are not my fiancée," he says.

"But I'm beautiful? I think that's what you're trying to say," I tease.

He comes to me, seeming more vexed than normal. "Roy was nervous. About the archives, no doubt."

"Maybe," I agree. "Though mentions of bloody entrails on the heads of children can also give people the jitters."

"His nerves spiked at my mention of the archives. But what does it matter? He is not a suspect."

"All information is valuable," I say.

"Disagree," he says.

I ignore this arguably fair point. "What is up with the archives, anyways? Just when we want that picture, the archives have suddenly been mysteriously hacked? And there's no backup? I mean, somebody who makes a living in photography doesn't use multiple backups? Come on! It's completely bizarre and frankly unbelievable to not back up your life's work. As in, I'm not buying it."

"Do you suspect Bo, now?" Alexandru asks. "You said yourself he wasn't at all of the weddings in question."

"It just seems super weird. And supposed mole-person Manny calling us back? Something's up with the Richardson Photography crew. And don't say serial killer group!"

"I will return to my residence now. You will choose a suspect tomorrow, or I will choose one myself."

"But May second is two days away," I say.

Alexandru doesn't answer. He seems a bit on edge.

I glance at the stairway up to our living quarters.

"There is something you're not telling me," Alexandru says. "What now?"

I wince. "Granabelle's services of detaining Roy came at a bit of a cost."

"If you need money to pay her something, you are free to do so."

"No. We have to go to the supper club with them."

"You said I would dine?"

"I told them you're on a one-meal-a-day fasting program, so we'll go and have a drink with them, and they'll go and dine."

His expression is thundercloud-dark. I'm really regretting this dining promise, trying to think how to finagle a rain check, but right then, Granabelle sweeps down the stairs wearing a mod, red and orange geometric-patterned mini dress with go-go boots. Very 1960s Austin Powers era. But she pulls it off. She takes Alexandru's arm. "Ready? Can we go in your fancy racer?"

"It's an Alfa Romeo," he bites out.

"Ooh!" Granabelle says as they head out the door.

I'm feeling a little sick. I believe Alexandru is good for his word that he'll hold off feeding and give us a chance to find the killer, but I can tell he's feeling feral tonight.

Damn.

Mom blows through the store, heading for the door. "I'm not riding in that. It's three blocks down for heaven's sake."

I don't bother pointing out that it's a two-seater anyway. "I'll walk with you," I say.

Granabelle has already commandeered the passenger seat of the Alfa Romeo by the time we've locked up. She waves, and they speed off.

"I don't know what you see in that guy," Mom says as we set out walking. "He's pushy and arrogant."

"He is pushy and arrogant, and we're not dating. Just FYI."

"Good."

"It's convenient for the mystery to let people think it. Unfortunately, a lot of people know we're investigating."

"And he's on board with all that?" she says skeptically.

"He is."

Mom wears a sour look. "And you're telling me he only eats one meal a day?"

"It's supposed to be good for you."

"Sounds like nonsense and nuttery to me."

I explain the principle behind it; naturally, I looked it up after the Tres Hermanas close call with the crab cakes and told a very non-plussed Alexandru that would be our excuse for him not eating.

We arrive at the Golden Stag Supper Club, and I immediately spot them seated like minor royalty at the front-and-center window table. The most prominent spot in the entire room.

Of course.

Granabelle waves us over with theatrical energy.

Alexandru rises smoothly as we approach, elegant and unreadable in charcoal gray. Granabelle beams like a floodlight. "There you are!"

We settle into our chairs, and Granabelle starts waving people over. She introduces each one with the same flourish. "Have you met the prince?"

Alexandru is the picture of ease as he fields questions in that devastating British accent of his.

"Yes, I'm settling in beautifully."

"No, I'm not terribly concerned about the cliff. One must respect geography, of course."

"It will be my assistant and I living there... for the time being, at any rate."

Folks are instinctively nervous around him, but the way he uses charm to get them to drop their guard? Breathtaking.

And scary.

It even happens to me at times when I forget what I'm dealing with.

Sitting there, I vow to never lose sight of the fact that

Alexandru is a monster, a predator who sees my kind as prey, who doesn't understand the problem with killing people. A beast who tolerates me because of what I can do for him but that if my usefulness were gone, or if I broke one rule in that contract, he'd kill me and everyone I love.

Without a second thought.

And he's hungry.

We need to settle on a suspect.

Is it Kip? His motive is the pleasure of the act and opportunity, being at every wedding. Another motive is pleasing the Snag Tooth Riders. But it's all so circumstantial!

Then there's Whitney, who likely has a history of sabotage and may have tried to conceal evidence. But again, it's not conclusive. And of course, there's Harlan. I can't imagine what his motive could be, but he has opportunity, being that he seems to be able to travel everywhere, like a charmed chess piece.

And what is up with the photo archives and the weird crew at Richardson Photography?

We need a break. Something.

Anything.

I check my phone after the waitperson takes our order, praying Sloane has sent that picture and that it's wildly incriminating.

Nothing.

I notice that my admin mafia galpal came through with a big fat file of photos of the champagne tower collapse from the insurance company, but we don't need those anymore. Bo showed them to us, and there wasn't anything interesting in them.

I text Sloane.

Any progress on the sparkler pictures?

She gets right back to me.

I text back the cowboy hat face. It's an ironic all-purpose shorthand we used in high school. In this instance, it means, "Carry on, cowgirl."

I hate myself a little bit for using it. The emoji feels like emotional begging. Please forgive me. Please like me again.

Josie and Derek drop by, too, Josie looking radiant in a floral wrap dress. She explains to a disappointed Granabelle that Angus is home with a sitter.

I discreetly trade wineglasses with Alexandru—his untouched red for my nearly empty one—while the attention is elsewhere.

It's fine. I'm fine.

I knock back half of it.

Derek, ever the golden retriever in human form, grins nervously at Alexandru. "We do a low-stakes poker night on Wednesdays. You should come. It's just a few guys—me, Maverick Cooper from the police station, Sam from Hardware Sam's, and a couple of teacher friends of mine, one who plays the lute."

"Alexandru doesn't play poker," I say quickly.

"Nonsense," Alexandru replies without missing a beat. "I rather enjoy a game of cards."

"Somehow I can't see you playing poker with the guys," Mom says, and truer words have never been spoken.

"Nonsense," Granabelle says. "They would be thrilled to have a prince play poker with them."

"Alexandru is extremely busy," I say.

"Doesn't seem that busy to me," Mom says.

"Where is that assistant of yours?" Granabelle asks Alexandru. "Sloane has been saying that he seems a very somber sort. I think he could use a night out on the town as well."

Alexandru swirls the bit of wine at the bottom of his glass. "Sadly, I have him scrubbing the dungeon with a toothbrush."

Everyone laughs uproariously.

❧

"ALEXANDRU, you better not actually be making poor Gregor scrub the dungeon with a toothbrush," I say once we're out of there. "Tell me that's not true."

Alexandru doesn't smile. "I don't typically discuss one servant's tasks and punishments with another."

"So you're punishing him?"

"I didn't say that."

I roll my eyes. "Where'd you park?"

"Down along the river. I dropped your grandmother off, but there wasn't a single space closer."

"Admit it—you can't parallel park."

Alexandru doesn't rise to the bait.

"And what's up with wanting to play cards?"

"Is it not advisable to put the villagers at ease?"

"Is that a threat?"

He turns his face to the sky as if to sniff the air. He's very bear-like, all of a sudden.

"It sounds like a threat," I say.

His posture shifts. Head tilts. Alert.

"Bat signal?" I joke.

He whirls around just as a man in a ski mask steps out from behind the parked cars. The man holds a gun in his gloved hands, and that gun is fitted with a silencer. "The lady's bag, and no one gets hurt."

I freeze and clutch my bag.

Alexandru takes a step forward.

"Back off," the man warns, gun steady. It's not a voice I recognize. "I'll shoot."

Alexandru takes another step.

"Alexandru, no!"

"Don't make trouble," the man says. "I just want the bag."

Another step.

"I'll do it! I'll shoot!"

"I heard you," Alexandru says, voice calm, almost bored. "Now pull the trigger."

The man flinches. Alexandru keeps coming. I don't know what the man sees in Alexandru's eyes—maybe hunger. Maybe something worse.

The gun fires—soft, muffled. Right into Alexandru's cheek.

I gasp.

Alexandru doesn't stop.

The man stumbles back, panicked. Fires again. Alexandru's body jerks with the impact, but he keeps going. It's like watching a horror film.

"What the hell," the man breathes. "What in the actual hell?"

Another shot—this one smashes into the car beside me. I scream, and my heel catches on a cobblestone. I go down hard, palm scraping, ankle twisting.

"Shit—ow!"

Alexandru turns to me, and that's when I see his fangs, gleaming white and fierce against his full, firm lips.

I gasp.

He just stares at me, nostrils flared, monstrous rage slowly softening.

"Don't worry about me! Go after him," I say. "Now!"

"Were you hit?" He kneels by my side as the bullet wound in his cheek knits shut with slow, grotesque precision.

"Hurry!" I wave him off, even as pain radiates from my ankle. The gunman's already bolting, vanishing into the alley's shadows.

"There's blood on your shirt." Alexandru's tone is murderous, even for him.

"I think it's from my hand—maybe? Doesn't matter. Go! Find him and find out who sent him."

Strong, sure fingers glide over my shirt, searching for bullet holes, presumably. His eyes are intense, and his face is a mask of concentration; his unruly hair tumbles over his brow.

It's so strange, this centuries-old killer turning the full weight of his powers on making sure I'm not hurt.

"You're wasting time. Can you follow his scent?"

"I am not a hound, Ms. Renfield." He continues his inspection, fingers sliding down my arm, touching every inch, leaving a trail of shivers.

"I said I'm fine!"

"Those in battle don't always know when they're hit."

"He had a silencer," I say. "That was next level."

"He was not a typical footpad; he asked for your bag, but nothing from me. I believe he was after your electronic ledger."

"Well, now he knows about you," I say, breathless. "Whoever sent him will know, too."

"And I will find them both and make them bitterly regret what they have done." He scoops me up like I weigh nothing. "Gregor will tend to your ankle."

"Gregor? No! I got it."

"You are injured and in shock."

"Just bring me home."

He settles me gently into his car. The soft leather smells of musk. We speed through the night, past old familiar landmarks, until we reach Kingston Manor, all stone and shadow and silence.

Alexandru carries me inside over my vehement protests. His fangs are gone now, but I can't forget the way they shone in the streetlight, deadly white against his lips.

"Gregor," he bellows as he lowers me onto a velvet-backed

settee in the front room. I glance past him and spot the foyer table, the one he bought from my mother's store.

Gregor appears—out of breath, streaked with grime, knees scraped raw like he clawed his way up from hell.

Alexandru barely glances his way. "Clean yourself. Then tend to her injuries."

I sit up straighter. "Actually, if you could just show me where your first aid kit is, I can manage—"

Gregor vanishes.

"We have to figure out who that was," I say. "I get that you can't follow a scent trail, but do you have any other superpowers that will allow you to track him down?"

"The power of my vengeance," he growls.

"Not a superpower," I whisper.

"You require another pillow." He storms from the room.

Less than a minute later, Gregor's back, impeccably clean, hair tied in his soldier's ponytail, and coat exchanged for a crisp black tunic, first aid kit in hand.

"W-what did Alexandru have you doing before that got you so dirty?" I ask.

"Chores." He sets down the first aid kit and extracts an antiseptic wipe packet and some bandages. "Your hand, please."

"It's just a little scrape."

"Allow me."

I give him the hand that took the brunt of the fall. "It's nothing."

He examines it. "This may sting," he says, grabbing the packet.

"That will be all, Gregor." I look up to find Alexandru watching from a shadowed doorway, pillow in hand.

He strides in like a soldier and plucks the antiseptic wipe packet from Gregor's fingers, sending him away with a wave.

He kneels in front of me and cradles my hand. "You're

injured enough without Gregor bungling the job of bandaging you," he growls.

Shivers race over my skin. "I'm fine."

He tears the packet open with his teeth. It's a brutal, violent movement, but his touch is startlingly gentle as he presses the pad to my wound. The sting makes me draw in a sharp breath.

His gaze lifts to mine then, intent with some emotion I can't decipher.

"Whoever did this will suffer for it, bled dry, broken, screaming."

My heart races.

Shivers skitter over my skin.

He's just really hungry, I think. Or more like hangry.

"To come after you in such a way," he adds.

"To be fair, they were coming after my tablet."

He grunts and finds a bandage, pressing it onto my palm with care.

And then it's time for my ankle.

He unzips the side of my ankle boot and slides it off.

"I can do it."

"Be still." Slowly, ever so slowly, he pulls off my sock.

He goes motionless when he catches sight of my toes; I'm guessing it's the red nail polish, because he looks up at my lips— same exact shade—and then quickly back down again.

Is it the red? Does it remind him of blood?

"It does not look swollen." He skims his fingers over my ankle, pressing lightly in a pattern that feels almost deliberate. "You will tell me where it hurts."

"Okay," I say, hyperaware of every bare inch of skin his fingertips graze. I'm trying really hard not to think again about his comment about giving women exquisite, soul-shattering pleasure with his so-called superior senses.

And failing.

What is wrong with me? What woman in her right mind

would view this arrogant monster with his polished manners and twisted morality in any kind of sexual way?

You would have to be so desperate. So foolish and—

"There!" I say when he touches near my anklebone. "It hurts there, but just a tiny bit."

"And when you stand?" He stands and puts out his hands.

I set my hands in his and let him pull me up. I test out the foot. "The tiniest pain."

"You will sit. I will wrap it."

"It's not that bad."

"Sit," he commands.

I sigh and plop back down, allowing him to wrap it, which he does with surprising skill.

"Okay, I got it from here." I finish up myself and roll my sock back on. "Don't you worry. Your Renfield is in perfect Renfield working order. No need to make the pesky switcheroo to an inferior Renfield just yet."

He stands, peering down at me. "Good." He calls for Gregor to bring a small bag of ice and a footstool.

I lean my head back on the settee, gaze drifting to the snake-writhing stairway woodwork. "We can't let somebody run around town knowing what you are. What if he tells people?"

"Nobody will believe him, and I'll find him soon enough."

"But he was wearing a mask!"

"The man was about five feet eleven. Hazel-green eyes. Two hundred some pounds with a rotten tooth, a penchant for bourbon, and a preference for offensive chemical-scented dryer sheets."

"Wow, that's a robust profile."

"It will do."

Gregor arrives with the ice and a small upholstered stool. Alexandru instructs me to put my foot on it, and he arranges the bag of ice over it and then settles himself on the other side of the settee in his usual princely way.

"We have to go back to Whitney," I say. "I'm going to try to get us in with her. Tomorrow morning before work, if possible. We have to ask about the sparkler picture, even if we don't have it."

"Very well," he says.

"Can I ask you a question?" I say.

"What?"

"Why did you order calling cards?" I ask.

He's silent for a while, and I think he won't answer. Then he says, "Habit, I suppose. Ritual. And they do strike terror in certain circumstances."

I smile. "Don't tell Sloane that!"

He seems lost in thought. "What happened between you?"

"It was a long time ago."

"You are ashamed."

Everything feels so raw, suddenly, like the world is spinning on a knife's edge. We were mugged, Alexandru's gotten too hungry, and he tended to my wounds in a gentle way that scrambled my brain, and I find myself telling him. "Sloane and I were good friends in high school. We worked on the high school newspaper together, along with our friend Jerome. I was the editor, the decision-maker on the paper. Sloane was a reporter, and she was a good one. She loved finding stories."

Alexandru nods, watching me, dark eyes steady.

"Anyway, one day she came to me with a scoop. Our championship swim team was practicing in dangerously cold water because of a broken heater. They didn't want to halt practice to fix it because of upcoming important competitions. It was a great story, the kind of scoop that a high school newspaper dreams of—the kind of story that big city newspapers would cover. I mean, it was people's children. Beloved athletes. Child endangerment to a certain degree. We started taking a series of temperature readings and quietly researching legal parameters. We even snuck into the maintenance office to try and find work orders about the heating system. And we did find a request. It was something, but it wasn't a smoking gun. Even so, Sloane and I built a damn good story."

"You were a team," he says.

"A great team. Josie pitched in from the student council angle, but it was Sloane's baby. She was an amazing reporter. And she loved doing that work. The paper went to press every Friday. Sloane felt we had enough data to run with the story."

"And you disagreed."

"I didn't want to get it wrong. People would've been hurt if I had gotten it wrong. Of course, kids were potentially getting hurt by being forced to swim in the cold water. But we needed more data."

Alexandru adjusts my sock.

"We fought so hard about it, Alexandru. We said things we shouldn't have. I decided we'd do cheerleader profiles on the front page and hold off on the pool story for another week."

"Did you run it the next week?"

"No. *Ashwood Gazette* ran with it on their front page the following Monday. They had their own sources. Or maybe they heard the buzz. The big Cleveland papers picked it up the next day. It would've been such a feather in Sloane's cap. It was even on the TV news."

"I'm sorry," he says to me. And I think that he is sorry.

"Thank you."

"It is a hard thing to lose a friend like that," he says. "To have a friend turn enemy."

I pull apart the sides of my boot, hoping I can fit it on over the bandage, and wonder if Alexandru had a friend turn enemy. Does a man like this ever have friends?

But then, he's not a man, is he?

Chapter Forty-One

Alexandru

We've spent what feels like the entire morning being shep-
herded through Whitney's wedding planning studio. There is
even an entire room dedicated to collage and fabric-based art
she calls "wedding vision boards." Another room holds a table
set for one, with no evidence of food anywhere. A third has
shelves of glassware.

Now we sit in what Whitney calls her "office," though I
can't help but notice that it's decorated like the parlor of a
brothel. The lights seem unnaturally bright, though it could be
the effects of hunger.

Ms. Renfield extracted a promise from me before coming
here that I would keep silent about the missing photograph. She
will ask the questions about it.

I agreed against my better judgment, distracted, perhaps, by
her injuries. Humans do take a long time to heal, and she is my
Renfield now; it wouldn't do to have her incapacitated in any way.

Though, as it turns out, her injuries are not so bad. She
walks with a slight limp, and her scraped palm shows no sign of
infection.

It was foolish of me not to go after the gunman and drain him. He would have the punishment he deserves, and I would no longer be hungry.

And Ms. Renfield is hardly helpless. She could have waited there for me. But something about the thought sits ill.

She speaks to Whitney with her bright, determined energy, a smile touching her red lips now and then. She's taking a long time to get to the point of asking Whitney why she asked the bride to remove the exploding sparkler wedding picture from her "Facebook," whatever that is.

Whitney has launched into a tedious monologue about "bridal experience flow." She's focused on Ms. Renfield, but her gaze flicks to me now and then, as if vaguely aware she should be careful around me.

"So I understand that you did the planning for the Bamberg-Greyhorse wedding where the sparklers exploded," Ms. Renfield says finally.

"You can't have it," Whitney announces bluntly.

"Excuse me?"

"Can't have it." Whitney smiles. "Sorry."

"Can't have what?"

"You can't have a wedding reception with exploding sparklers. I've had countless brides ask me to engineer something like that, and the answer is always no. It broke several city ordinances, and yes, the bride loved it. Yes, it was notorious. But it was some sort of mischief that should never have happened, and if I were to be party to planning anything like that, Maverick Cooper would haul me down to the station so fast. Now, I can certainly help you come up with other elements to create unexpected thrills."

Ms. Renfield smiles. "Roy told me that you got a lot of interest from the picture the bride posted on Facebook."

"Yes. Very unexpected!"

"If you don't mind my asking, then, why did you message her last week and ask her to take the picture down?"

"What?" Whitney stiffens. "I messaged the bride? No! I haven't interacted with her for months. I don't understand—"

"Are you sure?" Ms. Renfield leans forward. "She said you messaged her requesting that she remove it."

Whitney stares at Ms. Renfield like she's sprouted horns. "She said this to you?"

"A mutual friend."

"Well, it's not true. Why on God's green earth would I ask her to remove that photo?"

"So it wasn't you?"

"Absolutely not."

Well, this is interesting.

Ms. Renfield glances at me with a question in her eyes. *Do I think Whitney is telling the truth?*

"It sounds," I offer slowly, "like someone may have been impersonating you, Whitney."

Whitney's mouth falls open. "You're telling me that someone reached out to Vera Greyhorse *pretending to be me* and asked her to remove a photo of her own wedding from her own Facebook page?"

Ms. Renfield leans in. "That's what Vera told a mutual friend."

"I need to call Vera. She needs to know it wasn't me."

"You're sure..."

"Of course I'm sure!" Whitney frowns, thinking now.

"What is it?" I ask.

"Her mother-in-law *hated* that picture being up there. Said it was unflattering to the family. Could it have been her? But honestly, I just don't see it."

I exchange another look with Ms. Renfield. We need to get that photograph.

"I understand there were several interesting photos from

that wedding," I say. "We tried to get the photos from Richardson Photography, but their firewalls have been breached. Hacked."

Whitney laughs. "You wanted to start poking around in their archives, and they told you they got hacked?"

"You don't believe it?" I say.

She shrugs theatrically.

"Whitney," Ms. Renfield says. "Do you have thoughts?"

Whitney raises her brows. "I don't want to tell tales..."

Whitney very badly wants to tell tales; this could not be more evident. "Whitney," I say. "We told you the tale of somebody impersonating you, did we not? I believe you owe us a tale."

Whitney gives me a sly look. "You have a point."

I cross my legs and wait.

"Well, just between us..." Whitney taps her nose three times. "Let's just say a certain someone has a *very* specific interest in women's feet."

Ms. Renfield straightens. "I don't understand. Are you talking about Bo?"

"No, I'm talking about his employee, Roy LaRue." Whitney lowers her voice. "Roy takes the foot shots. But Bo's a digital hoarder—keeps *everything*. Which means there are a lot of foot pictures all through those archives that nobody wants to talk about. The photographers get cagey about the archive because it's all very inappropriate. I won't name names, but one of the other photographers, let's just say, she is *not* happy. It's like an emperor's new clothes thing—everyone pretends not to notice. Well, Bo doesn't seem to care. Bo just refuses to clean it up. He's so jaded."

"Foot worship," I say. "There was a monk in Avignon who whipped himself with rosemary switches at the sight of bare toes."

Whitney blinks. "Huh. Okay."

Ms. Renfield clears her throat. "Bo does seem a bit jaded."

"A bit? There's an understatement," Whitney says. "He photographs weddings purely for the money these days, and it shows. I don't recommend him anymore. Valerie is quite good, though."

"Whitney," Ms. Renfield says, "do you remember if Kip Kidderson worked the wedding with the sparklers?"

"Let's check." Whitney gets up and goes over to her desk. "If Kip worked it, he's in here. I keep it all in my book." She flips through the pages. "A-ha. It was Twist Mixology working that wedding, but a young woman named Jane Dawber was the lead, and the staffers were Ruby Gallagher and Verne Lee. Nope, it looks like Kip wasn't there."

"You're quite sure he wasn't there?"

"Quite sure," Whitney says. "If he were there, he'd be in my book. When Kip works a wedding, it's a Kip show. Though it's odd that he wasn't there. It was a somewhat high-profile wedding..." She pulls out her phone and taps it a few times. "That explains it. That was the weekend of the big motorcycle rally in Kentucky. He goes to it every year and makes much ado about it. And by much ado, I mean, he will not stop talking about it."

Chapter Forty-Two

Harriet

I trace the velvet piping of Whitney's fancy office chair, quietly freaking out.

Kip was at a motorcycle rally during one of the most obvious examples of sabotage?

The more we learn, the less progress we seem to make.

And Whitney isn't the one who messaged to have the photo taken down?

Alexandru seems convinced that she's being honest about not sending the message, and I'm inclined to believe it.

But nothing is adding up!

Bo said Whitney was at the curtain fire wedding. Is Bo lying about that? Is he lying about getting hacked?

But maybe the whole hacking thing has nothing to do with the accidents.

Or maybe it's Whitney who's lying. How do I know what's in her book?

And who sent the gunman to take my bag?

Nothing is adding up, and I feel like Alexandru is growing hungrier by the day. He's not saying anything, but he hums with something primal. I can feel it deep down.

I swallow and turn to Whitney. "You were at a lot of these weddings where accidents occurred. Can you recall anybody who seemed to be skulking around where they shouldn't have? Acting strangely..."

"Wait, so you're actually *investigating* this?"

"The number of unexplained accidents is very concerning and worth investigating, don't you think?" I say.

"Well, I mean, yes, of course." Whitney's words say one thing, but her tone is unconvinced.

Alexandru watches her closely. Is he picking anything up?

Whitney continues, "I honestly don't think we have more accidents here in the Silverton Valley area than other places. Weddings are large events, and large events are prone to accidents and mishaps, tragic though some of them have been. Surely there must be ways to compare. Wedding accidents per capita or something like that."

"There are ways, and I've run that comparison," I say. "And it's extremely unusual. Nine times what you'd expect."

She blinks. "Oh." But then she launches into something about how past events aren't predictive.

Alexandru touches his head. Is it possible that he has a hunger headache?

Two days left.

I pull my thoughts together. We need two things right now: To rule Whitney out once and for all, and to get hold of that photo from Sloane's friend.

I have an idea for ruling out Whitney.

I give Alexandru a significant glance. Under my breath, softly as I can, I say, "Please try to distract her. Please try to get her out of the room."

Alexandru furrows his brow. I think he's going to refuse, but then he stands, and in his cut-glass English accent, he says, "I'd like to see the vision board art projects one more time."

Whitney looks shocked and surprised. "You would?"

"We do not have such things in Karsovia. I want to know about them."

"Good idea!" I say.

"Well... Of course." Whitney leads us into the vision board room and begins to explain something about the process.

I pull out my phone. "I'm sorry, I need to take this real quick. Be back in a sec!"

Whitney gives me a gracious nod, already turning back to her wall of fabric samples and images. Alexandru pretends to be interested in some photos.

I step out of the room, ducking back down the short hallway to her office and around the desk, quick and quiet, heart beating like crazy.

Whitney's planner is closed but not locked. One flick of the magnetic flap and I'm inside.

I scan the pages for the date of the curtain fire wedding. Bo said she was there. The firefighters said she wasn't. I want to know the truth, and I want it straight from her book.

I find it. She was in Philadelphia that weekend. There are several Philadelphia addresses and even a hotel reservation number. I take pictures of everything, just in case I want to confirm things, but it seems pretty obvious to me.

She wasn't at the fire wedding. Not even in the state.

Bo was wrong.

Or he lied.

I snap the planner shut and rush back around the corner, rejoining Alexandru and Whitney at the vision board station.

"The prince's taste runs quite strongly to the gothic," Whitney says.

"Well, he is all about castles and dungeons, I guess. And bats!" I add. "He does love bats!"

Alexandru is not amused.

Whitney furrows her brow. She is definitely not a fan of the gothic direction. She encourages me to add my aesthetic, if and when we create an official wedding vision board. I'm guessing she senses a lot of potential publicity from the wedding of European royalty, and she doesn't want it to look like a Tim Burton movie set.

"This is all great food for thought," I say, "and we really appreciate it, but I need to get to work."

Alexandru puts on his day walking hat and gloves, and we get out of there.

I tell him that Whitney was out of town the entire weekend of the curtain fire wedding, effectively ruling her out. He seems very confident that it was somebody other than her who requested that the picture be taken down.

And she also supplied an alibi for Kip—a motorcycle rally. Totally believable.

He slips into the passenger seat, and I get into the driver's seat.

"I'm freaking out a little," I say to Alexandru.

"We do seem to be losing suspects."

I start up the car. "No chance of an extension?"

He gives me a dark look.

I pull out onto the sunny daytime streets, trying to drive fast to minimize Alexandru's exposure to sunshine. He's perfectly covered up, but I'm worried about the light, especially if he has a headache.

"All we really have is Harlan. But trying to stop an investigation isn't that conclusive. Though Maverick Cooper seems to think there's something there."

I stop the car in front of Alexandru's house. "I have to go to work, at least for part of the day, but I'm not giving up. We are going to find our culprit before tonight."

"That would be most advisable," Alexandru says.

Understatement of the year.

My phone pings. A text from Sloane. I open it up. "The forbidden sparkler wedding picture!"

Finally! I grab my tablet so that we can see it on a larger screen.

Everything is just like Roy described. The frantic people in action poses. Others crouching. The bride and groom, hands locked, jaws hanging open. The officiant ducking behind a lectern.

I zoom in on a man crouching behind a chair on the groom's side of the wedding. You really can't see much of him—just his hair and a tiny bit of his forehead. "Is that Harlan?"

"That is indeed Harlan."

"You can tell?"

"I can."

"He's not doing anything suspicious," I say. "Just hiding."

I inspect the areas around the sparkler decorations to see if anybody seems to be retrieving something incriminating.

Nothing.

I spot Whitney with her dramatic streak of white hair over her mane of black, gripping the arm of an elderly woman whose hat is askew. I zoom in to see if Whitney's maybe holding something weird, even though we ruled her out.

Nothing.

I zoom in on Manny, who's on one knee, shooting from the front, feed cap low on his forehead, stringy hair hanging over his shoulders. One sleeve is flopping loose, and you can see a tattoo of a camera with a giant yellow lightning bolt through it.

"Like a heraldic emblem on his skin," Alexandru observes.

"It's a tattoo," I tell him, zooming in on another part of the photo. "A tattoo shows what you love and who you are. So I guess it is sort of a heraldic emblem. They're very popular."

We inspect the photo quadrant by quadrant. There's some reason somebody wanted this hidden!

"In my time, men have lost their heads for wearing the

wrong emblem. Allegiance shifts with the wind—foolish to carve it into your flesh."

"That is definitely a problem for people. They don't lose their heads, but they feel stupid at the beach," I say, trying to keep things light, though in truth, I'm starting to feel unnerved by Alexandru's closeness, his heat, and his hunger.

"Do you have a heraldic emblem?" I can feel his gaze on me. Those liquid brown eyes that see too much.

"Me?" I ask.

"You," Alexandru says.

"That's for me to know and you to never find out." I focus back on the partial image of Harlan. "If only he were scrabbling suspiciously around on the ground or holding something incriminating."

Alexandru stays silent.

"Why would anybody go through such pains to hide this? What are we not seeing?"

"Send it to Gregor. He will present it to me, and I will study it more closely," Alexandru says. "You will proceed to your job."

I appreciate him intensely right then. Maybe he'll see something in it with his raptor-like vision. "Thank you."

THE OFFICE IS BUSTLING with energy when I get there. We just learned that InovaSpire's up for a big award, and Serena's whispering about buying a smaller firm out of Detroit. She asks me to crunch the numbers and ramifications with Malik, who's going to be an amazing replacement, though he'll definitely need somebody to assist him in the operations area.

He's not a Renfield, I catch myself thinking.

I'm also working on creating informational guides for people to consult when I'm gone, trying to prepare them for every possible situation.

306

I anticipate fielding a lot of calls... from my new home in Kingston Manor.

Whether or not we identify the culprit, Alexandru has played by the rules. He's allowed me to direct the hunt, and he's been more helpful than I ever dreamed.

Malik takes off, and I sit back and stare at the ceiling. What is in the exploding sparkler picture that we're not seeing?

I was hoping to hear some sort of a "Eureka!" message from Alexandru, but I guess that would be too easy.

I print out a copy of it on InovaSpire's nice high-DEF printer and study it with my microscope app.

Nothing.

I decide to examine the photos as a set, which can sometimes spur ideas. I send some of the other key images to the printer room: the shot of Kip so mesmerized by the curtain going up in flames, an image of the collapsed cake that Berky baked. I never got the champagne tower collapse image from Bo, but then I remember my friend sent me the duplicates that the insurance company had, so I download that file and go through it.

That's when I see something interesting.

Or more like a whole lot of interesting *somethings*... namely, about seventy extra photos that show the collapse in the background unfolding in slow motion.

I zoom in on the corner where it's all happening. The shots are magnificent, like catching an upside-down waterfall of light and glass and motion.

Why would Bo not want to show us these awesome photos?

I send the whole group of them to Gregor with an urgent message to show Alexandru.

Then I crop a dozen of the champagne tower collapse photos so just the tower part is showing and send them to the printer room.

A few minutes later, I have the photos arranged on my desk.

The curtain fire shot taken by Manny. The cake collapse photo taken by a wedding guest. One of the champagne collapse photos taken by Bo. The sparkler mayhem photo taken by Roy.

Nothing makes sense.

KC the intern strolls by. I call him in. "What strikes you about these photos?"

He studies them for a while but can only comment on the superior quality of the professional photographs. A couple more people wander in. Nobody sees anything new.

And then Serena comes by. "Secret meeting?"

People mumble excuses and clear out.

"You're a photographer," I say to her. "What do you notice about these four photos?"

"I'll play." She comes in and leans over the desk. She can tell the three professional shots from the wedding guest shot. "But the three pro pictures... Two of these photos are not like the others."

"Really?"

She slides the sparkler picture to the side, leaving the champagne tower collapse and the curtain fire at the center.

"These two were set up. The other two weren't."

I stiffen. "Set up? How can you tell?"

She picks up the curtain fire photo. "Look at the exposure. The color balance. The shadows falling just behind the flames. This wasn't luck. This fire got big really fast, and people are only just reacting. The photographer would've had to know in advance that there'd be a fire."

I peer over her shoulder. She's right. A couple of people haven't even noticed the fire.

"You're sure about that? It would've had to be anticipated?"

"You don't get a shot like this in automatic on accident. This was manual—high ISO, wide aperture, shutter just fast enough to catch the flame's curl without freezing it. The depth, the focus—" She exhales, low and sharp. "This person was ready."

"Wow." The photographer was Bo's anti-social nephew, Manny, of course.

"And this one—" Serena straightens the champagne collapse photo. "Are there a lot of these, do you know?"

I grab my tablet and show her the full photo series with the guys moving around in the foreground.

"Right. This was shot on burst mode. Look how tight the interval is—glass shattering, midair, splash. Whoever took this was holding the shutter down."

"Burst mode."

"Clever. He's pretending to be documenting the grooms-men, but the falling glasses are his real subject. If you're a photographer, I promise you, you're not shooting these assholes on burst mode. You're not wasting memory on that."

"The photographer knew it was coming," I say.

"That would be my admittedly hobbyist assessment."

"It's a great assessment," I say.

The only problem is that they're from two different photographers. The photographer for the curtain fire was Manny. Whereas Bo was the photographer for the champagne glasses falling.

God, *could* it be a duo? Is Bo the alpha and Manny the beta?

I need to talk to Alexandru. "Can I take a half day?" I ask her.

She studies my face like she's searching for the answer there. "Is this part of it? Why you're going to work for him?"

"Part of it," I admit.

Her mouth curves—not quite a smile, but close. She likes this. It makes my move make more sense, I suppose. "Take the half day," she says. "And be careful."

I smile. "You know it."

I pull up my spreadsheet. Bo or Manny were present for every one of the accident weddings.

It's entirely plausible. Everything adds up.

Maybe jaded, judgmental Bo just needed a touch of violence and death to fall back in love with wedding photography.

Chapter Forty-Three

Alexandru

I sit in the library, distracting myself with a favorite book, the pages soft with age. Gregor watches from his usual corner, his nervousness strung tight.

He says nothing—he wouldn't dare. It is not his place to tell me to feed.

Still, I feel the weight of his silence.

The truth is, I've forgotten what real hunger feels like. I haven't gone a full month without feeding since 1345.

I set aside the book, and once again, I pick up Gregor's tablet to study the picture of the exploding sparkler wedding.

Somebody went to some trouble to conceal this photo, impersonating Whitney in a message, and then scrubbing it from the internet, as Ms. Renfield termed it.

I finger-swipe to make the glowing screen display the champagne tower photographs. So many of them, so similar.

The front doorbell chimes.

"It is Ms. Renfield," I say to Gregor. I sense her excitement blazing through the door from where I sit.

Not a minute later, Ms. Renfield rushes in, eyes sparkling, cheeks flushed. "Take a look!" She goes to the long table and sets down a series of photographs. "We were looking at the content of the photographs when we should have been looking at the quality, the technique. Luckily, Serena is a photography geek."

Breathlessly, she explains what her boss told her: the way Bo and Manny took the pictures proves that they had to have fore-knowledge of the accidents.

I straighten, relishing this new clue as I once relished the first bite of warm bread after three days riding through snow.

"That's why Bo didn't show us the really good champagne tower collapse shots," she says. "I bet those were for his personal pleasure only. But somehow, the insurance company got hold of the full set before he could split them up."

I nod. "And Bo could not help but show Kip one of his very best ones. It is one of these that Kip saw. His report about their quality was correct."

"Yes!" Ms. Renfield says excitedly. "And that's why you picked up on all of that annoyance from Bo! Because he wanted Kip to shut his biker-nacho hole."

"So... both of them knew the accidents would happen before they happened," I observe.

Ms. Renfield shows me her electronic ledger. "According to this, every single one of the accident weddings was photographed by either Bo or Manny. Maybe they are a duo."

A smile touches my lips. "As luck would have it, my dungeon is big enough for both of them. I'll drain one and keep the other alive for a while. Let's go."

"Hold on, though," she says, ignoring my order, and I experience a startling frisson of delight in spite of my hunger.

"What?" I growl.

"Do you think it was Bo who came at us with the gun? Or Manny?"

"It was neither."

"Are you sure? It was dark, and maybe your scenting ability was scrambled by your hatred of smelly dryer sheets."

"The one who came after us was shorter in stature than those two. He weighed a bit more. Perhaps Bo and Manny hired somebody to take the electronic ledger."

"Why would they want it?" she asks. "What's the point? Even if they somehow hacked into it, what does it get them?"

"I'll get it out of one of them easily enough."

"Right," she says, hesitant.

"What now?"

"It's just a big step to kill people or throw them in a murder dungeon. And aren't you curious about which one is the ringleader and which is the follower? I know it seems logical that Bo would be the leader, but Manny is such a cipher in a way, it really could be him. If you spend any time around the true crime world, you know that it's the one who keeps to himself and is very quiet that turns out to be the maniac."

"What does it matter? Bo and Manny knew the accidents would happen before they happened." I stand, hunger gnawing at me. "It is time."

"But what if one is coercing the other? What if Manny has Bo's beloved dog in a camper van somewhere, and he's threatening him? And how does Harlan fit into this thing? Maybe Harlan's compelling them both."

I close my eyes. "We will put them both in the dungeon. We would get our answers then."

Ms. Renfield exhales, frustrated. "I'm so sorry. I know this is a liability of mine, but I would love a confession. Or just some certainty."

I pluck the photos from the table, one after the other. "Let us pay a visit to Bo's studio. I'll see that you have your certainty."

Chapter Forty-Four

Harriet

"I should get tinted windows," I say, speeding down the road. "Do you think tinted windows would help?"

"Marginally," Alexandru says.

"You're okay, though, right?" I say.

He turns. Our eyes meet, and I feel his heat. He's like a bear roused from hibernation—dark hair tousled over his brow, eyes sharp. Hungry. Dangerous.

My heart stutters in my chest, and for one wild moment, I think he's become more beautiful, somehow.

I focus back on the road. It's probably some kind of glamor or mystic vampire thing. Or maybe the allure is part of his hunter's weaponry, like his fangs.

"I am really hoping that Bo or Manny is there. It would be great to question Manny."

"The questioning phase of our investigation is over, Ms. Renfield."

"Right," I say nervously. "I'd like to present him with the photos, and then you see what sort of read you get on him. Can we at least do that first?"

"You'll want to be quick about it."

Bo is in his studio, thankfully, standing at his three-giant-monitor workstation.

We walk in like we own the place, but Bo's wary eyes are on Alexandru. "Hey, terrible timing," he says. "I'm just about to go out on a shoot."

"This will not take long," Alexandru says.

I try to look confident and not nervous.

I'm more of a spreadsheet type than a judge-jury-and-executioner type.

"We have some questions that require a photographer's explanation." I walk around to his side of the desk and set down a few of the really good champagne tower collapse photos. "Why didn't you show us these?"

Alexandru comes to stand next to me.

Bo looks outraged. "I showed you the champagne tower set out of courtesy, and now you're here complaining that I left a few of them out?" He slings his bag over his shoulder, indignant, but his hands tremble as he rolls up his sleeves. "I need to lock up and be across town."

I set down the sparkler photo. "Somebody messaged the bride impersonating Whitney and asked for these to be taken down. Can you think of any reason for that?" I put down the curtain fire photo. I'm about to make a comment about how beautifully done that photo is, but that's when I see a familiar tattoo on Bo's forearm.

The camera with the lightning bolt through it.

Bo has the same tattoo as Manny.

I look over at Alexandru. He sees it, too.

I slide my gaze back to Bo's tattoo.

And Bo sees me see it.

In a flash, he has me by the hair. He pulls me backwards, away from Alexandru. The sharp edge of a knife bites into my throat.

"Look at you, too clever for your own good," Bo growls.

It all comes to me then in a flash: Roy's comment about how Bo seems to avoid Manny, which is another way of saying they're never in the same place at the same time.

And Manny's weird feed cap and long hair and sunglasses.

A disguise.

The blade feels like it's broken skin.

Alexandru's face is shadowed with something lethal. Eyes gleaming.

Everything slows.

My blood goes cold.

The fake happy brides all around us seem just menacing, now.

"Please," I whisper.

Alexandru's gaze sharpens as he prowls a little closer.

Bo holds my hair more tightly. "S-stay away."

Ow.

"Release her," Alexandru says, low and deadly.

I can feel the fear in Bo. Like he's stiffer, somehow.

"Please, Bo," I say, pulse whooshing in my ears. "You have my word we won't turn you in to the police. We promise."

"Somehow that doesn't convince me," Bo says.

"You killed those people," I say. "The groom who died falling off the balcony. The deputy mayor."

"You figured it out. Good for you. You want a medal?"

I blink. I have my certainty. Cold comfort.

Alexandru prowls nearer to us, slow and coiled, gaze fixed on mine.

The air feels charged, like a thunderstorm might start raging.

Alexandru's eyes slide down to the blade pressed against my throat. And finally, to the blood I can feel trailing down my neck.

My blood.

I can feel his fury like heat on my skin, radiating off him in waves. I can feel Bo's fear escalating behind me, his breath faster now.

The knife bites in more. The pain is precise, intimate.

My pulse keens in my ears. I can't think. Can't breathe.

I am so scared.

So scared.

I try to keep my voice from shaking. And maybe it's stupid, but I have to know. "Why send a gunman after us?"

"A gunman?" Bo lets out a snort. "Wasn't me. Maybe you two are just that annoying."

It wasn't him?

"Hey!" Bo jerks my hair. "Not one more step, Alexandru. You so much as twitch, and she dies."

Alexandru stills. Too far away. A car length away. Maybe more.

Too far, probably, even for vampire speed.

His unruly hair tumbles over gleaming eyes that are ruthlessly focused on a single point. He's like a large, powerful panther. There's a looseness to his muscular body, but I know it's deceptive; I know he could spring at any moment.

He tips his head a fraction lower, focus intensifying.

Bo tightens his grip on my hair. "Now here's what's going to happen. I'm taking your girlfriend for a little ride. You're going to wait and stare at that clock. For a full hour. When it chimes—"

In the span of a breath, Alexandru is on us, yanking Bo's knife hand from my throat.

I stagger away on shaking legs.

I hear a sickening pop that sounds like a shoulder socket, and then the unmistakable crunch of a bone as Alexandru twists Bo's arm up and back.

Bo's screaming.

Alexandru clamps a hand around Bo's neck, and Bo's body suddenly slumps, unconscious. But not dead, I think. Choked out. Blacked out.

He lets Bo drop to the floor and comes to me.

He takes my hand, liquid-brown eyes feral with emotion.

He's trembling with hunger, I think.

He turns my hand so that my palm is facing up. It's the one that wasn't scraped. What is he doing?

My pulse hammers. I'm sure he can feel it. "I'm okay," I say.

Did he understand that? Or is he too far gone into beast mode...

He brings my palm toward his mouth.

For one terrifying moment, I think he's going to drink my blood, like maybe from my wrist.

But then he simply presses his lips to the tender center of my palm, kissing me there.

Just a touch of his lips, cool and soft and achingly intimate, his breath ghosting over my fevered skin.

Shivers slide over me, and I have a thought that my palm must be the gateway to the most sensitive and forbidden places inside my body.

This monster.

This kiss.

This shudder of pleasure.

I yank my hand away. "Thank you for saving me."

He blinks, as though he's having difficulty understanding my words.

My gaze darts to Bo, lying there, unconscious, broken, defenseless.

Bo's going to die now. No trial. No jury. Just Alexandru.

"This isn't how it's supposed to work," I whisper. "It feels wrong."

He comes to me and touches my throat, a touch light as air.

Holding my gaze all the while, he slides his finger down my neck, alongside the trail of blood that I know is there.

"For this," Alexandru says softly, "he dies."

I swallow.

He tears his gaze from me with seeming effort, turning to the door. "You will exit the front, turning out the lights as you go, turn the open sign to closed, and drive home."

He's going to do it. He's going to kill him. This was our agreement. This is what saves people.

"Okay," I breathe.

"Unless you need more ducks in a row?"

"No, I'm good. Enough ducks."

"Go."

"What about you? There's a body and fingerprints and—"

"Ms. Renfield!" His face is hard to read, and I have the sense he's losing his grip on what shred of humanity he possesses. "Go!"

Pushed by some sense of self-preservation, I find myself rushing to the door, palm buzzing. I turn out the lights, flip the sign, and get in my car.

I drive home, hands shaking.

The headline at this point should be that Alexandru is sucking all of the blood out of local wedding photographer Bo Richardson.

But I can't stop reliving that kiss—Alexandru's lips pressed to the center of my palm.

The impossible tenderness of it.

The fierce intimacy of it.

How one brush of his lips dropped through me like a roller-coaster plunge, stealing my breath.

And I can't stop thinking about how I saw him suddenly, terrifyingly, as something other than a monster.

Chapter Forty-Five

Harriet

"Hold on, you're going to what?" Josie gawks at me.

"I know it sounds kind of weird."

"Kind of? When I said you should move out of that antique store, I was imagining... oh, I don't know, a fabulous condo on the river? Or maybe one of those cute little cottages up by the music conservatory?"

"I know." I sip my champagne cocktail. It's three days after Bo "disappeared" and we're just catching up.

"But to move into Kingston Manor with your boss?"

"I'll have my own entire wing."

"Dude."

"My bedroom will be in a turret. And there's a lavish sitting room all my own, a state-of-the-art office, and a porch with a great place to grow flowers."

This is how Gregor described it. I haven't seen my supposed wing yet, but it's not like I can say no to moving into Kingston Manor at this point.

Josie is just shaking her head.

"It'll be amazing! Liz the monstera will have plenty of room to grow weirdly huge, and the quiet there is incredible. Also, there's a massive library in that place. It would completely blow your mind. The central turret spirals three stories high with books. It's unbelievable."

Josie regards me suspiciously. As well she should.

The truth is, I don't want to leave Mom and Granabelle. And if I decided to leave of my own accord, it wouldn't be to move into a windswept gothic mansion on a hill because if I don't, a murderous vampire will start killing my friends, family, and neighbors.

"It's so beautiful and luxurious."

"You're not a luxury girl," Josie says.

"Maybe I've come to like a little luxury."

"Don't bullshit me," she says. "You quit your job to work with this guy, and now you're going to be living with him? You're not into him, are you?"

"Not in the least," I say.

Josie positions the base of her cocktail glass in the very center of her napkin, pondering.

I've been dreading this conversation. Josie is too smart, and she knows me too well.

"It took you five months and three spreadsheets just to change your brand of multivitamin, but now you're suddenly moving up there for no apparent reason?"

"There are reasons. For example, it's really convenient when you're managing a massive worldwide empire to run it from somewhere like that, where you can hop on with Brussels from a state-of-the-art office before breakfast."

"You can hop on with Brussels from your laptop at Berky's."

"Not like I can at Kingston Manor." I grab a breadstick and swipe it through the artichoke dip. "Look, this is the choice that I made, and you need to respect it." I stuff it in my mouth, chewing with determination.

She watches me, unconvinced.

"You need to respect it," I repeat with more conviction than I feel.

She looks away.

"Is that a no?" I ask.

"Harriet," she says in a small voice, "I just don't want to lose you."

"I'm not going anywhere. I'm still in Ashwood. We're still neighbors."

"It's not the physical distance," she says. "I feel like I don't know your mind right now. Or your heart. What you are doing makes no sense."

"You know my heart—you *know* you do. *And* my mind."

She shakes her head. "There's something you're not telling me."

I grab another breadstick, but I don't eat this one. I just focus on it, trying to think of what to say.

I'm not ready to tell her the truth. I don't know if I'll ever be ready.

"I promise you—you *will* understand. And in the meantime, after I get settled, I'm going to have you over for a fabulous dinner in my new digs, and you'll be so jealous."

"I guess I wouldn't mind seeing that library."

"There's the spirit!" I say.

I ask her about Angus, and she fills me in on his new fire truck phase.

We're acting *as if*.

It's the best we can do right now.

"Also, I think congratulations are in order." She lifts her glass. "To the one very brilliant and amazing person who called it on the wedding accidents."

"Thank you!" We clink glasses.

After Bo didn't show up for work, Valerie went to his home,

looking for him. She discovered a room decorated with the accident photos he had taken, displayed like museum pieces.

They discovered a workshop in his garage where he made all of the little devices that helped him stage the accidents. They found his research, too, on how to use chemicals to create metal fatigue that mimics rust, and use lye to weaken wood supports. They found a 3D printer and plans for a tiny heating device that could be stuck under a table holding a cake. And there were prototypes for the hydraulic device used in the grand stairway collapse that killed the deputy mayor.

They also found a "Manny" disguise—a cap, wig, and dark glasses, and even a selection of clothes. The going theory is that Bo worked some weddings as Manny in order to throw off suspicion, just in case somebody noticed he was present at all of the weddings where there were accidents.

Valerie has been telling people that she thinks Bo staged the accidents as a twisted way of seeking authentic moments.

When I heard she was saying that, I remembered the cynical way he talked about people he'd photograph for weddings, how they'd "pretend to feel emotions they didn't feel" and so on. How even Whitney had stopped recommending him because of how jaded he was.

At any rate, Maverick and his team were able to pin every single one of the wedding accidents on Bo.

There was nothing in the news about anything amiss in the photography studio. No traces of blood, no signs of a struggle.

No drained body.

What happened? Did Alexandru spirit it away? Did Gregor come and help?

Valerie has taken over managing duties at the studio. Perhaps she'll purge the archives of Roy's obnoxious foot photos. Or maybe she'll talk to him about it.

Some people say Bo disappeared to Rio de Janeiro, because

he had vacationed there some years back. Others think he went to Qatar or maybe the Philippines.

Apparently, he's also in the national "Most Wanted" databases.

I haven't seen Alexandru since that night.

Since Bo.

Since the palm kiss.

Sometimes I tell myself I'm making too big a deal of it. Alexandru kissed my grandmother's hand after all. Yes, he kissed my palm instead of the back of it, but it's still the hand.

It changes nothing. He's a monster, and I'm managing the situation the best I can.

Maverick Cooper came by our store on Saturday to apologize for ridiculing my theory.

"I should've known if you were saying it, it wouldn't be bullshit," he said. "I should've looked at it harder."

"Well, it was outrageous," I said to him. "Kind of unbelievable."

"No, I should've had an open mind," he said. And then Granabelle wandered up and asked him about his grandmother and cajoled him into buying a paperweight in the shape of a lighthouse, and that was that.

A small package came for me that day. Inside was a key, a remote control for the gate, and Alexandru's calling card. Written in heavy scrawl above his name were two words.

It's time.

"Oh, hey, I forgot to tell you the new city council gossip!" Josie says.

I lean in. "Spill!"

Josie smiles. "I found out why the mayor flip-flopped on Harlan's horrible park-ruining development."

"What? I haven't even been following. There was another vote, and the mayor changed his mind?"

"Yeah." Josie leans back. "That vote was the day before the

324

news about Bo came out, and to everybody's utter shock, the mayor lobbied for Harlan, and it was on the verge of passing."

"No!" I say.

"Right? They had to take a recess to do some stuff to finalize the zoning, but it was all but done. Then, just yesterday, the mayor called an emergency session to change his vote back to 'no.' He got all the people he had strong-armed to change their votes back to 'no,' too. He made sure that Harlan's proposal got killed."

"That's a pretty massive about-face."

"No kidding, right? What changed, you might ask?" Josie holds up a fork. "What changed is that everyone found out Bo was behind the staircase collapse murder. Because, as it turns out, the mayor thought Harlan was the one behind it, and he was scared out of his mind that Harlan would kill him, too."

"He thought Harlan engineered the stairway collapse?"

"Yes. The mayor literally thought Harlan killed his deputy and might kill him due to their opposition to the project, so he changed his vote. Out of fear! But luckily, the news about Bo came out in time, before things got finalized."

"Thank goodness! It's weird that the mayor would assume Harlan was the one who did it."

Josie's eyes sparkle. "I got it from a good source that Harlan actively said things to imply he was responsible for it. Little comments here and there, sort of like, 'Shame about that collapse. Just a couple more accidents to go…'"

I sit up, shocked. "Harlan was trying to take credit for the stairs to scare the mayor into voting his way?"

"Yup! And it almost worked!"

"Whoa."

"That guy is the worst. They're both the worst." Josie goes on about the cowardice of the mayor and the awfulness of Harlan.

Meanwhile, a few more pieces come together in my mind.

The mayor must've said something to the police about Harlan's vague threats, and that's why Alexandru sensed that Maverick had suspicions about Harlan.

I push the plate toward Josie. "Last bit is yours."

"Don't mind if I do."

"You will be such a better mayor," I say to her. "I can't wait."

She grins. "I know, right?"

We always talk about *when* Josie will become mayor, not if. She's just biding her time for now. Gathering allies. Waiting for the right moment.

We still don't have answers about the gunman who shot Alexandru during that mugging.

Who sent him?

Alexandru says that Bo was telling the truth when he said he didn't send the gunman.

I agree. Bo's words had a ring of truth to them. Also, why would Bo deny sending a gunman after us when he'd already basically confessed to two murders?

Which leaves the question: Who *did* send the gunman? Harlan?

Did Harlan think that mugging us and taking my tablet would slow down the investigation? Maybe buy him enough time to get that project passed?

It makes a little bit of sense, I guess. Not a lot of sense, though.

Could it have been some random mugger who picked the worst victim ever?

Either way, the man shot Alexandru right in the face—three times—and Alexandru is currently walking around fresh as a daisy.

That's got to raise an eyebrow or two to whoever was involved.

Did the gunman chalk it up to hallucinations? Or does he think that Alexandru is some kind of supernatural being?

Did he tell the person who hired him what happened? Did he tell anybody else?

Though when you think about it, a tale that features you shooting a person in the face three times is probably not one that you'd tell just anybody.

Rita comes by just then with a plate of cheesecake slices. It's a new dessert she's developing in the kitchen—salted caramel pretzel cheesecake.

"We'll test!" Josie moves over so her mom can sit down, and we dig in.

Chapter Forty-Six

Harriet

I load the last box into the van and shut the doors, and then take a good, long look up at the last window on the third floor of Mrs. Morgan's Curios. My bedroom window for these past thirty-two years.

One of Josie's main problems with me living with Mom and Granabelle all this time was that she believed I was staying there out of guilt.

She's not wrong about that.

My failure to follow the rules and pick up James on time that day led to his disappearance.

Mom insists that she was way wilder than I was at the age of twelve; she's always telling me how she never followed the rules. And Granabelle constantly reminds me that James's disappearance was not my doing. "You were just a kid, too!" she says.

It doesn't take away the guilt.

My fingers go to the pendant around my neck. James's key.

I know they desperately want me to stay. The idea of abandoning them twists something in my gut.

I'll always feel guilty. Always.

But now that I've hauled the last box out to the van Serena

so graciously lent to me, I can feel the smallness of that place. Of my cramped little bedroom, of that little world.

Mom comes out and stands beside me. "I don't know about this whole thing."

That makes two of us.

Mom and Granabelle couldn't believe I didn't want to take all the furniture from my bedroom. But that furniture was never really mine. It was just a rotating cast of pieces hauled up from the store, depending on various display and collection needs.

I very much doubt I'll like whatever furnishings are in my new space, considering Alexandru's taste runs more to *Saw* than *Elle Decor*.

Granabelle comes out and gives me a hug. "When are we coming over?" She's still gunning for that photo shoot, and I guess she's going to get it now.

"Tuesday. I'll give you the full tour!" I've already warned them about Alexandru's "offbeat" tastes. Granabelle cannot wait. She's already teasing it on her Instagram feed with a special caption: Countdown to the great Kingston Manor reveal!

She adjusts her hat.

"Off to mahjong?" I ask.

"Wish me luck!" She turns and heads down the sidewalk.

"Okay." I turn to Mom. "I'll see you at Sunday dinner," I say.

"What are you talking about? I'm riding with you. I'm not going to let you haul those boxes in all by yourself."

"There aren't that many," I say.

"Don't be an idiot. Half the time with twice the people. Ruth can close up."

This is a surprise—a pleasant one. "Okay, then! Let's do this!"

I get into the driver's side while Mom hops into the passenger seat.

I pull out onto the road, asking more questions about Ruth, their capable new shop assistant. It looks like her hours will be expanding now that I won't be around to jump behind the counter every two seconds on nights and weekends.

Luckily, as Alexandru's business manager, I gave myself a big salary bump and move-in bonus, half of which I used to shore up the antique store bank account, so paying Ruth will be no problem.

I turn the van up the steep road that leads to the bluff.

"Does Ruth get on with the customers okay?" I ask Mom.

"Well, she's not you," Mom says gloomily. "How's your replacement at InovaSpire shaping up?"

"There are two of them replacing me, and they're doing great so far. But I'll go in for consulting now and then."

"I hope you know what you're doing, quitting that place," she says.

"I do!" I say. "I enjoy being in control of this massive business entity, moving around the pieces and delegating and organizing and tweaking."

This is somewhat true. I do enjoy running Alexandru's empire—it's letting my inner spreadsheet goddess run wild—but in the end, it's only about making money. In that way, it's not that much different than my job with Serena.

But solving a mystery and stopping a killer? That was invigorating.

Bo would have kept escalating, of that I have no doubt, and other people would have died. We stopped him.

I head past the music conservatory with its old, gothic architecture and up to the road that runs along the bluff, higher and higher past all the fancy houses until we come to the end.

"Welp. Good for you trying new things—*I guess*," Mom says morosely.

I snort. That's as big a vote of confidence as I'll ever get from her.

"It does seem a bit isolated, though," she says as the huge iron gates slowly creak open to allow the van through.

"Literally seven minutes from you," I say as we ramble down the drive, flanked on either side by burr oaks whose branches look like gnarled fingers. We round the curve, and there's Gregor—severe coat, severe face, severe ponytail—waiting in the doorway like he's been standing there for centuries.

"Who's this guy?" Mom asks.

"Gregor. He's Alexandru's butler, kind of."

"The prince has a *butler*?" Mom says it like it's the stupidest thing in the world. "Can't the man tie his own cravat?"

"Alexandru doesn't wear a cravat," I say.

We hop out, and I go around back and fling open the doors, revealing my carefully packed boxes and Liz the monstera plant, who has thankfully survived the trip without tipping.

Gregor comes and takes the largest, heaviest box and leads us in, through the main foyer, past the serpent-coiled-wood-work stairway, and off to the left down a rather elegant hallway.

We arrive at what I presume is my suite of rooms. The living area is awash in late light from soaring windows that frame the Silverton River and all of Ashwood beyond. A low fire burns in the carved marble fireplace, and shelves line the walls —rows of worn leather spines, with numerous shelves left for my own books.

A comfy-looking blue sofa is flanked by two boxy mid-century armchairs with squared wooden arms. There's a lovely Persian rug and French doors that lead to a stone patio over-looking the river.

But it's the chest that stops me cold.

It sits near the French doors, an old oak thing bound in blackened iron. It's completely out of place in the cozy, colorful environment.

And I don't need to open it to know what's inside. I can feel them.

The ledgers.

Their presence hums against my skin—silent, heavy, alive.

My father's hands touched those ledgers, and possibly the hands of Renfields before him. His mind carved its patterns into their pages. Even from across the room, the knowing coils through me.

"Wow." Mom sets her box on the floor and lowers herself into one of the chairs. "These are real," she says, running her hand along the armrests. "Nice."

"Yes, milady," Gregor says, setting his box next to hers. I follow suit.

"*Milady?*" Mom says. "I'm not yours, and I'm definitely no lady. You can call me Lorna."

Gregor bows from the neck. "Gregor."

They regard each other strangely for a moment. O-kay.

Over the fireplace hangs a gilt-framed 19th-century landscape of storm clouds rolling over a craggy Carpathian valley. I'd bet Alexandru chose to remind me exactly whose house I'm in.

That's not staying.

I wander into the next adjoining room—an office with a massive slab of black walnut for a desk, a leather chair that looks like it was lifted from some midcentury CEO's corner suite, and built-in shelves.

And then there's the bedroom. The bed dominates the space—an enormous platform frame in pale wood, dressed in layers of cream linen and a charcoal cashmere throw. Another fireplace faces it, this one in pale marble veined with gold, with a low armchair pulled close as if someone's already sat there reading. The rug is thick enough to swallow my bare feet, and on the nightstand sits a blue vase with a bunch of yellow flowers.

"This is some real princess shit right here," Mom says. "Not too shabby."

She's right. It is princess shit, all shockingly wonderful, right down to yellow flowers. I love yellow flowers and velvety soft things, and there's not an art farm in sight.

But that chest of ledgers. I can feel the tendrils of them already trying to hook into my subconscious. I hate how badly I want to go out there and start going through them. It feels unhealthy. The kind of fascination that will lead to no good.

"I don't want the ledgers here," I say to Gregor while Mom is inspecting a side table.

"Milady?"

"The ledgers," I say. "Get them out of here. I want you to put them in the dungeon, and then send them back to Karsovia tomorrow. They don't belong here. I'm not going to want or need them."

Gregor inclines his head.

"Right away."

"Understood." He goes and gets the chest and leaves.

Mom and I bring in the rest of my boxes and Liz the monstera plant, with an assist from Gregor once he comes back. Afterward, Mom insists on a tour.

I exchange glances with Gregor. "Alexandru is probably working in his study," I say.

"What? His study isn't the whole rest of the mansion, is it? Harriet, you said something about a library. Let's see it."

In the end, we show her the library, the front room, where some of the stuff from the antique store ended up, and the dining room with the weird, giant sculptural chandelier.

Mom loves the library, but she's not so sure about the weaponry chandelier. "Very pugilistic," she says.

I return from driving her home a little while later with some groceries from Gables, and I'm relieved to find that there is a full kitchen. I wasn't sure, being that Alexandru doesn't eat food, and Gregor restricts himself to gruel. I put my stuff away, except for a nice big family-sized bag of Bugles, which I take to my office for a nice Bugles dinner.

Feeling at a loss for what to do next, I set up my computer and get everything connected. That's when I catch sight of the calendar on the desk.

There is one date circled—the day we caught Bo.

The date of Alexandru's last meal.

I pick it up. It's been four days since then, which means we have twenty-six days until we have to catch the next killer.

I count out those twenty-six days and write five exclamation points on a pink sticky note, sticking it on the last possible day before Alexandru's hunger turns dangerous.

I feel the charge in the air before I see him.

He's in the doorway, leaning on the frame, immaculate as ever in a gray suit, eyes gleaming with the promise of trouble.

I press my palms together. The ghost of his kiss still burns between us.

"You can't just come in here," I say.

He nods at the calendar. "Best to not leave it to the last minute next time."

I swallow. His control had frayed toward the end, but how badly? And was that kiss part of the unraveling? What happens if he finally snaps?

Best not to find out. I grab the calendar and move the sticky note up a couple of days. "There. A little extra cushion."

"Do you have anybody in mind for my next meal?"

"Not yet." My gaze slides to the window. It shouldn't be hard; there are probably plenty of killers around.

"Tick-tock, Ms. Renfield." With that, he turns and leaves.

"Still not my name!" I call after him.

~ THE END ~

Author's Note

Thank you so much for reading! I hope you enjoyed Alexandru and Harriet as much as I did!

And there's more!

Alexandru has some opinions on his new live-in underling (of course!) in the bonus epilogue you can get with my newsletter here:

> **https://geni.us/MoreAlexandru**

Will Alexandru and Harriet be able to find a serial killer before Alexandru goes all beastly and feral?

Pre-order the next book!!

The next Ms. Renfield Immortal Boss #2:

> **https://geni.us/ImmortalBoss2**

This book is part of the Immortal Boss series, a group of standalone Vampire Mystery Romance books, though it's best to read in order.

These books are also available in AUDIO.

>> https://geni.us/ImmortalBoss1audio

Also by Annika Martin

Acknowledgments

I'm so grateful to have so many generous, creative authors and readers in my corner. You're always up for reading my work at different stages and bringing fearless insights, and it means the world—especially to this book.

Big thanks to Jessica Lourey—for brainstorming in the early stages, reading pages, and helping make the mystery sing. Major love to my husband, Mark—your read was wildly wonderful; you brought so much fun and smarts to this text, and turned nowhere lines into the best jokes. And to Veronica Wolff—thank you for your insights and for reconnecting me with the fun and magic of this tale. I am indebted to Molly Fader—your brilliant read and ideas delivered some truly delicious hero moments. And Joanna Chambers—your generous notes and smart suggestions deepened the tension and sharpened the coherence of the story just when I needed it most. Thank you also to Zoe York—for reading this book helping me decide all the things with your usual clarity.

Big love to Melody Pate—who swooped in with support and crucial tweaks—and to Molly at Novel Mechanic—for editing and proofing with such care. Special thanks to Judy at Judy's Proofing—for stellar work—and to Shelley Charlton—for eagle-eyed typo catches.

I'm beyond grateful to Erin Tolbert—my everything, my second brain, endlessly creative with graphics yet flawlessly organized—and to Kelly Reynolds—for social media brilliance and fun. Huge thanks as well to Becca and Shauna at The Author Agency—for helping me spread the word far and wide.

I owe so much gratitude to Maria at Artscandare—your cover design blew me away and captured the exact vibe I dreamed of. Huge thanks as well to Denise and Marnye at Audio Sorceress for making the audio sparkle in every detail. And to my amazing narrators, Candace Fitzgerald and Benjamin Sands—you didn't just read the story, you embodied it.

To my ARC crew—you are the absolute best. Every time you dive in, share your thoughts, or spread the word, it lights me up. And my Fabulous Gang on Facebook—you crack me up, you cheer me on, and you are the best.

And finally, to my readers—there aren't enough thank-yous in the world. You pick up these books, you talk about them, you leave reviews, and you keep me going. You make me laugh, you make me dream bigger, and you give my characters a reason to scheme, swoon, and love hard.

About the Author

Annika Martin is a New York Times bestselling author who lives in Minneapolis with her husband; in her spare time she enjoys taking pictures of her cats, consuming boatloads of chocolate suckers, and tending her wild, bee-friendly garden.

newsletter:
annikamartinbooks.com/newletter

Facebook:
www.facebook.com/AnnikaMartinBooks

Instagram:
instagram.com/annikamartinauthor

website:
www.annikamartinbooks.com

email:
annika@annikamartinbooks.com